Other Books by Frank McKinney

The Tap

*Dead Fred, Flying Lunchboxes,
and the Good Luck Circle*

*Burst This! Frank McKinney's Bubble-Proof
Real Estate Strategies*

*Frank McKinney's Maverick Approach to Real Estate Success:
How You Can Go from a $50,000 Fixer-Upper
to a $100 Million Mansion*

*Make It BIG! 49 Secrets for Building a
Life of Extreme Success*

THE
OTHER
THIEF

THE OTHER THIEF

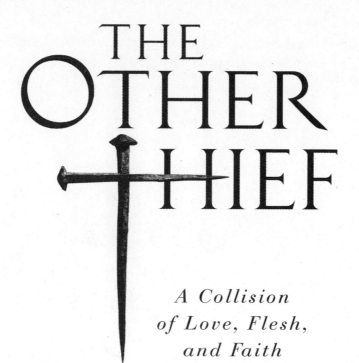

*A Collision
of Love, Flesh,
and Faith*

FRANK McKINNEY

Health Communications, Inc.
Deerfield Beach, Florida

www.hcibooks.com

Library of Congress Cataloging-in-Publication Data
is available through the Library of Congress

© 2018 Frank McKinney

ISBN-13: 978-07573-2123-8 (hardcover)
ISBN-10: 07573-2123-2 (hardcover)
ISBN-13: 978-07573-2124-5 (ePub)
ISBN-10: 07573-2124-0 (ePub)

HCI, its logos, and marks are trademarks of Health Communications, Inc.

Publisher: Health Communications, Inc.
       3201 S.W. 15th Street
       Deerfield Beach, FL 33442–8190

All Biblical quotes taken from the NIV Bible

Cover design by Erik Hollander, www.ErikHollanderDesign.com
Interior design and formatting by Lawna Patterson Oldfield

Dedicated to a world in desperate need of grace, mercy, forgiveness, love, and redemption. And to you, the reader who is deserving of the same, with hope that you'll also want to extend it.

ACKNOWLEDGMENTS

Of all of my six books, *The Other Thief* was the most challenging for me to write. In the pages that follow, you'll discover the ride, like your favorite roller coaster, is both mercurial and exhilarating.

It's not a work I could have undertaken alone, as it challenged my own faith and the forces surrounding it. Thanks to the following, *The Other Thief* became a reality.

I want to thank God for the strength, courage, patience, and enlightenment He gave me to write *The Other Thief.*

I have to start with Lisa McCourt, who collaborated with me on every word you're about to read. Lisa is a superhero and a dream come true for me. She helped me with more breakthroughs than I can count! Without her, the book you're holding wouldn't exist.

I want to thank the team at HCI Books, and what a team it is! Christine Belleris, my editor, and Camilla Michael, an editorial intern, both offered invaluable input and refinements to the manuscript, opening my eyes to important aspects I was not seeing. As HCI's in-house publicist, I'll have Kim Weiss to thank for bestseller status, as her genre direction, placement, and promotion will certainly get us there. Thanks to Lawna Oldfield, the interior design and layout of the book is simply fantastic! The book you're holding is a business, and on the business side of publishing, there's no finer partner than HCI's Executive VP, Christian Blonshine. Of course, there would be no HCI Books without the man who signed my publishing contract, Peter Vegso, the owner and founder of HCI. Thanks, Peter, and also Anne Vegso, for all you do in our community.

I want to thank the supremely talented Erik Hollander, the graphic artist for my last three books. The jacket image and layout took nearly as long to perfect as the book did for me to write. Just look at that cover image!

I needed frequent spiritual guidance throughout the entire year it took me to write and publish *The Other Thief*. The devil covets those who are precious to God. I want to thank Pastor Tony Durante and Dr. Jan Ganesh for keeping my passionate heart from separating from my soul.

I want to thank my mom, Katie McKinney, for never giving up on me when I was a child, nor when I grew into a child at heart.

And finally, can you imagine what it would be like to marry your guardian angel? How beautiful and romantic would that be? Well, I was blessed to be able to do so by marrying Nilsa nearly thirty years ago. Thank you, honey, for your understanding of this work of passion.

Ironic? Coincidence? A "Tap Moment?" There were twelve people who helped *The Other Thief* become the novel it is.

CHAPTER 1

We circled and made our second pass, buzzing just above the narrow grass and broken asphalt landing strip in Cap Haitien, Haiti, the wheels of our small private plane scuffing the runway. "Hail Mary, full of grace, the Lord is with thee, blessed art thou . . ." Tracy's voice trailed off into a mumble, her long guitarist's fingers gripping her hand rest, her eyes squeezed shut.

"Don't worry, Tracy. God wants us to give this concert, and I'm praying He'll protect us," I assured her with false confidence.

The oxen, roosters, and goats finally decided they'd seen and heard enough of our turboprop engines. They scurried off the runway into the rocky hills, giving our plane a small window of opportunity to land before they returned to graze again.

Heavy with all our instruments and gear, our plane slammed down, jolting Rikki from his sleep. Instinctively he grabbed his drumsticks from the seat pocket in front of him and started hammering away, only half awake.

"I'll never get used to this," I yelled into the mayhem. "But you've got to admit it's exciting!"

Even though it was our fourth visit to Haiti, the harrowing bumps and grinds of our landings on this gravel and weed-covered grazing area-turned-runway still terrified me. I couldn't help but think it was entirely likely that one of these times the pilot wouldn't be able to stop, sending us careening off the edge of the runway into the sea two hundred feet below. Luckily, this wasn't that time.

"Bravo!"

"Way to go!"

"We made it! Thank God!"

We all took turns directing our relief toward the cockpit.

Arriving in Haiti for a benefit concert of this magnitude felt surreal to me. I pinched myself, imagining what was about to go down. "Do you guys realize that in less than twenty-four hours the largest soccer stadium in all of Haiti will be filled with over ten thousand fans?"

"While most of these will be Haitian locals who get to attend the show for free," added Stephanie, "some big celebs will risk hitting an ox and fly in from all over the world just for the benefit concert. God is good!"

I silently thanked Jesus for sending me a faith-filled manager so skilled at keeping track of all the necessary details along our arduous journey to fame. Stephanie continued, "If all goes according to plan, the live show and telecast back home will raise over a million bucks, and we'll be able to build our third self-sufficient village, this one hopefully on a much larger scale, in Cite Soleil. God is so good!"

Yes, God is good, I mused. And sometimes He certainly works in mysterious ways. As grateful as I was for our recent meteoric rise to superstardom, it was a far cry from what I had originally envisioned. I shook my head, recalling how I had come up with the band's name, Justus, that foretelling New Year's Eve of 1999. When the guys questioned my choice, I explained my reasoning to them by sharing a personal biblical interpretation.

"Justus was almost the thirteenth apostle," I told them. "When Judas took his own life after betraying Jesus, in order to fulfill the scriptures, the remaining eleven disciples were to choose a replacement from one of the men who had been with them the whole time Jesus was living among them. Justus was the unsung loyal follower of Jesus—one of presumably only two who had been with the Lord from the time of his baptism to the time of his death—but other than in one verse out of more than 31,000, the guy's not mentioned anywhere in the Bible! When it came to filling that vacant seat, he lost out to Matthias, basically, by the unfortunate flip of a coin."

I had wanted us to take the same approach to following Jesus that Justus had taken: not looking for any recognition or acknowledgment, just expressing my love for Christ through our music in our small hometown Lutheran church of 162 congregants in Keeler, Indiana. The band had been born out of the concept of not needing fame or glory, yet somehow in the last year, ironically, we'd gone platinum.

We piled out of the plane and were immediately rushed by dozens of excited barefoot children in tattered colorful clothes. They swarmed us, their twiglike arms wrapping tightly around our waists. *"Bon Papa! Bon Papa! Bon Papa!"* they cried. Knowing that this nickname they'd given me meant "kind, benevolent godfather," I gratefully drank in their love.

A ragtag marching band with dented, damaged instruments paraded among the scattered livestock, playing what sounded like

"Stars and Stripes Forever." I scanned the joyous madness for Mary and the kids. Like our plane, theirs had been required to dust the runway several times, waiting for the wildlife to clear a landing path.

"Daddy! Daddy!"

My heart leaped to hear my kids' voices and spot them running toward me, Heather with her arms wide open and little Eddie tripping over an exposed root in his attempt to keep up with his big sister. As they approached the cluster of Haitian children surrounding me, I felt their frustration at not immediately finding a clear route to their dad. A few of the Haitian kids looked curiously at Eddie as he pushed his thick glasses up from where they had slid down his nose in the intense heat. It was rare for the Haitian kids to see white faces, and even more rare to see a Down syndrome face like Eddie's. But these were children who loved unconditionally, so they embraced Eddie and Heather with the same affection they afforded me.

I gently peeled the small dusty hands from my jeans and belt as I waded through the crowd to hug my darlings. "How's Daddy's little girl?" I crooned, scooping Heather up into my arms. "Whoa, you aren't as light as you were when I left! You're not growing up on me, are you?"

Heather giggled. "Look, Daddy, I brought the new doll you gave me for my seventh birthday!" Heather held the baby doll a few inches from my sweaty face. "I did what you asked, Daddy," she whispered. "I took good care of Eddie the who-o-ole month you were gone."

I gave Heather an extra squeeze and a kiss on her forehead, then turned to Eddie. "How's my little cowboy?"

4

"Cowboy good. Bang-bang, chicken." Eddie shot his toy gun toward the roosters pecking away at the grass by his shifting feet. In his other arm he clutched his favorite stuffed animal, his purple octopus, Rosey.

Basking in this reunion, I longed impatiently for Mary to emerge from the plane. Finally, I spotted my beautiful sweetheart walking down the plane's stairs, the sunlight bouncing off her honey-brown hair. Her five-foot ten-inch frame hunched slightly, straining under the weight of her camera and a backpack full of gifts for the Haitian children. I watched her, dressed in her signature comfortable country-girl attire, hug the pilot and copilot as she thanked them and said good-bye. The band had been on tour for a month, but it felt like so much longer, and I couldn't wait to catch up with Mary. It had been hard to spend so much time away from my family, and I was grateful we'd all have a chance here to reconnect.

Our eyes locked, and Mary's smile lit up the landscape as we hurried toward each other. Swinging her big Canon camera around to her back, I pulled her into a tight, full-body hug, relishing the familiar scent and feel of the woman I had given my whole heart to. I cradled Mary's head in my hands, drinking in her beauty. "How's the love of my life?"

"Hi, baby," she whispered. "I missed you so much."

Silently thanking God for bringing me this angel—the most loving woman I'd ever known—I pulled her close to me again, wrapping her in my love as she melted into my chest. Electricity running through us both, I lifted her chin and kissed her, just as I'd done when we were pronounced husband and wife. The giggling of our children and some of the little Haitian faces finally popped our private bubble, reminding us to open our hug to include all of them. Our family was back together at last.

Once our gear was loaded into beat-up old Ryder trucks belching thick black smoke from where their mufflers should have been, we all piled into two large cargo vans and headed to the hotel. Mike didn't trust the overpacked cargo bin with his bass guitar, so he perched it awkwardly between his knees. I knew I'd never get used to the sight of the beautiful Haitian children precariously lining the road, nibbling at wafers resembling pressed bread while barely avoiding the speeding vehicles that seemed so indifferent to their existence.

Heather looked troubled as she took in the scene. "Daddy, why do those kids' bellies stick out so far, and what are they eating? I thought you said they don't have enough food here."

"They don't, sweetheart. I know it looks like cookies, but what you see in those kids' hands is really dirt. Their mothers flavor mud with salty water and lemon juice, then press the mud into shapes that look like food. It kind of tricks the brain and body into thinking they're eating something real. Believe it or not, sweetheart, their round bellies are actually a sign of starvation. These kids have parasites in their stomachs from eating the dirt, and the parasites create a gas that makes their tummies stick out."

Heather quietly took in my words while Eddie, cozy in Mary's lap, ran his toy car across the van window. Mary snapped photos of the chaos outside. Being born on a small farm in a small, one-road-in and one-road-out Indiana town, she had a unique appreciation for beauty in nearly every setting. Watching Eddie's happy face, I was grateful, for once, that he was oblivious to his surroundings.

"Why aren't they in school?" Heather asked.

"They don't have one, honey. That's why we're here; to put on a concert so these kids don't have to eat dirt anymore and can have a place to live and go to school. Just like you. Just like Jesus would want."

Heather fell silent, and I wondered if I had burdened her too quickly with more worldly knowledge than she could comfortably process. Heck, even after several visits here and all the good we had started to do, *I* could still hardly process the cold reality of it all. Each time I arrived, I felt full-throttle culture shock all over again. I wondered if it would wear off one day, but I suspected that this would never be the case.

The only sense I could make of our first studio album going platinum was to attribute it to divine intervention. From the minute *Sanctified* had started bringing in significant dough, I'd known it was our responsibility to share it. Our credo, then and ever since, was rooted in the biblical passage Luke 12:48: "From those to whom much is entrusted, much will be expected." Regardless of religious preference, I had always believed this was a beautiful life mantra.

We'd been blessed to have built two self-sustaining villages in Haiti so far, and the next one promised to be the most extensive of all, built to reflect the success of *Sanctified* and the proceeds from this benefit concert. A huge step up from the 10-house and 20-house villages we'd started out with, this one would have 100 houses, a large community center, a school, a church, and two water wells. Best of all, it would include a fishing cooperative as a source of renewable food and commerce, as well as 200 sewing machines so the villagers could make and sell textiles and clothing.

As I looked into the hollow eyes of the children we passed, I thanked the Lord for the privilege of being able to help them at this level.

We checked into our modest hotel—considered the height of grandeur in Haiti—and I reluctantly left Mary and the kids to head over to the stadium with the band for rehearsal and sound checks. On the way over Stephanie slipped into her mother-hen mode, offering her well-worn preconcert advice.

"Okay, Francis, you know what to expect tomorrow night, right? Even though this time we're in the poorest country in the world, plenty of your regulars are flying in. That means the usual round of star-struck groupies shoving their room keys at you and inundating you with inappropriate offers that I'll never understand how they reconcile with their Christian faith."

I chuckled. "You know none of that is ever a problem for me."

"I know. But I still don't like it. The devil is at work everywhere, especially in Haiti with all this voodoo talk, and his presence is likely to increase at the same rate as Justus's fame."

I gave Stephanie a reassuring pat on the arm. Once the receptionist at the small Lutheran church where we'd gotten our start, she'd been with us every step of our journey, always assuming the self-appointed role of spiritual protector in addition to being our manager. We parked at the loading deck and brought as much of our gear as we could carry through the backstage door.

The aroma hit me right away. It had been a long day without much opportunity to grab a bite, and the savory smell of homemade cooking immediately made my mouth water.

"Whoa, check out the spread," said Mike, the first to reach the buffet that had been thoughtfully laid out for us. Steaming tinfoil trays were piled high with chicken, rice, beans, plantains, and salad—the very best of what the Haitians had to offer.

Tracy grimaced, noticing that the cooked chickens remained in full possession not only of their feet and toenails but also of their heads—complete with eye sockets and crispy little beaks. Shooting me a look that implied she didn't want to offend the staff of Haitian servers we'd been provided along with our meal, she discreetly pulled a granola bar from her purse.

The rest of us put down our equipment, excited to dig into this fortuitous feast we had not been expecting. I grabbed a plate and dug a serving spoon into the rice and beans. But as I scooped out a generous portion, I felt my heart do a flip-flop in my chest. Even though we were in the backstage area, nothing in Haiti is secured, and I could see the eyes of curious local onlookers peering through the curtains—starving onlookers, undoubtedly. What were we doing? How could we eat all this when people right outside the stadium were starving to death? I dropped the spoon back into the dish, feeling uneasy.

I looked at my bandmates happily chowing down on a delicious meal—just as all of us did practically every night of our lives. I knew better than to doubt the mysterious ways of the Lord. Still, I wondered, as I often had before, how it could be God's will for children to starve to death in the streets. Once again I heard in my heart, *From those to whom much is entrusted, much will be expected.*

"Guys, that's enough," I said, waving Rikki away from the buffet, where he was heading for seconds. I pulled aside one of the Haitian servers. In the broken Creole I'd managed to learn in the past few months, I said, "Take this food outside to the people who are hungry." The server hesitated to honor my request. He'd clearly been told this food was for us. But once I was able to make him understand my earnest desire, he conveyed this turn of events to the others, and they hastily began packing up the food.

I hadn't meant to shame my bandmates, but everyone looked a little guilty as they wiped their mouths and resumed unloading the gear.

"Just trying to make sure we remember why we're here," I said with a shrug and a smile.

CHAPTER 2

The Arizona sunshine felt delightfully dry after Haiti's stifling humidity, and we all were filled with gratitude to be back in our luxurious Scottsdale surroundings. Slouched comfortably in our van, we couldn't stop grinning at one another. The benefit concert had been an incredible success.

Stephanie tossed the lumpy gray duffel bag to Mike. "You look the least exhausted out of us all," she said. "Why don't you count out the ten thousand dollars that's due to each of the band members? You guys certainly earned it, and you may as well take your portion from this cash before I deposit it into the account."

I chuckled at the absurdity of us carrying around a duffel bag containing more than $100,000. I knew I'd never forget the sight of the beat-up old water buckets that had been balancing on the heads of the Haitian villagers being passed around the arena, the dollars flying into them from all directions. Although the pay-per-view telecast was raising an unprecedented amount of money, I'd felt a divine nudge to announce from the stage how easy it was, financially, to change lives in Haiti. To save lives even. I'd told the crowd how every dollar they could spare would buy ten meals for a starving child and how $5,000 would build a new concrete house, and so on.

The volunteers wading through the crowds with those water buckets saw them fill to the top and turn into money buckets. They'd never seen so much cash in their lives. Heck, none of us had. So here we were, lugging home this duffel bag of bills, in addition to the million-plus bucks raised through the website, phone calls, and ten-dollar texts. We'd raised enough for our 100-house dream village, with a bit to spare. After the twenty years of hard work we'd put into Justus, our faith was paying off in glorious ways.

Mike folded four leftover flyers into makeshift envelopes and began counting out the $10,000 each band member would receive as the agreed-upon payment for the performance. I closed my eyes and let my thoughts wander to the new village in Cite Soleil, so desperately needed by the people we'd just hugged good-bye. Knowing it was coming was a comforting thought, but I still couldn't shake the pain of all I'd witnessed there. The new village couldn't happen soon enough.

The van rolled up to my house, and I was disappointed to see that Mary and the kids hadn't arrived yet. I couldn't wait for us all to be at home together. As I grabbed my bags from the back, Mike came around to help. He put his hand on my shoulder, looked me squarely in the eyes, and, handing me an envelope, said, "Dude, none of this could have happened without you. Here's what you deserve." He seemed to be wanting to convey something that went beyond his words. His eyes were saying, "This is yours, buddy. Thanks for taking care of us. This is for you."

I gave him a brotherly whack on the back and said, "Jesus had his disciples, and I've got mine. We're all in this together, man. Just like God intended us to be."

I watched the van pull away and dragged my luggage into the house.

I couldn't wait to show Mary the pile of money I'd been able to bring home even earlier than anticipated. We were behind in our annual $35,000 tuition payment to Eddie's school—the best in the area for addressing his special needs. I thought I'd have to wait a few days for the accounting to take place before I'd have my check, but now I'd be able to get this money to the school before we got another embarrassing late notice. Even though *Sanctified* had gone platinum, the royalties had only begun to start trickling in. I opened the envelope and fanned out the stack of bills, curious to see what $10,000 in cash looked like. The number of bills was amazing! Too amazing, in fact. It seemed like there were far too many bills. I counted out the cash.

Then, confused, I counted it again, coming up with the same number.

Mike had put $30,000 in my envelope.

I sat looking at the money. Could it have been a mistake? Could he have accidentally counted out my share three times, or given me someone else's? I thought back to the somewhat awkward exchange we'd shared at the back of the van. He had definitely been trying to tell me something. Taking that whole scene into consideration, I came to the uneasy conclusion that Mike had intended to put this extra money in my envelope. I mean, none of us knew exactly how much was in that duffel bag. We had done an approximate tallying in Haiti, but the exact figure had not been established. Had Mike simply taken it upon himself to decide that I deserved a cut way above the previously established amount of ten grand?

Had he put extra money in anyone else's envelope? In his own?

Scratching my head in amazement, I heard the back screen door slam shut and Mary's boot heels stomping across the kitchen floor as she came running in. "Honey, are you here? You won't believe the shot I got of the sunset in the desert today! It's my fiftieth one. Only two more to go to complete my collection this year!" As Mary rounded the corner into the office with the view-finder of her professional camera plastered close to her face, I quickly piled the money back up and stashed it in my desk drawer before she saw it.

"I vote for Mommy's famous baked ziti," shouted Heather.

"Me too, with a lot of cheese," chimed in Eddie.

"I gotta go with the smart money. I love your baked ziti, too, honey," I said.

"What about my all-time favorite, a burrito bowl from Chipotle? I guess I lose, three to one. Who's gonna help me in the kitchen?" Mary said as she ran the water to boil for the pasta.

The evening at home with my three favorite people was filled with hugs, laughs, and stories about what each of us had been up to over the past month. Mary showed me the beautiful sunset photos she'd taken while I was away, and the four of us shared some meaningful conversations about what we'd witnessed in Haiti.

Watching Mary and me cuddle on the couch, Heather came over and nestled in between the two of us. "Tell us again about how you and Mommy met, Daddy," she begged. The story was a family favorite, and I hadn't been asked to share it in a while.

"Well, it was Valentine's Day and I was just twenty years old," I began. "I'd just sung all by myself at the morning church service in our old church, Trinity Lutheran, back in Keeler, Indiana. Some of the people from church would always gather in the parish cafeteria afterward, and I liked to go there to grab a doughnut, some coffee, and some conversation after we all prayed together. I had just picked up Daddy's favorite kind of doughnut, a jelly one, and was headed across the room to sit down when I saw what I thought was a real angel, the most beautiful woman I'd ever seen."

Heather blushed as she looked at Mary, who was radiating the same pink hue. Eddie twisted Mary toward him, checking her back for wings.

"She was tall, with auburn-brown hair, wearing a flowing red dress and matching red shoes. She was sitting with an older woman I later learned was Grammy, and it was their first visit to our church. I walked toward the pretty woman in red, intending to welcome her and Grammy, but Daddy was so overcome with her beauty, I tripped over the metal leg of a cafeteria chair, sending my jelly doughnut tumbling to the floor right in front of her. Before I could regain my balance, I stepped right on the doughnut, squirting a ton of red jelly all over the shoes and legs of the lovely woman I had wanted to impress!"

The kids were doubled over in laughter, in spite of having heard the story many times before. Mary rolled her eyes, but her smile let on that she was loving it.

"Mommy is an angel," shouted Eddie, checking again to see if she had sprouted wings.

"Say the funny part," pleaded Heather.

"Daddy was so embarrassed that I just blurted out the first thing that came to me," I continued. "I said, 'I'm so sorry! I re-e-eally hate jelly doughnuts. That's why I step on them. At least they match your pretty shoes.' That could have been the end of it right there. She could have never spoken to me again. Lucky for me, she laughed instead and shyly said, 'Thank you for the compliment, and extra jelly. What kind of doughnuts *do* you like?' And that was the moment I figured out that Mommy was probably the kindest, most loving woman on the planet, aside from being the most beautiful."

Mary wrapped her fingers through mine and rested her head on my shoulder. I looked around me and felt completely overwhelmed by my blessings. Yet even while enjoying a perfect evening with my family, I found it hard to relax. The money in the desk drawer kept sliding its way into my consciousness, no matter how much I tried to temporarily banish it.

Once we were stuffed with Mary's special baked ziti and the kids were tucked into bed, Mary settled into my chest on the couch. She knew me better than anyone, and I was afraid she had sensed something was going on with me. Why hadn't I told her? I told myself that I didn't want to burden her with it. But part of me knew there was more to it than that. Part of me knew that I hadn't fully decided yet what I was going to do.

How could I even think of keeping this money? On one hand, I was the front man, the guy who had started the band, the lead singer and the band's most recognizable figure. I even wrote all our songs. That got me a higher percentage per song download, so why shouldn't it get me more from the stage, too? Everyone in the group would agree that I was its leader, so didn't that mean that maybe I deserved a bigger cut, especially when we'd just had such a successful show? Heck, if it wasn't for me tugging at the hearts of the audience from the stage, we never would have raised this kind of money. Was that what Mike was trying to tell me earlier?

On the other hand, why the secret padding of the envelope? If I deserved a bigger cut, shouldn't that be something we all discussed together? Maybe it was time for all of us to take a bit more for ourselves, even though we had always agreed that we were doing this for Jesus and that our common goal was to use whatever excess money we made to help those less fortunate. If we didn't have that goal—if we were just your average band—we'd each have earned several hundred grand instead of a measly $10,000! Didn't I deserve something at least a bit closer to what the average leader of a mega successful band earns?

I thought about all the expenses that had built up in the twenty years Justus had struggled financially. I thought about how expensive it was to get the best care for Eddie and how this extra money would make our day-to-day lives so much more comfortable. What if there would never be another hit album like *Sanctified*? What if this would be the only fantastically lucrative year we ever had as a band?

I decided to sleep on it.

Fortunately, Mary seemed oblivious to my preoccupied state of mind, luxuriating in her own bliss at having all of us under the same roof—our roof—for the evening. With a sly smile, she took my hand and led me to our bedroom. She locked the door, kissed me deeply, then nudged me onto the bed, peeling away my jeans and T-shirt so she could show me just how much she had missed me. She delicately traced the tattoo on my upper chest as I melted under her touch, powerfully answering her longing with my own.

Gently, reverently, I undressed my remarkable wife. She had given up her modeling career when we started our family, but she still had the most impressive body I'd ever seen on a woman. I drank in her natural beauty, her sensuous curves, her loving, playful smile. I brushed her silky, long brown hair away from her ample breasts to better appreciate their perfection. Overcome with devotion for her, I took her into my arms, reveling in the sensation of her naked body against my own, losing myself in her lips, her skin, her exquisite tenderness. As I'd done countless times before, I silently thanked God for the gift of my Mary.

After an extended and explosive reunion of our souls and bodies, we kissed good night, drenched in dopamine and oxytocin, delighting in the opportunity to resume the comforting rituals that marked our blessed life together.

As I listened to Mary's soft breathing and watched the rise and fall of her lovely, full chest, my mind went to one of my favorite verses from Proverbs: "Let your fountain be blessed and rejoice in the wife of your youth. A loving doe, a graceful deer—may her breasts satisfy you always, may you ever be intoxicated with her love." But after several hours, sleep still eluded me. I wanted to join Mary in blissed-out slumber, but a shot of something dark had taken residence in my bloodstream, and it noisily coursed through my veins and my soul. Was I really going to keep the extra money taking up sinister space in my dresser drawer? What would Jesus do? I looked adoringly at my angelic wife. Never mind Jesus. What would Mary do?

As if my thoughts themselves had woken her, Mary opened her eyes and took in my restless, anguished face. "What's wrong, baby?" she sleepily whispered.

"Something happened today," I said, sighing deeply.

I told her everything. I told her about the duffel bag full of cash, how Stephanie had asked Mike to distribute it, Mike's strange interaction with me at the back of the van, and my discovery of the overpayment. Mary listened with loving concern, her soothing hands caressing me all the while.

When I stopped, she asked, "Where is the money now?"

"In my desk drawer," I replied.

"Oh, so you haven't returned it to Stephanie yet? Or talked to Mike?"

And there it was. The clarity I'd struggled all evening to find. Of course that was what I'd do. I would return the money to Stephanie and speak to Mike about his lapse in judgment. That is what I would do! A tremendous burden lifted from my shoulders. I felt $20,000 lighter, and it felt amazing.

"Right. No, I haven't done that yet. That's what I'm going to do tomorrow," I said to Mary, as though that had been the plan all along.

"Of course you are," she said, snuggling into that space under my arm where she fit so well. She stroked my temple. "Assuming it wasn't just a math mistake, I'm surprised Mike thought you'd ever be on board with something like that. I know he's a good man and you all have been together a long time, but he obviously doesn't recognize the depth of your character. Go easy on him. Everyone makes mistakes, and this could simply be one of poor arithmetic.

If not, all this new fame is bound to create a few ripples until you guys get used to it."

I squeezed her close to me, thankful she couldn't see my guilt-creased face in the dark room.

"Temptation like that must be hard for mere mortals to resist," Mary teased, playfully running her fingers through my long hair. "I'm so lucky the guy I married is no mere mortal."

We nestled together, and I let our synchronized breathing finally lull me into a sleepy trance. Where would I be without my guardian angel? Having grown up with a cold and distant mother, I never ceased to be amazed by Mary's abundant generosity of spirit and unconditional love. I never thought I'd find a woman who could satisfy my interpretation of Proverbs 31:10–31, but Mary exceeded it. A wife of noble character . . . worth far more than rubies. Like chanting a mantra over and over, I thanked the Lord for my Mary.

I woke up resolute and ready to plan my day. I'd go do everything exactly as Mary had said. First, I'd ask to meet Mike and straighten things out, being sure to offer him grace and promise to keep his poor math between us, yet insisting it never happen again. I'd make sure Stephanie included that extra money in the funds that were going to Haiti. It felt good to be myself again—to know I was doing the right thing.

I couldn't help but think, though, about how close I'd come to slipping down a dangerous path. Vanity and pride had made me believe I deserved more than my bandmates. I'd felt envious of the lead singers of other successful bands who accepted much more money than I did. And greed had even tempted me to keep money that was meant to help the poor.

I was so blessed to be with a woman as special as Mary, a woman so pure she never gave a moment's thought to the path I came so perilously close to being led down.

I needed to shake this feeling of self-loathing, so I went to one place I knew I could count on to make me feel better. A small stream of fan mail had trickled into my inbox ever since Justus's earliest days, but in recent months the trickle had become a deluge. My policy had always been to answer all fan mail personally, but that task had begun to prove insurmountable. I decided to catch up on a bit of it before moving on with my day, in the hope that it would pep up my spirits.

Over the years I'd developed a system. The mail could usually be sorted into a few dependable categories. There were the gushers: those who just wanted to let me know how much they loved our music, how much they, too, loved Jesus, and how impressed they were with our charity work. Then there were those who wanted to join our cause by helping in specific, financial ways and those who were seeking something from me. Finally, there was the dying-breed category: actual envelopes with letters in them instead of e-mails! I decided to start there, since there were only eleven of them and hundreds of e-mails.

My interest was piqued by a letter from a Paulina Zakharova with colorful postage and a Moscow return address. I knew we had international fans, but I'd never received anything from Russia before. Opening it, I noticed a faint hint of musky perfume. I'd always had an extra keen sense of smell. Curious, I unfolded the letter and read:

Dearest Francis Rose,

You do not know me but I am very much aware of you. I have listened to Justus from its earliest beginning, and all of your lyrics are burned into my memory and into my heart. You have a talent for writing what the soul needs to say.

I am well-known Russian actress turned playwright and I am currently work with my first musical that I have hope to debut in Los Angeles. As you could guess, my skills lie more with spoken word, and I am having trouble to convey the full power of my message through the vehicle of song.

To my mind, you alone possess the rare talent to provide the opus to my life's work. Would you consider to meet with me to discuss potential collaboration? My email address is pzakharova@gmail.com.

Your loving fan always,

Paulina Zakharova

A headshot accompanied the letter, and I found myself gazing into the nearly black eyes of a breathtaking woman with a soul of fire shining from within her stunning exterior. It felt good to be acknowledged for the complexity of my lyrics and musical compositions. My songwriting talent was one of God's greatest gifts to me. It was the one area that was often overlooked when people raved about how wonderful the band was. It was easier to focus on the vocals, the skill of the musicians, and the overall message and packaging. Not many fans understood how meticulously I labored over each note and each lyric. I felt I should share my gift with this woman who needed my assistance.

I opened my computer and started typing: "Dear Paulina . . ."

CHAPTER 3

I stared into my own green eyes in the rearview mirror. It wasn't like me to be excessively concerned about my appearance, so why had I taken extra time with my hair and swapped out my customary white clothes for my most ripped pair of jeans, a dark shirt and jacket, black boots, and larger-than-usual earrings? I looked more like a heavy-metal bad boy than a Christian rocker. But everything about this meeting felt different. My queasy stomach signaled an equal blend of excitement and anxiety.

After a bit of correspondence had passed between us, Paulina told me she'd be coming to Los Angeles to meet with her musical's potential producers and would love the chance to meet me while she was in the western United States. I suggested she make the short flight and come to the Ritz-Carlton in Paradise Valley, about ten minutes away from my house. As I drove there, I wondered why I hadn't just told her to come over. She could have met Mary and the kids. We could have talked on the back patio.

There was no denying that Paulina and her project intrigued me. Her e-mails had been strictly professional, and she'd been straightforward about her interest in me laying primarily in the added value my name and talent could bring to her production.

The LA producers she'd lined up were high-profile. They'd no doubt been impressed by her celebrity status in Russia as one of its most sought-after actresses. Not long ago she had been the star of nearly every acclaimed Russian film, and she was still getting plenty of leads. As a playwright, however, she was utterly unproven. She had stepped out from in front of the camera because she wanted to take her creativity in new directions, she told me. She believed that if my name were attached to her production, that would weigh the play favorably in the eyes of the producers she was meeting, and she was probably right. I guess I'd become kind of a big deal.

So why the sweaty palms? This was just an ordinary meeting with a potential new business partner. I'd had dozens of meetings like this before. Of course, writing songs for a theatrical production would be a pretty cool new extension of my creativity and talents. It would put me in front of new audiences and give me more clout as an artist. It was exciting to think about stretching my professional gifts in this direction, and I was curious to find out more about the musical. Maybe Paulina would be open to me weaving some Christian values into the production. Surely any work of art that glorified the kingdom of God would be something I could get on board with!

Yet to be honest, I knew it was primarily the image of Paulina herself that had brought me to the parking lot I was about to turn into. I couldn't get her face out of my mind. If the same request had come from a pudgy, balding, bearded dude, I probably would have blown it off or asked for some kind of compensation up front. The realization felt a little like lead in my gut.

I pulled up to the front entrance and handed my keys to the

valet. He did a double-take, then his face lit up like Christmas. "Hey, aren't you Francis Rose?"

I grinned. "The one and only."

"Man, I love your stuff! Could I get a selfie with you?"

I threw my arm around the skinny kid and put on my rock-star face. He nervously fumbled with his cell phone, then leaned into me like we were old buddies. A few flashes later, I finally made it into the lobby.

Even with my sunglasses on, I was immediately recognized by a few more people. One woman nudged her husband, and they smiled and nodded at me from a distance. A shy teenage girl asked me for an autograph. I greeted each interaction warmly, but my usual pleasure at being recognized by fans was taking a backseat to my anticipation of finding the face I'd come here to see. A quick assessment of the lobby told me I'd arrived before Paulina. As I selected a spot along the couch-lined wall, I overhead a kid telling his sister, "That guy from Justus is here!"

I wasn't sure what to do with myself, so I was relieved when a lobby waitress stopped at my table to see if there was anything she could bring me. I told her, "I'm meeting with a very special client here today. Please bring us a tray of cheeses and exotic fruits. And a glass of your best champagne for the lady."

As the waitress scurried back to the kitchen, I caught my first glimpse of Paulina. I had missed her entrance, but there, in the center of the lobby, she stood. She was a radiant sun, with everything and everyone around her caught in its orbit. The bartender stood frozen with his rag in a glass. The girls at the front desk whispered, wide-eyed, to one another. The piano player held his note a bit too long as he took in her magnificence. She hadn't spotted me yet, and I was grateful for the opportunity to collect myself before she did.

I had known Paulina would be stunningly beautiful, but nothing had prepared me for the unparalleled grandeur she exuded, having just sucked every drop of oxygen from the room. Her suit was the epitome of haute couture, her countenance regal, her red lips parted slightly in a self-assured smile that took center stage on her luminescent, flawless face. Behind her, a well-groomed young man juggled portfolio cases, boxes, and a collapsed easel. He studied her closely, apparently waiting for his next cue on how to best serve her.

Before I could decide how to signal her, our eyes met, and I felt a jolt run through me. *Showtime*, the jolt seemed to be saying. Without losing eye contact with me, Paulina signaled to her lackey and strode confidently in my direction. She stopped in front of the table where I was sitting, arm outstretched, and said, "You are Francis, no?"

I nodded my affirmation of this, standing to shake her hand. Her handshake was strong and firm, but that didn't stop me from noticing her silky skin and upscale manicure.

"It's good to finally meet you," I said, my rocker persona in full force.

"The pleasure is mine," she replied. She was all business. "I know you are a busy man, so I am grateful for you take this time to hear of my longing to work with you." Her buttery voice was made even more intoxicating by her Russian inflections and broken English. This was a woman so accustomed to adulation that she seemed utterly oblivious to the effect she was having on me and every other human in the vicinity.

Paulina sat down in the chair across from me, her long legs distractingly visible beneath the small glass table between us. She crossed them gracefully, flexing and twirling her foot in rhythmic circles. I noticed that the bottoms of her Manolo Blahniks showed no wear; this was apparently the first time they'd been worn. She signaled to her assistant, and he began setting up the easel he'd hauled in.

"While Anton prepares the storyboards, why don't I tell you of the musical, yes?"

"Can't wait to hear about it," I said. "If it's anything like your acting career, I'm sure it will be a huge success."

It was clear who was in charge, and in this case, I was happy to sit back and be led. As Paulina spoke, I took her in—the way an art enthusiast experiences a masterpiece. I watched her mouth wrap sensuously around the English words she so carefully selected. I watched the winsome dance of her hands as she explained plot-lines to me. I watched her expressive, dark eyes widen at the more provocative moments of her storytelling. And as I watched, I detected an unexpected nervousness beneath her cool professional exterior.

In addition to her personal charms, the story she was spinning held me captive. The main character in her musical was a beautiful oligarch from Kiev who becomes romantically entangled with a rough-and-tumble, corn-fed country boy from the American Midwest. He's a struggling documentary filmmaker from the Rust Belt with nothing more than a YouTube channel to his credit; he found his way to Russia by working on a film he believed would be his breakthrough accomplishment, his pièce de résistance. The ridiculously unlikely lovers are from completely opposite worlds yet are irresistibly drawn to each other. After overcoming monumental obstacles that nearly destroy them both, they end up marrying in a satisfying, reverse-Grace Kelly turn of events.

As Paulina unraveled her grand romance, Anton turned the pages on the intricate charcoal-illustrated storyboard he had set up on the easel for my benefit. When he turned the page to first reveal the male romantic lead, I had to gulp back my surprise. It was *me*. Right there, on the paper. I mean, sure it was only a sketch, but the guy depicted bore such a striking resemblance to me that I expected Paulina to comment on it and offer some sort of explanation.

She didn't even pause, however, and I soon realized there would be no mention of the resemblance unless I brought it up. My curiosity was on fire, but I didn't want to interrupt her monologue, and I certainly didn't want to declare my observation if the resemblance were purely coincidental. Just when I was thinking I couldn't be more intrigued! Before the image had even been unveiled, I'd sensed that Paulina was describing me when she talked about this guy. He certainly shared my commitment to artistic expression, and he even had my background and mannerisms, too. I leaned in on my elbows as Paulina concluded her presentation.

"How do you like?" she asked, looking at me out of the corner of her eye. There was something in the glance that again hinted at her vulnerability. It was a stark contrast to the polished, controlled facade she portrayed.

"It's good," I said, "but I know I can make it even more spectacular for you." The waitress had delivered our cheese tray, complete with olives, yogurt, and rolled prosciutto in addition to an elaborate presentation of papaya, mango, passionfruit, and starfruit. I popped an olive into my mouth in an attempt to appear more casual than I felt. "How many songs do you think it needs?"

Paulina looked relieved to have gotten my approval. "All I need from you is eight songs. Half of them already I have partially written. With your talent and insight, you will easily be able to complete this, no?"

Her words warmed me, and I felt a genuine longing to make her happy by agreeing to her request. I briefly imagined her delight when I would deliver the private performance of the songs I'd composed just for her, her lovely face filled with gratitude. I had to snap myself out of my reverie. Before I could open my mouth to respond, she interjected, "I will pay you, of course. Not right away, but I am prepared to offer you twenty-five percent of the advance from the producers, and twenty-five percent of all the proceeds thereafter. For you, or for your charity work, which I know is important to you. Wait. I will show to you the projections."

Paulina spoke to Anton in Russian, apparently dismissing him from the meeting. He handed her a folder, gave me a farewell nod, and disappeared through the lobby doors. Paulina brought the folder to my side of the table and sat next to me on the couch. Acutely aware of her thigh touching mine, I scooted a few inches away to give her more space.

She began going over financial figures. She was unbearably attractive, and she sat so close to me that I felt an excitement that was foreign to me. I breathed in her perfume, recognizing the intoxicating scent I'd noticed in her very first letter.

Wrapping up her financial projections, Paulina turned her face toward mine. "So you will help me, yes?" Our eyes met, this time in close proximity, and the spark igniting our gaze was immediately palpable. We held the gaze, spellbound, until I forced myself to break it, looking down at the table in astonishment at what I was feeling.

"Yes," I heard myself say as I popped another olive in my mouth. "Yes, I will help you."

"You will not regret your decision," Paulina replied, her voice dripping with seduction. Or was that just in my mind? I watched her take a longer drink of the champagne she'd been sipping.

A wave of reality swept through me, startling me awake. I looked urgently into Paulina's eyes. "Are you sure about this? I need you to understand that if I agree to work with you, I'm *all in*. When it comes to the songs, it's gonna be my way; I'll need complete control and final say over the music. I want to make sure you're ready for this, because this is a wild ride you're jumping onto. I mean, look at you. Look at me. That bowl of yogurt right there has more culture in it than I have. Are you sure I'm the one you want on this project?"

Paulina seemed surprised at how forcefully I had turned the tables and taken charge of our encounter. I watched her melt a bit before my eyes, and I realized how refreshing it must be for her to interact with a man who's not just another fawning fan. She bit her lip, and in a voice thick with magnetism replied, "I am certain, Francis Rose, that you are the one I want."

In a vain attempt to recapture some control of the situation, she began gathering her papers and folding the easel. She couldn't quite regain her professional composure, however, and flipped her hair repeatedly as she gulped the last of her champagne and prepared to end our meeting.

"Let me carry that for you," I said, sensing that our time together was coming to an end. With her easel and briefcase under one arm, I followed Paulina through the lobby. She walked regally, several paces ahead of me, affording me the opportunity to sheepishly appreciate the view. I expected her to head through the lobby doors, but she turned instead down a hallway toward the elevator.

"Oh, are you staying here?" I asked.

"Yes," she replied as we reached the elevators. "I've finished my meetings with the producers in LA and will be heading back to Moscow in the morning." She pulled from her Gucci bag a plastic room key—the kind that was only necessary at the elevator for a top-level VIP suite.

Too quickly the elevator doors dinged and opened. I stood frozen, having no idea what she expected of me. Should I assume I was going up in the elevator with her?

Paulina leaned in so close I could feel her champagne-scented breath on my face. "We have the chemistry to make this unforgettable," she said. She pulled me forcefully toward her, kissing my mouth and sending a flood of arousal coursing through my body. I let my hand run down the back of her hair as her lips lingered on mine. Then she pulled away just as quickly. She took her possessions from me and stepped into the elevator just as the doors were closing, leaving me swirling in a pool of bewilderment.

What in the world had just happened?

For the next three weeks I ambled through my life in a blur. Because of the time difference, Paulina was hard to reach in Russia, and I had little guidance in creating the songs she wanted. When we were able to correspond, she was all business again. I convinced myself that I had imagined her romantic interest in me at the Ritz-Carlton. I convinced myself that my motives for working on the musical were all about stretching my creativity and extending my professional reach. My bottom-line artistic motivation had always been to spread the Word, and I reasoned that anything that gave me additional exposure would indirectly give it to Justus as well.

I wrote the songs Paulina wanted, but they didn't flow forth from me the way our Justus songs did. When I wrote songs for Justus, it was as if Jesus himself were cocreating with me. The act of writing Justus songs usually left me pumped up and full of energy. It was as if the Holy Spirit flowed through my guitar, filling the empty pages of sheet music with pure melodic goodness and light.

Writing the songs for Paulina didn't feel that way. I started with the love songs, holding Paulina's image in my mind for inspiration. The music and lyrics did flow through me then, but after completing a song this way I would realize it was filled more with lust than with genuine love. For the first time in my songwriting career, I was fueling my creativity with lustful fantasies that held me in their grasp more inescapably than any other inspiration I'd experienced.

Wanting the songs to be more pure of spirit, I tried using Mary as my muse. But Mary, in all her virtue, failed to spark the gush of creativity I could get by flowing with my imaginings of Paulina. After all that Mary had been to me and done for me in our beautiful twenty years together, Mary—bless her soul—was a kingmaker.

Paulina was a queen.

Finally, the time came for us to meet again. The LA producers were ready to sign a production agreement and had requested a meeting with both Paulina and me. I had told Mary about my work on the project and explained how it was an important step up in my career. Trusting and supportive, as always, Mary had bought me a new jacket and new pair of shoes for the meeting.

It was an easy, quick flight to LA for the final pitch, but I couldn't get comfortable on the plane. I had realized only days before that the trip would cause me to miss Eddie's first T-ball game. He'd been so excited to join the Miracle League, on a team specifically for kids like him, and he'd been so looking forward to the start of the season. It broke my heart to know I wouldn't be there to watch him.

I tried to shift my attention to the meeting with the producers. I knew a lot was hinging on it. Just based on Paulina's screenplay and my reputation, they were apparently ready to agree to a production run, and this meeting with all of us together would be the deciding factor. The execs we'd be pitching had A-list shows all over Broadway, London, Tokyo, and every other theater capital in the world. I knew they wanted to meet me before agreeing to the $1 million commitment Paulina was asking of them.

I arrived at the conference room in the Viceroy L'Ermitage Beverly Hills before Paulina. It gave me a chance to introduce myself to the producers and engage in a bit of small talk before we got down to business. It turned out that about half the gathered production execs knew who I was; the other half only knew that I was some Christian singer, and that didn't seem to impress them much.

Paulina was as poised and radiant as ever when she made her entrance, flanked by Anton and another assistant. If she was nervous, she hid it well. Her expression, her royal air, left nothing to be desired. Her audience was clearly captivated by her as she began the final pitch she'd prepared.

But as she continued, I couldn't help but notice a few of their faces glazing over. Paulina was a well-spoken woman in her country, but her English was not perfect, and she occasionally used a word that didn't quite fit in the context of what she was discussing. I knew these guys had scheduled only a half-hour meeting, and they were starting to look bored. The accountants were there, along with the marketing team, the creative team, and, most important, the head of the company. He sat in the back like a mob boss, and I got the impression it would all come down to a yay or a nay from him.

I couldn't shake the feeling that things were deteriorating fast. Seeing no alternative, I jumped up and joined Paulina at the front of the room. She looked surprised, but not unpleased, by my bold move. When she came to a pause, I interjected, "Let me tell you how the songs are going to enhance Paulina's story line." I just ad-libbed from there, but I had definitely shifted the energy in the room. The producers were looking a bit more alive, so I continued talking about the fantastic and moving interplay between the script and the songs. I could see they were hanging on my every word, so I decided to wrap up by singing some of the lyrics from the show's main theme song.

The fat cat in the back stood up, and with a gleam in his eye began slowly clapping his hands. I knew that signaled two things. One, the meeting had ended. And two, we'd won them over. "With you two at the helm," he said, "this is going to be the next *Wicked*."

Taking their cue from their leader, the others all started talking at once, shaking our hands and slapping me on the back. The look on Paulina's face was priceless. Relief, excitement, and gratitude all rolled into one exquisite expression. I had saved the meeting, saved her show, and all-around saved her ass. And she knew it.

There was a flurry of paperwork, pen passing, and celebratory follow-up conversation with the production team before everyone filed out, leaving Paulina and I alone in the conference room. It quickly became apparent that Paulina's business demeanor had also left the building. She threw her arms around me and melted against my body in a hug of profuse gratitude and happiness. "You were amazing! Simply magnificent. How shall we celebrate?" she asked, her black eyes dancing with excitement, her now-familiar perfume filling my senses.

I had left my return travel plans open, and now it seemed like a celebratory meal with Paulina before heading home was the only appropriate thing to do. "We're going to find the best restaurant in town," I told her. "And then we'll—"

My planning was interrupted by a jingly tune from my cell phone. I glanced down and saw a FaceTime alert from Mary. A rush of guilt ran up my spine, and I instinctively stepped away from Paulina. She'd seen the screen and also stepped back, clearly annoyed by the interruption. My heart heavy, I swiped Mary's sweet face to ignore the call.

"Your wife?" asked Paulina. "Perhaps she can wait until we have finished our celebration."

"Sure. I guess so," I answered, my insides swirling. I tried to put my party face back on, but the moment was gone.

Another beep from my phone indicated a text. Sheepishly, I opened it. "Hi Daddy! I'm using Mommy's phone. I got an A on the math test!" A huge, involuntary smile took over my face. "It's my daughter! She got an A!" I exclaimed to Paulina, who didn't even try to feign enthusiasm. "You don't understand what a big deal that is," I told her. "Math is Heather's kryptonite!"

Paulina forced a dry smile. "If you need to leave . . ." Her voice trailed off, but her irritation was palpable.

"Just give me a second," I said, sensing that my opportunity to enjoy Paulina's intoxicating company a bit longer was now in jeopardy. I hastily texted a reply to Heather. "I'm so proud of you, sweetheart! I'm in a meeting now but I'll call you soon. Why don't you tell Mommy to take you to Chipotle to celebrate?" With feelings of intermingled remorse, guilt, and excitement, I stuffed my phone back in my pocket and held my arm out for Paulina.

"I'm all yours," I told her.

Paulina smiled triumphantly. When we reached the hotel lobby she leaned in close. "I have a room here," she said. "And I want to go there now to change my clothes for dinner." Her eyes locked on mine. Was she suggesting I go with her?

"I'll wait here in the lobby, then," I said.

She seemed amused. "Suit yourself," she replied, sauntering toward the elevator.

I sat on a bench and took some deep breaths. I didn't know how to reconcile what I was doing with the man I knew myself to be. The mission had been accomplished; the contract was signed. If I hopped on the next flight, I'd make it home in time to tuck the kids into bed. I'd already missed Eddie's game, but at least I could be there in person to congratulate Heather on her math test. In my heart, I heard James 4:17: "So whoever knows the right thing to do and fails to do it, for him it is sin."

I could explain it to Paulina. I could still do the right thing. I felt myself leaning toward goodness; leaning toward the impulse for right action that had served me so well all my life. I slid my phone out of my pocket and dialed Mary's number.

"Hi, Daddy!" Heather's bubbly voice filled my soul with sunshine.

"Hey, sweetheart! How's my math genius?"

"Can you believe it, Daddy? Me! I got the highest grade in the class!"

"I always knew you could do it," I told her, beaming with pride. "What have I always told you? You can do *anything*, my superstar girl!"

"Mom's making a special dinner tonight to celebrate. I wish you were here, Daddy! When are you coming home?"

I wanted to tell Heather I would be there just as quickly as I humanly could. I wanted to tell her I was rushing to the airport right then and there. But before I could form those words, the elevator doors opened. And what I saw knocked all reasoning out of me.

When Paulina said she wanted to change out of her business suit, I assumed she had packed a classy, casual cocktail dress. But nothing prepared me for the vision that now appeared before me.

From top to bottom, Paulina was scantily adorned in black leather. The soft, thin, sensuous leather wrapped her slender legs and barely draped over her uplifted breasts. Her back was entirely bare, and she arched it ever so slightly when she caught me staring. My eyes caressed her from head to toe, my body electrified.

"Daddy? Daddy, are you there?" Heather's sweet voiced bolted me back to our conversation. "When will you be home, Daddy? I miss you!"

"I'll be there soon, sweetheart," I heard myself saying. "Daddy's got a bit more work to do here, but I'll be home soon. I love you so much. Goodnight, big girl."

"Bye, Daddy," came the disappointed voice as I hurriedly closed my phone and stood to greet Paulina.

"Wow," I said, taking her in.

"You like?" she replied flirtatiously. "This is how you rock-and-rollers like your women, no?" She was clearly teasing me now, her eyes playful. She slid one finger down my arm and pointed toward Cut Lounge. "We start there," she said, sauntering toward the hotel bar without waiting for my reply. All I could do was follow her, trying to keep my eyes aimed at her stiletto-heeled Giorgio Armani boots, yet feeling my gaze slide involuntarily up her leather-clad legs to the gentle sway of her waist and sensuous curves of her bare back and cascading black hair.

Once we were seated on a couch in a semiprivate room in the far back of the lounge, Paulina ordered a bottle of Cristal champagne and a tin of her favorite Russian caviar, Prima Osetra. Scanning the options, I chose some chips with guacamole and a root beer. I was about to close the menu when I noticed Paulina's caviar was priced at $3,000. As if reading my mind, she handed the waiter a black AMEX Centurion Card. Staring deeply into my eyes, she said, "You are my guest tonight. My gratitude for what you did in that meeting is boundless. My debt to you never can be repaid."

Basking in her praise, I tried for a false air of nonchalance. "I didn't do much," I said. "You had already won them over with the script. I just stepped in to offer a few words about the music in case that might help." I was lying, and we both knew it. My articulation of the songs I was writing had totally stolen the show and clearly been the deciding factor for the producers.

"You are a very special man, Francis Rose," she said. "I am looking forward to discovering all the many more ways you are this special."

We clinked glasses, hers filled with sparkling champagne, mine with root beer, and I marveled once again at how different we were. Even with her attempt to dress like me, we were from completely opposite worlds, much like the star-crossed lovers in her play. Had I been her muse? Would I ever find the courage to ask her? Just the mere idea of that being the case sent ripples through me.

Glancing at the table, I laughed out loud at the juxtaposition of her caviar to my guacamole. "See that stuff right there?" I asked her, gesturing to the shimmering mound of iridescent, wet spheres. "That is you. And see this glob of green goop, and these salty, edgy, fried things here? That's me."

I searched her expression, hoping she understood the metaphor. She smiled, reaching slowly for one of my chips. She plunged it deeply into the juicy caviar, scooping a generous, glistening mound onto the pointed corner of the chip. Holding my gaze, she lifted it to my lips. Obediently, I opened my mouth, allowing her to place this metaphorical combination of the two of us onto my tongue. Her finger brushed my lip as she drew back her velvety hand. I savored the decadent, luscious taste sensation while Paulina watched my pleasure with delight. "You see?" she said. "I am right. We together make very, very fine team, no?"

As the line marking the champagne in Paulina's bottle moved steadily down toward the table and a cloud of intoxication began to surround her, I consciously focused on being a gentleman. I stood when she went to the restroom, tried to keep our conversation professional, filled her glass whenever it was empty, and fought down each impulse I had to touch her. I was surprised to learn that despite my internal uneasiness, I was able to project a casual and charming exterior.

Paulina seemed to have different ideas, however. She scooched closer to me on the couch, her thigh touching mine, and ran her slender fingers through my hair. "I know this hair," she whispered. "This is the thick blond hair of my story's hero. In my mind, I have touched it many times. You. Him. They are the same. Did you know?"

"I did see some similarity," I admitted, lost in the sensation of her fingers on my scalp. Slowly her hand circled down behind my ear and slid across my neck. She turned toward me then, her breast brushing my arm, her thigh wrapping over mine. I looked around the room, embarrassed about who might be watching. I wanted to stop her, but I was rendered helpless by the ecstasy of the moment. Her silky warm hand slid inside my shirt, unsnapping each snap on its way down to my navel. I looked into her dark eyes and watched her pupils enlarge as she took in my rigid chest and abs.

"This body is even more magnificent than it appeared in my private thoughts," she said, running her hands down my chest.

She stopped at my jeans, pulling on the button as if it were another snap. Her fingers dipped inside the low waistband, causing my ever mounting arousal to threaten the containment of my zippered fly.

Paulina seemed to like the fact that other patrons were enjoying the R-rated show we were putting on, as it inched toward becoming X-rated. My conscience screamed, *Resist,* but she took my open shirt with both hands and pulled me into a deep kiss, our tongues hungrily encircling each other. The room fell away, my life at home fell away, and it was as if we were the only two beings on the planet. Touching, kissing, we melded ever more deeply into each other.

Paulina slid off me and took my hand. "Come," she said, leading me out of the lounge. She led me to the elevator and as soon as the doors closed we fell immediately back into our embrace, her body pressing fiercely against mine, her hands on my lower back, pulling my waist up against hers.

We stumbled into Paulina's room, and she slid my already open shirt down my arms, tossing it to the floor. I kissed her urgently as her hands caressed my bare skin, working their way toward my waistband. The desire coursing through my veins was nearly unbearable. As Paulina tore open the zipper on my jeans, she moaned her delight in discovering I wasn't wearing underwear. I leaned my chin on her shoulder, my breath hard, my eyes adjusting to the dim light. A display of minibar offerings through the glass refrigerator door behind Paulina caught my eye: Bloody Mary Mix.

Mary.

Mary.

The word pierced my consciousness like an anvil. As if jolted awake from heavy sedation, I jerked back from Paulina.

"No."

It was the only word I could find.

I groped for the wall switch, flooding the room with the bright light I needed to snap me back to myself.

Paulina's tragically beautiful face was clouded with confusion. Her barely-there top had shifted, partially freeing her large left breast from its leather adornment.

"No," I repeated, zipping my jeans and scooping my shirt off the floor.

"Francis, please," Paulina began.

I held my hand up to stop her from saying anything further. "This is a mistake, Paulina," I said, with more conviction than I felt. "This has all been a terrible, terrible, terrible mistake."

"But Francis—"

I couldn't look at her as I fled the room, the booming sound of the slammed door reverberating down the hallway. I must have looked like a madman, my hands clasped in despair behind my head, tears running down my face as I repeatedly jammed the down button at the elevator. In the elevator, with my shirt still unbuttoned, I shook uncontrollably as I internalized the full impact of how close I'd come to destroying everything I loved and everything I stood for. My chest heaved in racking sobs.

CHAPTER 4

By the time I got to the airport, I was emotionally spent. All flights out that night were booked, so I bought a ticket for the first available flight late the next morning and hunched down uncomfortably in an airport chair for the night. It was better than I deserved. Paulina tried texting and calling, but I couldn't bring myself to answer. Again and again I replayed the events of the evening in my head. How could I have let myself be led so astray? Was I that desperate for love and attention?

I recalled how in the band's early years our manager, Stephanie, would often read Proverbs 7:1–5 to all the male band members: "My son, keep my words and store up my commands within you. Keep my commands and you will live; guard my teachings as the apple of your eye. Bind them on your fingers; write them on the tablet of your heart. Say to wisdom, 'You are my sister,' and to insight, 'You are my relative.' They will keep you from the adulterous woman, from the wayward woman with her seductive words." I realized that to make any sense of what had happened, I'd have to go back to the first letter from Paulina. That was truly when this downhill turn had begun. My mind was ablaze with the anguish of it all, and I tried my best to shut down my tormenting thoughts.

Throughout the night and during the flight home the next morning, I drifted uneasily in and out of tortured slumber. It felt like part of me had died; like I was walking through quicksand, half hoping it would swallow me up. How could I face my family? I was almost relieved to see that no one was home when I finally arrived later that afternoon.

Then I saw the note on the counter in Mary's lovely handwriting: "Can't wait to hear all about your meeting! We've gone a little early to the Down on the Ranch fundraising event. Come join us when you get in."

The rodeo benefit! That was today? With everything I'd had on my mind, I'd completely forgotten about Mary's annual charity event for kids with Down syndrome that she hosted at the Down on the Ranch facility. It was her favorite cause, and she had chaired many similar activities, all of which had raised significant funds for Down syndrome research and treatment. Mary knew from our experiences with Eddie that letting Down syndrome kids immerse themselves in an activity like horseback riding on a dude ranch can be hugely therapeutic.

Today's event would have a Lone Ranger theme, with more than 600 attendees expected, many of them high-profile community members. At $500 a ticket, and with Mary having gotten all the expenses underwritten through numerous sponsorships, the event was sure to be a huge success. I needed to be there to share the fruits of all Mary's hard work. I needed to be there for my family. Besides, I was one of the prizes.

It had been Mary's idea to offer me up as the grand prize in her live auction. The winner would have a private concert from Justus, followed by two of us cooking dinner in the winner's home. My kitchen skills were legendary, and so were Rikki's. I was sure that Mary hoped I would mingle with guests during the late afternoon to get the crowd pumped up for the silent and live auctions that evening. I had promised to perform an unplugged set of Justus's greatest hits, hoping that it would help Mary meet her target goal of $500,000, which would underwrite a one-week stay at the ranch for fifty Down syndrome kids and their families.

I pulled up to the ranch's rodeo corral, autographed my Uber driver's notebook, and set off to find my family amid the crowd of clowns, horses, and adorably dressed-up cowboys and cowgirls, with and without Down syndrome, all running around popping their tiny pistols at one another. The smell of the horses blended with the burning mesquite from campfires, the smell of Southwest barbeque, and all the dirt churned up in the air by enthusiastic little feet. I spotted Heather first.

She ran into my arms and I hugged her extra hard. For her, it had only been a day since we'd seen each other, but on my end, it felt like a lifetime. "I'm so proud of you for your math grade, sweetie," I told her. "And I'm sorry I wasn't here to celebrate it with you."

"That's okay, silly Daddy," she said, oblivious to my emotional pain. "Look, I'm a junior hostess!" She pointed proudly at her star-shaped badge. We walked together toward the big-top tent, passing sharpshooting and archery contests on our way. Mary had done an exceptional job, as always.

As one of the hayride trucks rode past us, I spotted Eddie. He was dressed half as Tonto and half as the Lone Ranger, tightly clutching his faithful companion, Rosey the purple octopus, by four tentacles. Mary sat behind him, her loving arms holding him in place for the ride. Balancing Eddie in one arm, Mary swung her camera around and snapped a picture. They both waved enthusiastically at me and Heather, but it was difficult to meet Mary's loving eyes. How, how, how, could I ever have been so foolish as to jeopardize my life with her?

I went through the day with a painted-on smile, doing all I could do to cover the anguished guilt I felt. Wherever I went, the big question floated out in front of me in a hazy blur. Should I confess my sins to Mary and seek her forgiveness, or was it kinder to shelter her from my inexplicable behavior? Both options fought furiously within me, each having an edge over the other at different times.

My mind wandered to the pastor I'd known back at Trinity Lutheran in Keeler—a kind, wise, old soul I had gone to many times for spiritual counsel. What would Pastor John tell me to do? As much as I hated to admit it, I felt like he would probably want me to be honest with Christ by being honest with my wife. I toyed briefly with the idea of calling him, but my shame ran too deep. I thought of Proverbs 3:5–6, which said, "Trust in the Lord with all your heart and lean not on your own understanding; in all your ways submit to him, and he will make your paths straight." I said a quick silent prayer to affirm my trust in Jesus to guide me and to somehow straighten this treacherous path I'd found myself on.

Mary had been so busy throughout the day that we'd barely spoken when it was time for my unplugged set to start. I always felt my best behind a microphone, but the heaviness in my heart refused to be lifted, even as I performed my original songs to a crowd of cheering fans. I'd saved one of our biggest hits, "Love

Never Fails," for the end of my performance, and the time had come for me to sing it. It was a fan favorite and one of our oldest songs. I'd written it in the early days of my relationship with Mary, and the lyrics could be applied to a love for Christ or to a pure romantic love relationship, depending upon one's perspective.

As I sang the lyrics taken from 1 Corinthians 13:4–8, my eyes rested on Mary in the back of the room cuddling Eddie. He squirmed in her lap in his half-Tonto, half-Lone Ranger getup as I sang, "I'll always love you near and far away. You alone occupy my heart, a love so deep I could never betray." It was too painful to look at Mary while I sang those lyrics. I'd written them for her. They described the devotion I felt for her—a devotion I'd callously almost thrown away.

I averted my eyes from Mary's loving gaze, panning the crowd to distract myself from the gravity and guilt of what I'd done. A woman with long silky black hair was swaying to the music; seeing that hair jolted me back to the bar lounge with Paulina, to the elevator, and to the hotel room. Frantically I searched for Mary again. I felt a tear roll down my face as the chorus came back around. "I'll always love you near and far away. You alone occupy my heart, a love so deep I could never be—"

The word *betray* was too much for me to utter, and my voice cracked as I tried to keep my fingers moving across the frets and the strings, hoping to distract the audience from my emotional collapse. I couldn't hold back the tears any longer, and they streamed freely down my face. As I panned the crowd through tear-blurred vision, many in the audience seemed to become emotional as well, assuming I was moved by the music and my love for Jesus.

I was officially living a double life.

I wiped my eyes and apologized to the audience while taking a quick bow and exiting to the roar of a standing ovation. Disgusted, I felt like a complete fraud.

Instead of going around the tent to join Mary after leaving the stage, I slipped out the back and headed for the stables. With the auction going on, no one was back there, and I needed a private place to try to regain my composure. I found a stool inside one of the stalls and straddled it, letting my head hang down in front of me. Staring into the pale blue eyes of the rodeo horse I'd barged in on, I sobbed, watching my tears disrupt the dry dirt until I had nothing left inside. The words from 1 John 1:9 kept circulating in my head: "If we confess our sins, He is faithful and just and will forgive us our sins and purify us from all unrighteousness." I looked up, wiping my eyes, and uttered, "I'm so, so sorry" to the horse standing before me, as if she were God Himself. She dropped her head and picked it up quickly, in tacit acceptance of my apology. I wanted desperately to go home, but I knew I had one more rodeo obligation to fulfill.

I ambled back to the tent, mustering the best fake cheerfulness I could summon. "Where have you been?" asked Mary. "You're up next!" She excitedly nudged me toward the stage for the grand finale of the live auction: me. I stood next to the auctioneer as he offered up the opportunity for one lucky bidder to win a private Justus concert followed by a home-cooked dinner with the band. Although my soul was crumbling, I tried with all my might to project a rock-star exterior. I wanted Mary to be proud.

The bidding started at $3,000 and jumped quickly by $1,000 increments. Some of the bidders were our friends, but there were several people I'd never seen before. A consistent bidder was

Mary's good friend Cindy, and she smiled and winked at me each time she raised her paddle. Cindy and Mary had seen each other through many milestones over the years, and it was now Mary's turn to take emotional care of her friend as she went through a painful divorce. I hoped Cindy would win, since Mary and I had been looking for ways to cheer her up.

The auctioneer's prattle sped up and slowed down in a steady rhythm until the bidding seemed to stall at $20,000. Mary hopped up and down in the back of the room, silently clapping to show me how excited she was that I'd earned her charity that amount. But just as the auctioneer was ready to bring down his gavel, Cindy leaped up from her seat, shouting, "Twenty-five thousand dollars!"

The crowd gasped at the substantial jump in price, and everyone turned to look at the other bidder, a dad with teenagers all sporting Justus T-shirts. They clasped their hands imploringly, but he just chuckled and shook his head in a gesture of defeat, giving a thumbs-up to Cindy.

"Sold! To the gorgeous blonde woman in the pink cowboy hat in the back of the room!" said the auctioneer as the losing teenagers groaned dramatically. "Hey, can I come with you?" he playfully added.

Cindy let out a little yelp as Mary ran to hug her. "He's all mine," she barked back at the auctioneer, shaking her head. The sight of my beautiful wife showering love on her girlfriend got me choked up again, and I discreetly left the stage.

For the next hour I made excruciating small talk with our friends and acquaintances while waiting for Mary to be finished with her obligations. I asked our neighbor Christina if she would take Eddie and Heather home. Her kids and our kids were friends, and she said she would gladly take Heather and Eddie to spend the night at her house, since all the kids were exhausted. I wanted to be alone with Mary for the drive home, although the thought of it filled me with dread.

Always more comfortable in the background than in the spotlight, Mary helped the waiters and busboys clear tables and remove the beautiful floral centerpieces, stopping only to give each of the Down syndrome families hugs and centerpieces as they departed. As the dishwashers, waiters, and cooks handed in their aprons and cowboy hats, Mary thanked them sincerely for the fine jobs they'd done, discreetly slipping each of them a small envelope containing a $50 bill, probably more than they'd each made working that night. I had helped her stuff them, so I knew that each envelope also contained a small card with a simple handwritten note from Mary that quoted John 3:16: "For God so loved the world that he gave his only begotten Son, that whosoever believes in him should not perish but have everlasting life." She'd added the line "God loves you!" to each note. Her goodness made my transgressions additionally painful in contrast, and I told her I'd meet her at the car.

Sitting in the passenger seat, I watched Mary through the windshield, reflecting on the passage from Matthew 25:40: "Truly, I tell you, whatever you did for one of the least of these brothers and sisters of mine, you did it for me." Mary was a shining example of demonstrating Christ's love to all people equally. And who was I? I was hiding out in the dark car, a pathetic example of a lyric from another Justus song taken from John 3:20: "Everyone who does evil hates the light and will not come into the light for fear that their deeds will be exposed."

I knew in that moment, as much as I wanted to avoid it, that I would have to confess my near sin to Mary. If I tried to keep it to myself it would eat me alive. I only hoped and prayed it wouldn't destroy her—or us.

Finally, my beloved Mary slid into the driver's seat, leaning over to give me a quick kiss before starting the car. She was exhausted, but I was even more so, having barely slept the night before. Besides, Mary knew I didn't like to drive, and she did. She began cheerfully recounting the night's events, thanking me for my beautiful performance and passing along the many compliments she'd heard about it. I couldn't focus on her words, though. I stared out the passenger window, flipped the air-conditioning on and off, and turned the radio volume up and down. Mary grew silent.

As I adjusted my seat for the third time, she turned to me and softly asked, "What happened when you were singing 'Love Never Fails'?"

She alone had seen through me. Everyone else thought I'd broken down simply because of the emotionality of the song, but Mary knew that although I was sensitive and compassionate, that was out of character for me.

"I wanted to talk to you about that," I began.

"Okay," she said tentatively, taking my hand.

"It's about Paulina, Mary. The woman I've been helping who wrote the musical."

Mary kept her focus on the road, but her face became strained. "I saw her picture online," she responded. "She's very attractive."

"Yeah," I said, slowly pulling my hand from hers as my words stuck in my throat. "I'm afraid our professional relationship grew into something forbidden, something I deeply regret. I was not a good husband to you last night, Mary."

Mary sat up straight in her seat. Her eyes filled with tears, but she fought them back, silently waiting for me to continue. The tension in the car was unbearable. "I never meant to hurt you," I gushed, the tears now flowing from both of us. "And I did not have sex with her, Mary. I didn't. I would never do that to you."

We both cried for a moment; Mary never dared to look in my direction. In a muffled voice she asked, "What, then? What do you mean by 'forbidden'? What is it you regret?"

"Do you really want me to tell you?" I asked.

"Did you touch her? Hold her hand? Did you kiss her? Did you go to her hotel room? What? What did you do?" Mary's voice was steadily rising in tone and urgency. She wasn't leveling accusations at me; she was asking the painful questions that had to be asked.

"I did. Yes. I kissed her and went to her hotel room."

Finally she jerked her head to look at me, the horror and disbelief on her face stabbing through my heart like a hot knife. Her eyes were wild, her soul visibly shattered. I had broken the most valuable thing in my life.

"No-o-o-o!" A deep tortured wail escaped Mary's throat.

I didn't realize she had veered off the road until I saw the enormous trunk of the Joshua tree collapse the driver's side of our front hood and smash against our windshield. I felt the rough airbag violently shove me against my seat as our Range Rover tumbled down the desert hillside, rolling over again and again, like clothes in a dryer, sending all the contents of the car and broken glass flying. The rearview mirror hit my head as it tumbled past me through the airbag dust.

"Please, God! Please, God, don't forsake us!" I begged.

One more sickening lurch, and the car came to a stop on the passenger side.

I saw my Mary suspended motionless in midair by the seat belt around her neck, blood dripping from her mouth and ear onto my left cheek, soaking the collar of my torn shirt.

Then everything went black.

CHAPTER 5

I watched anxiously as Mary's heart-rate monitor beeped in unison with the jagged image on the screen. Her breath was shallow, her lovely hands intertwined on her rising and falling stomach. Where her wedding ring had been for the past fifteen years, there was only a white tan line now. I couldn't escape the sickening cycle of emotional pain.

The physical pain was still strong despite all the medication I'd been given, and I barely recognized my reflection in the hospital room's mirrored cabinet. My right arm was in a sling, my head was wrapped in gauze, my face was covered in small bandages from the flying glass, and I knew the dried blood on my shirt collar was not mine. Oh, dear God. Isaiah 53:9 pierced my memory: "For your hands are stained with blood, your fingers with guilt."

Again I pleaded with God for a way to understand how I could have walked away with just a sprained arm and a slight concussion while my Mary had to be brought here unconscious in an ambulance, brought back to life after she had flatlined twice. She had come close to dying, with a punctured lung and multiple internal injuries. I was the one who deserved to suffer, not my innocent Mary. I winced, noticing the dried blood still in her ear and recalling the terrifying ambulance ride, when all I could do was hold her hand and pray as she labored to live.

Pastor Vance from Scottsdale Lutheran came as soon as I called him, and he softly uttered prayers on the other side of Mary's bed while holding hands with Catherine, Mary's mom, who had driven in from Flagstaff. Pacing the hall and crowding the small waiting area were Stephanie and all the members of Justus, along with Cindy and a few of Mary's other close friends, each taking their turns in the room with us as space allowed.

Stephanie waved me out into the hall. "Where are the kids?" she asked. "Do you need me to get them?"

"Thank you," I said, "but they're still with the neighbor who brought them home from the rodeo event. Christina is great with them, and her house is like a second home to Heather and Eddie."

"Well, I'm here if they need me," Stephanie replied. "We all are."

"I know," I said, getting choked up again. "Heather was so brave on the phone with me. She promised she'd take good care of Eddie, but I know she's a wreck inside."

Stephanie put her hand on my shoulder. "I know you'll be spending most of your time here with Mary, so let me pick things up for you. You know I drive right by your house on my way home, and I have the key you gave me, so it's no trouble at all. I want you to know you can lean on me."

"I do know that," I said. "I always have." I swiped at my wet eyes with the back of my hand and excused myself to be with my wife.

The room was particularly full when Pastor Vance guided us to all lay hands on Mary while silently praying together for her healing. We'd been ignoring the small TV in the corner, but the silence of our praying made the low volume now seem loud. We all looked up when we heard the reporter announce, "Christian rock sensation Francis Rose and his wife, Mary, were lucky to survive their one-car crash on East Camelback Road around midnight last night. The Range Rover they were traveling in is a total loss. Circumstances are being investigated."

Together we watched as the shaky news camera showed the mangled wreck of Mary's Range Rover being pulled by a winch onto the back of a flatbed tow truck. It was so demolished that not a single tire was able to rotate as it was dragged across the pavement while leaving fluids like a trail of blood behind it. After all the tumbles it had taken, it looked like it had just come out of a junkyard car cruncher. This was not the wrecked vehicle of survivors. That should have been a coffin, and it nearly was for Mary. We all stood mesmerized, mouths agape, comprehending the miracle that had occurred. It could so easily have gone another way.

"It's only a car," said Pastor Vance, soothingly. "You were protected by the Lord because it is not your time. Be comforted by 2 Corinthians 4:15, which states, 'All this is for your benefit, so that the grace that is reaching more and more people may cause thanksgiving to overflow to the glory of God.'"

We all paused to let the pastor's words sink in. The TV again mentioned my name, but before I could tune in to what the reporter was saying, my attention was diverted to Mary, who seemed to be regaining consciousness. I squeezed her hand. "Dad—Daddy?" she mumbled, her eyes still closed, her throat raspy.

Catherine rushed to the bedside to respond to her precious daughter's request. "Daddy's not here, Mary, but I am here and Francis is here, and lots of other people who love you." Mary's dad had been dead for less than a year, and it was clearly still a struggle for Catherine to talk about her deceased husband. This poor woman had long ago suffered the losses of two of her infant children; then, more recently, her husband. Mary was all she had left in the world.

The beeping from Mary's heart-rate monitor changed cadence as she mumbled incoherently, still asking for her dad. The doctor came in to clear out the crowd of nurses and visitors now gathered around the TV. I pleaded with him to let Catherine and me stay, and he reluctantly agreed. Catherine wept openly at Mary's repeated requests for her father, and each of us held one of Mary's hands.

Slowly Mary opened her eyes. Staring vacantly at me, she asked, "Daddy? Daddy, please help me." Then her eyes closed and she drifted back to sleep. Mary's father had been her rock, the one she'd have gone to with a broken heart. She must have been looking for him because I'd broken her heart and betrayed her trust. The thought was so painful that I was almost relieved when the doctor insisted we clear out for the night and let Mary get some rest.

I arrived at the hospital early the next morning and found Catherine already there. "How's she doing?" I asked. I'd barely slept, wracked with worry about Mary's condition. I couldn't imagine my life without her, my torment compounded by the thought of me being the cause.

Catherine and I had always been close, so I was surprised to sense a distinct coldness from her. She didn't smile or look at me when she responded, "She's doing well. She woke up a little while ago, but she's asleep again now."

"How long have you been here?" I asked.

"About an hour," Catherine replied tightly. Something was clearly bothering her.

My blood ran cold in my chest as the possibilities slowly dawned on me. If Catherine had been there for an hour and Mary had woken up, she'd have had plenty of time to tell Catherine the whole story of my betrayal. Catherine would now know that I was the cause not only of her daughter's heartbreak but of her life-threatening injuries as well. Catherine wouldn't look at me. I wanted to take the seat on the other side of Mary, to hold her other hand, but I knew I didn't deserve that position.

"Look, Catherine, I never—" I began. My voice cracked, and I realized I had no idea what to say. I wanted desperately to explain myself, but I knew there was no justification for what I had done. I pushed through my resistance and walked over to take my wife's hand. She was still my wife and I still adored her, and even if she never forgave me I knew I would love her as long as I lived.

"I'm disappointed in you, Francis. How could you?" said Catherine.

Tears streamed down my face. "I know. I'm so sorry. I'm so very, very sorry." They were the only words I could find.

"How dare you, Francis Rose?" Catherine jabbed me with a convicting look.

"I wasn't thinking clearly; I got carried away. I should have never—"

Catherine interrupted my painful apology, saying, "You knew how tired Mary was. She'd been working for days and nights on end to get that event planned and executed. How could you have let her drive? What were you thinking?" Catherine looked up, her eyes boring through me, full of accusation.

I blinked back tears, confused by her words. Her face and her accusing energy felt right, but her words didn't match. If all her anger was about the fact that I'd let Mary drive, then maybe, just maybe, she didn't know about the infidelity!

"You're right," I said, trying to pull myself together. "I never should have let Mary drive. I'd give anything to go back in time and change that."

Catherine's face softened. "I know you would, Francis," she said. "You're a good man. I just wish you'd been aware enough to not let Mary get behind that wheel."

Though overwhelmed with grief and devastation over my wife's condition, I felt a trickle of relief run through me as I realized Catherine didn't know. She'd called me a good man. She still thought I was the man her daughter had married. A good man. I'd give anything to believe that about myself again.

I had to ask. "Did Mary have much to say? When she was awake, I mean? What did you two talk about?"

"She wasn't very coherent," Catherine replied, "But Dr. Shapiro said that's to be expected. We didn't talk about anything, really. She seemed confused about where she was, so I told her the two of you had been in a car accident. She was awake for only a few moments before drifting off again, but the doctor said it was a good sign that she's ready to come back to full consciousness."

As if on cue, Mary started to stir. She opened her eyes and let them rest on my face. I was half expecting her to ask for her father again, so I was relieved when she mumbled my name: "Francis?"

The heart-rate monitor began beeping wildly, and I winced, only barely able to imagine the trauma Mary must be feeling as she started to remember our last conversation. Was she going to tell me to move out? Ask for a divorce? I couldn't hold back my tears as they dampened Mary's hospital bedsheets.

"Oh, Francis, look at you," she said weakly, struggling to speak, her beautiful eyes full of love. "What have I done to you?"

What? I couldn't imagine what she was talking about. Then I remembered the bandages, cuts, and bruises she was seeing on me for the first time, along with my arm in a sling. I slowly realized I was wrong about the cause of her distress. She wasn't upset *with* me; she was upset out of concern *for* me. Breathing heavily in her attempt to speak, she whispered, "Mom told me about the accident. I crashed the car. Francis, I'm so sorry. Are you okay?"

I inhaled deeply, blinking back my disbelief that she could be so gracious, so selfless, so *Mary*, at a time like this. "Sweetheart, I am fine. It's you we're all worried about. You have nothing to apologize for; this was all my fault." I wanted to continue but I was too choked up to find the words.

"Your fault? But I was driving. Of course it was my fault."

"Francis never should have let you get behind that wheel," Catherine interjected, full of motherly protection. I was just so relieved that this was the only accusation being hurled at me. Catherine was obviously as distraught over Mary's frail state as I was. She needed an outlet for her emotion, and I was it.

"Nonsense, Mom," murmured Mary. "Francis hates to drive, and he knows I'm always happy to do it." She turned toward me. "Darling, how was your meeting? Did you wear the new jacket and shoes I bought you? Did the producers sign off on the musical?" The effort of speech was draining her, and she closed her eyes.

The questions felt so terribly insignificant after everything that had happened, but I tried to wrap my mind around the direction in which Mary was taking the conversation. Was she just waiting until we were alone to level the bigger concern? She seemed so much her usual, kind, compassionate self. Was it the medication? The head injury?

"I did wear the new things you bought me, sweetheart, and the producers did sign off on the musical, but none of that is important right now." I squeezed Mary's hand and searched her face for some glimmer of acknowledgment of our situation, and maybe, God willing, even some glimmer of forgiveness.

"Oh, Francis, the kids! How are they? Are they worried? When can I see them?" Mary's countenance clouded over, and she became distressed. "I can't seem to remember my last conversation with them. I guess it was before I left to pick you up from the airport. I guess that's when we had the accident—coming back from the airport? Right? Tell me that's right. It's so strange that I can't remember."

Catherine and I exchanged glances. It was becoming apparent there was a gaping hole in Mary's recall of the events leading up to the crash.

"It was actually after the fundraiser, sweetheart," I told her, trembling at the realization that I might be prompting her to recall our conversation in the car.

"The Down at the Ranch fundraiser! I hope we can get at least $10,000 for your live auction offering, Francis. I need to go and pick up the centerpieces and get Heather's and Eddie's costumes ready. And all the name tags and the hayride trailer. And those Boy Scouts were going to monitor the fire pit; I need to call the Scoutmaster. How much longer will I be in the hospital? There's so much I still need to do for the fundraiser tomorrow!"

Mary's agitation was using up what little strength she had, and the heart-rate monitor acted up again. The nurse came in and told us Mary was jeopardizing her recovery and needed to get some rest. I asked him if I could speak with the doctor, and he jokingly said he'd be happy to arrange that in exchange for an autograph. I smiled wearily. I wasn't in the mood for fans, but this guy was taking exceptional care of my wife, so I honored his request and took down his address, promising to send him some CDs when I got home.

My conversation with the doctor was sobering. After leaving no stone unturned in discussing Mary's fragile medical condition, I moved on to the more delicate question about her apparent memory loss, describing the unusual exchange we'd had.

"Doc, what's going on here?" I asked.

"Mary nearly died and has a brain injury, among her many other injuries," began Dr. Shapiro. "Fortunately, it's not TBI—traumatic brain injury—but it might be causing a type of amnesia called dissociative or psychogenic amnesia. It stems from emotional shock or trauma, such as being the victim of a violent crime or other deep shock to the emotional system."

Dr. Shapiro paused just long enough to glance at me with what I perceived to be a glare of accusation.

"It seems she's only lost about a day of memory," I told him. "Are you saying this is a onetime thing, and her memory will be fine in the future? Will the lost memories ever return?" I tried to ask these questions objectively and not as though they determined the fate of my marriage. A part of me wanted to confess the whole situation to this doctor, a stranger, but I couldn't bear the thought of his condemnation.

"Aside from the accident, did your wife suffer any emotional trauma recently, Mr. Rose?" he asked dispassionately.

Frozen by his direct question, I stalled as long as I could before responding. "She took the death of her dad very hard. But that was almost a year ago. She was asking for him when she started to regain consciousness."

"It's unlikely to occur from a trauma that old," said Dr. Shapiro, "It must be from the trauma of the crash." I couldn't help but think that this doctor saw right through me and knew I was covering up the other blow my Mary had endured. He started to walk away.

"Doc," I said, reaching for his arm. "Is there any chance that at some point in the near future she'll regain the lost memories?"

His eyes bore through me. "There's a fifty-fifty chance."

As I watched Dr. Shapiro disappear down the sterile hallway, I buried my face in my hands and attempted to get my bearings. The options swirling around in my brain made me weak in the knees, so I found a bench in the waiting room where I could sit and process all that had happened. In the event that Mary did not remember my confession, was I obligated to confess again? Was I really doing it for Mary or just to relieve my own unbearable shame? Did I just want to clear my conscience by eliciting forgiveness from her—a forgiveness I knew I didn't deserve?

Telling her of my indiscretion had nearly gotten both of us killed. In hindsight, I realized that I had not chosen the best circumstances for revealing my betrayal. But would there ever be good circumstances? No matter when or how I did it, it would mean emotionally destroying the person I loved most in the world. It was agonizing to think of going through that again. Had the Lord offered me a gift, a merciful blessing and show of His grace? Was I being given a second chance to get this right? Sitting there, I pulled up my Bible app and found 1 Peter 4:10: "As each has received a gift, use it to serve one another, as good stewards of God's varied grace."

I decided I would not burden my angelic wife with my sins. I could handle this on my own. It was a onetime, horrible lapse in judgment, and I would *never* allow anything like it to happen again. If the memory returned to her, I'd deal with it then. I knew I'd carry the weight of my shame for all of eternity, but at least I wouldn't intentionally make Mary suffer with me. She was far too good for that. She was an angel—my own guardian angel sent to me by God.

CHAPTER 6

The day Mary was well enough to come home was one of the happiest days of my life. I had been by her side nearly around the clock at the hospital and the rehab facility, praying, loving, and holding faith like I'd never done before. The fact that she'd come through the most difficult parts of her recovery from her punctured lung and brain injury, and was able to resume life at home with me, felt like the best answer to a prayer I'd ever received. I was still having trouble processing the fact that her heart had stopped—twice.

"Stop staring at me like that, Francis," she teased, as I draped a light quilt over her on the sofa. "You're freaking me out." Her playful smile was the most beautiful thing.

"I can't help it," I told her. "I'm just so excited to have you home. You have no idea how empty this house feels when you're not here."

"Well I'm here now," she said, squeezing my hand. "And I can't thank you enough for all you handled while I was out of commission. Look at this place! It's spotless! And the kids have been fed and getting to school every day. You've even kept up with my room-mom obligations! Maybe I should crash the car more often.

You can take that big *S* for Super Husband off your chest now."

"Never," I said, returning her beaming smile with my own. "The doctor said you have to take it easy until that lung fully heals and you stop having such intense headaches, and I'm going to make sure that happens. Can I bring you some more tea?"

"What's giving me a headache is you waiting on me!" Mary laughed, enjoying my doting even as she protested it. Taking in her natural beauty, I thought of Galatians 5:22–23, which she exemplified so well: "But the fruit of the Spirit is love, joy, peace, patience, kindness, goodness, faithfulness, gentleness, and self-control. Against such things there is no law."

"What would you like me to cook for the PTA meeting here next week?" I asked her. "The RSVPs are in, and almost everyone can make it. I think most of them are just anxious to see you again."

"I could always make my baked ziti, but in this case I trust you to come up with a menu. I know whatever you make will be fabulous, but you know how much the ladies love your croquettes."

"Speaking of cooking," I said, strapping on Mary's favorite apron, "I have a surprise for you tonight. All your favorites for your homecoming dinner."

Mary shook her head and laughed as I retreated to the kitchen to begin preparing her feast, and I realized how much I'd been craving the sound of her laughter.

Mary's apron featured two fish and five loaves and the words "I, too, feed thousands. Just not all at once!"—a reference to Luke 9:16. It was so appropriate, not only because of the charity work we did but because of our household as well. Even though I was the one with the mad cooking skills, Mary had always prepared most of our meals so I could be freed up to concentrate on Justus.

I was committed now to reversing those roles. I needed to make sure that all of Mary's energy went toward her healing. I passed my hand over the apron's fishes and loaves, appreciating the fact that I was here.

As I pulled spices down from the cabinet, I felt my phone buzz in my pocket. It was Paulina again. I had ignored all her texts, e-mails, and phone messages while Mary was recovering, but they were becoming increasingly urgent and I knew it was time for me to man up and face that situation. I had never before failed to uphold my end of a business agreement, but after I'd made such a mess of things, I didn't trust myself to know how to keep my interactions with Paulina strictly business. During Mary's hospitalization, I was simply too fragile and preoccupied to deal with her, but now that I had Mary home, my emotional strength had returned. I vowed to call Paulina at the first opportunity.

The opportunity arrived later that night after I'd drawn a bubble bath for Mary and tucked the kids into bed. I'd been dreading the moment, but it was time to take my man-pill and do what had to be done. For strength, I opened my Bible to Ephesians 6:10–12: "Finally, be strong in the Lord and in his mighty power. Put on the full armor of God so that you can take your stand against the devil's schemes. For our struggle is not against flesh and blood but against the rulers, against the authorities, against the powers of this dark world, and against the spiritual forces of evil in the heavenly realms." Resolute, I stepped out onto our back patio and dialed Paulina's number. She answered on the first ring.

"Francis!" she exclaimed. "How could you avoid me like this? I thought I'd never get through to you! After all you promised me, and all the specialness that took place between us! Please tell me you just were busy with your band. When we're working together, you must do a better job of communicating with me, yes?"

The sound of her voice sent electricity through my veins, reminding me of how it felt to be in her presence, her image flooding my senses. I felt weak, so I took a moment to sit down and steady my resolve. Mentally I went back to Ephesians 6:14 for strength: "Stand firm then, with the belt of truth buckled around your waist, with the breastplate of righteousness in place."

"Paulina," I began. "You have every reason to be angry with me. I should have been in communication with you sooner. Mary and I were in a terrible car accident, and Mary was nearly killed—"

"Francis, no! Are you okay? Please tell me nothing has happened that will prevent you from finishing our project together! Are you hurt?"

"I was. But I'm all right now. And that's not even really the point. The truth is I simply did not have the emotional strength to speak with you until now."

"I've missed you, too, Francis," Paulina cooed, her voice oozing sex appeal.

Even with the breastplate of righteousness protecting me, the sound of Paulina's voice was like a needle that found the tiniest chinks in the armor of God. She needed me, and those small openings in the armor were making me want to help her. I had never been able to resist being a savior, even when I shouldn't be.

I shook my head violently, bringing myself back to my senses.

"No! That's not what I'm saying! Paulina, our romantic involvement was a mistake. A terrible mistake—the worst of my life—and one I will never, ever make again. I'm sorry to have gone down that path with you, and I'm sorry to have to end my involvement with your work as well, but I simply can't have this in my life right now."

There was a long pause before Paulina replied, "You signed a contract, Francis." The sudden chill in her voice startled me. She was all business now.

"I delivered half the songs you wanted. I'm sorry, Paulina, but that's all you're going to get out of me. My interactions with you nearly caused my whole life to implode. I could easily have lost my marriage, and even lost my life! I won't take that chance again. You can rip up our contract and keep my share of the proceeds from the musical. I know I didn't completely fulfill my end of the bargain, so I forfeit my rights to any payment. Consider the songs I've already written a gift. But this all must stop here. There's nothing in the world that could make me risk my marriage again. This is our last conversation."

"But Francis! We're so good together! We could make such beautiful work and memories!"

"Goodbye, Paulina." I was shaking as I pushed the button to end the call. I hated the way my body had responded to her voice, to the memory of her. It was as if my body were betraying my soul—the soul I had vowed would belong to Mary for all eternity.

My phone buzzed in my hand. A tremendous part of me longed to answer her call, hear her voice once more, and assure her that I would make everything all right for her. I resisted, and eventually the call went to voice mail. I knew what had to be done. I opened my contacts file to block Paulina's number. But even as my finger hovered above the button, I hesitated. Why was this so damn hard? I barely knew this woman, and I wished that she had never even entered my life! But the reality was that she had. And I would never be able to erase the memories and the feelings she had stirred in me.

Her number, though, I could erase. I allowed my finger to fall on the button that removed Paulina from my phone forever. If only it were that easy to remove her from my mind.

During the days after my final call with Paulina, I felt a lightness I hadn't experienced in months. I'd always been a believer that we're given a certain amount of energy to use each day, and it felt so good to once again be devoting all of that energy to my family and to Justus. I delegated most of the band's responsibilities to Stephanie, canceling several gigs to make sure I was available to nurse my precious wife back to health. Although the majority of my time was spent caring for Mary, the kids, and our household, I was walking on clouds.

There was just one recurring snag that repeatedly dragged me down to despair. Mary was regaining glimpses of her memory. She would suddenly clap her hands and excitedly report that she remembered what Eddie had worn to the rodeo or an interaction he'd had with one of the horses. Each time she remembered some snippet of the day she had lost, I froze in panic. And those occurrences were now happening with more frequency.

If her memories were coming back, how long would it be until she remembered our car ride?

The memories she regained all seemed to be happy ones, though, and she was generally in good spirits in spite of the considerable pain she was still suffering. She never complained, even when I made her coffee too strong, emptied the dishwasher when the silverware still had food stuck on it, or washed the white clothes with the reds, resulting in a lot of new pink clothing for us all. No matter how much I messed things up, Mary showered me with gratitude and love.

One day, after I had mindlessly packed an unopened can of tuna with two pieces of plain bread for Heather's lunch and had also picked Eddie up from school without noticing that he'd left his shoes, socks, and backpack there, Mary sat me down for a talk. I thought she was going to point out all the mistakes I'd been making, but I should have known better than to expect that from Mary.

"Francis, I can't tell you how much all this effort means to me. But you don't have to take on so much. I think you're trying to show God how grateful you are that our lives were spared, but God doesn't need you to do that." She opened the Bible and read to me from Ephesians 2:8–9: "For by grace you have been saved through faith. And this is not your own doing: it is the gift of God, not a result of works, so that no one may boast."

Mary then turned to another page she'd earmarked and read Titus 3:5: "'He saved us, not because of works done by us in righteousness, but according to His own mercy, by the washing of regeneration and renewal of the Holy Spirit.' See, Francis? God saved us according to His own mercy. You don't have to do anything to deserve it. You're trying too hard, darling. Relax."

She laid her hands on my heart, then wrapped them gently around my neck. "I love you just the way you've always been, and so does God."

Tears welled in my eyes. Even without knowing my secret, Mary had tapped into a part of me that I had failed to recognize on my own. She was right about me overcompensating; she just didn't know what it was I was overcompensating *for*. It hit me that everything I'd been doing was an attempt to relieve my guilt and shame. I'd been subconsciously thinking my good deeds would wash away my sins, but all my shallow prayers and efforts were doing little to ease my emotional pain, especially as I watched Mary still suffering with her physical pain and the pain of losing the memory of a day of her life.

I decided the best way to seal my closure with Paulina would be to reach out to Pastor John from Trinity Lutheran back in Keeler, Indiana. He had always been my rock as a spiritual advisor. That night I sent him a text. "Pastor John, it's me, Francis. I know it's been a while, but I could sure use your ear and some of your guidance right about now. Can we talk sometime soon?"

The reply text came immediately, just as I knew it would. "Francis, I am always here for you. I will call you this week." I breathed a deep sigh of relief. Slowly but surely I was becoming me again.

I'd been refusing all offers of help from Catherine, Cindy, Stephanie, and pretty much everyone else we knew, but they were having none of it. They all began stopping by with food, offers to pick up the kids, and healing advice for Mary. Stephanie was the only one who noticed something different about me.

"What's up with you, Francis?" she asked, cornering me in the yard as I walked her out to her car. I shrugged, avoiding eye contact, but she pressed on. "I know you've been under a lot of stress, but I get the feeling something is going on that you're not telling me."

"Nope," I said, looking down. "It's just a lot to deal with, you know? The accident, Mary suffering so much." I hoped I sounded more convincing than I felt.

"Okay," she said. "I'm here. Whatever it is, you can always talk to me about it, okay? But remember, Luke 8:17 states: 'For there is nothing hidden that will not be disclosed, and nothing concealed that will not be known or brought out into the open.' I'm here for you, Mister."

I nodded nervously, giving Stephanie a quick uneasy hug and opening her car door for her. Sometimes it was hardest to be around the people who knew me best.

On the day of the PTA meeting, Mary said, "Francis, when you told me about the rodeo, did you mention anything about a hayride? I just had a flash of a memory where I was holding Eddie on a hayride. We waved to you and Heather, but you looked distraught. Am I dreaming that up, or did it really happen?"

I gulped back my panic, terrified she had remembered the part I wanted to stay forever forgotten. I was growing weary of this recurring terror.

"Yep! You and Eddie did wave to me and Heather from your hayride," I told her with forced casualness. "And I don't think I had mentioned that to you. It's great that you remember." Could she detect the fear in my voice?

"But the most wonderful thing is your live auction result!" she cheerfully replied. "I just wish I could recall your unplugged performance that night. I'm sure you were amazing. And I'm so glad Cindy won the auction. I spoke with her yesterday, and she said she would be happy to come help you set up for the meeting today, if you'd like."

"That's kind of her, but I think I'll have plenty of help. Since it's an after-school meeting, Heather is anxious to play waitress, and of course Delia will be here to help me in the kitchen." Delia was our part-time housekeeper, and she was always willing to lend a hand with the cooking.

"I wish you would let me *do something*!" Mary said, for the hundredth time.

"You are doing the only thing you should be doing," I said, kissing her forehead. "Healing. Now what can I do for you?"

Mary laughed. "What you can do for me is stop doing things for me. I mean, you've always been a helpful husband, but Francis, this is crazy. I feel like royalty."

"That, my love, is precisely how I want you to feel."

"Mommy is the queen!" said Heather, bouncing into the room in her waitress costume and snuggling up to Mary on the sofa. "And I'm the princess!"

"Yes, you are," I said, going in for a tickle. "Daddy's princess forever!"

"And I'm the Lion King!" said Eddie, adorably chiming in with his favorite movie character role. "Roar!" He circled his paws in the air, with Rosey the octopus dangling by four tentacles.

After Delia and I had done some cooking and last-minute cleaning, the ladies began arriving for the PTA meeting. They all fussed over Mary, expressing their love, friendship, and gratitude that she was home and doing so well. Mary, naturally, gave all the credit to me for organizing the meeting, printing the agenda, and handling all the details.

Cindy found me in the kitchen and said, "There's the husband of the year!" She held her arms out to hug me, but my hands were covered in egg-soaked bread crumbs, so I raised my arms in a goofy hug-surrendering gesture. Cindy seemed taller than usual as she leaned against me for what seemed like an awkwardly long embrace. I chalked it up to her gratitude for all I was doing for Mary, and as I pulled away I noticed she was teetering on four-inch heels. Her skirt was shorter than usual, too, and her neckline more plunging. I guessed this must be part of her new divorcée transformation.

I stuck my hands back into my bowl of breading as Cindy whisked her platinum-blonde hair out of her azure blue eyes and said, "You are such a marvel, Francis. What would that lucky Mary do without you? I can't believe you put this whole meeting together yourself."

"I am but her humble servant," I teased. "And grateful for the position."

"She's the one who should be grateful," Cindy wistfully replied.

I felt bad talking about our happy marriage when Cindy's had just fallen apart. "How are you doing?" I asked her, lowering my voice to show my concern.

"Some days are better than others," she said. "Mary's been wonderful. But maybe you and I could talk sometime, Francis. You have such wisdom about these things."

I immediately felt that tiny stab of panic that overcame me whenever I feared anyone might know my secret. What did Cindy mean by "these things"? Did she mean I had experience with a troubled marriage? Nah, that had to just be my mind running wild. I stared blankly at her, unsure how to respond.

"You seem to have a spiritual answer for every problem," she continued. "Your lyrics are so uplifting, and you're so full of positivity and hope. I guess it just feels good to be around you. You are such a blessing."

I smiled sheepishly. Cindy didn't know my secret. She just thought of me as a source of spiritual comfort and solace to someone going through a rough time.

"I'd be honored," I told her. "But first, the croquettes!"

Cindy and Delia helped me finish the food prep and keep waitress Heather's tray full as she proudly made her way through the crowd to serve hot hors d'oeuvres. The PTA ladies raved about the spread I'd laid out for them. I kept their plates and wineglasses filled until a few of them switched to coffee, and then I kept their coffee cups filled. It really did feel good to be of service to these women on Mary's behalf.

The PTA agenda was well underway when my phone rang, and I glanced to see that it was Pastor John. It wasn't the best timing for our call, but I didn't want to miss the opportunity to speak with him, so I told Cindy she was in charge of hosting while I excused myself to our den. I closed the door and answered my phone.

"Pastor, thank you so much for your time."

"Of course, Francis. I always have time for you. It's good to hear your voice in person—that beautiful voice I listen to so often on your albums."

"Wow, that means a lot to me," I replied. "It's great to hear your voice as well. I've been wanting to talk to you about something but hesitating to call."

"Tell me everything, my son. That's what I'm here for."

I took a deep breath and began pouring my heart out to this warm, compassionate man who had taught me what it meant to be a Christian. He listened intently, never judgmental and never condemning as I confessed every detail of my encounter with Paulina. When I had finished my story and assured him that I had suffered greatly and would never let anything similar happen again, Pastor John said, "I'm glad to hear that, Francis, because you did violate one of the Ten Commandments."

"No! No, I didn't commit adultery, Pastor!"

"That's not the one I'm talking about. What about the Tenth Commandment, 'Thou shalt not covet'?"

My face flushed hot with shame. I knew he was right and there was no point in trying to defend myself.

"Francis, is there something in your marriage that could have caused you to behave in this manner? Sometimes the faithful spouse may be doing something that leads to unfaithful behavior in the other. I can't imagine this from Mary, but I have to ask."

I took a deep breath. "I love Mary," I replied, "but it's not like it was in the beginning. You remember how we were fifteen years ago, right, Pastor? Mary sacrificed so much for me during the lean years of Justus, and we never would have reached this level of success without her tireless support. But so much has happened since then."

"What kinds of things have happened?"

"Mary's so wrapped up in Eddie and his condition, Pastor. I don't know if you know or remember, but Mary was the only child of her parents to survive. Her older sister, whom Mary insisted we name Heather after, died two days after birth, and the younger one was stillborn. That's why Mary's so close to her mom, why she's such a loving person, and also why she's so overprotective. I know she learned her hypersensitivity to the fragility of life from her own upbringing. I understand it and think it's a beautiful characteristic. I do. Her loving nature is what drew me to her, especially since it was in such stark contrast to my own mother's nature."

"Francis, you know it's not an uncommon occurrence for a man who grew up without sufficient maternal love to subconsciously seek women to fill that void. It happens almost involuntarily, kind of like a moon in the strong gravitational pull of a larger planet," said Pastor John.

"And for years, Mary filled that void," I agreed. "But it feels like she hasn't had as much time or energy for me since Eddie's condition has evolved. I hate to complain, because she's made so many personal sacrifices to raise our family. She'd been modeling since she was a kid and always loved it, but she had to give that up. I know she's a great mom, and I should be more focused on that. I often feel so bad about thinking that Mary doesn't pay attention to me like she used to, or that Eddie takes too much of her time, but Pastor, that's how I feel sometimes. But with me and the band—we've really hit it big now, you know? We're selling out arenas everywhere, and we've sold more than a million copies of the last album."

"It sounds like you may be forgetting to whom the credit for your success belongs, Francis," interjected Pastor John gently.

"Oh, yeah, of course I meant that we've done all this by the grace of God," I said. "But it just feels like ever since Justus made it into the big league, things haven't been the same between—"

I stopped midsentence because I suddenly heard a small, stifled cough just outside the den door. The light coming through the bottom of the door frame revealed the shadow of feet. Was someone standing outside the door listening?

"Please hold on for a second, Pastor," I said, stepping toward the door.

When I was a few feet away from opening it, I saw the shadow move and heard the quick shuffle of steps down the hallway. I threw open the door, but no one was there in either direction. Looking down the hall, I caught a glimpse of a disappearing silhouette reflected from the glass of Mary's framed photography that lined the hallway walls.

Rattled, I returned to my phone call, but I couldn't concentrate on Pastor John's kind words of wisdom. Someone had been listening. What if it was Mary, or—just as bad—Heather? It suddenly seemed that taking Pastor John's call during the PTA meeting had not been such a good idea. How much had the person heard? How long had someone been standing there?

I hastily thanked Pastor John for his time and returned to the gathering, searching every face for clues. Had it been Delia? If so, would she tell Mary? Heck, every person in the house was a dear friend of my wife's! Now at least one of them knew that I was not what he, she, or the world thought I was. And I had no way of knowing who it was.

As the wine flowed, the PTA meeting turned into a social event that lasted well into the evening, giving me plenty of time to converse with every guest in the hope of gaining some sort of a hunch. To my great relief—and also confusion—no one treated me any differently than they'd been treating me before the phone call with Pastor John. I was especially relieved to find that this was the case with Heather, as she happily scurried around the house picking up empty glasses and plates. When the last of the guests finally exited our home, I sat next to Mary, desperate to be sure she had not been the one listening.

"How are you feeling, sweetheart?" I asked her.

"A little worn out," she admitted, "but happy. I don't know how I'll ever repay you for all this, my darling Francis."

I took her in my arms, thanking God that she still felt that way about me. Although she easily could have walked to our bedroom, I picked her up and carried her there. "Get some rest while I clean up," I told her. "I'll be back to check on you in a bit."

"We'll put Mommy to bed!" said Eddie, running up behind us wearing Mary's fishes-and-loaves apron, which was dragging across the floor, with his sister at his heels and Rosey the octopus clutched in his hand.

They crawled into bed on either side of Mary, creating the most perfect, blessed snapshot I could ever behold.

"I wanted Mommy to get some rest," I told them, but Mary interrupted.

"This is just the tucking in I need!" she said, weary but delighted to have an arm around each of her cherubs.

I washed the dishes, cleaned up all the party mess, and returned to find two sleeping angels flocking my beautiful wife. She beamed lovingly as I lifted them, one by one, and carried them to their beds.

When I came back to our bedroom, Mary was waiting for me in a sheer white Fleur du Mal negligee she hadn't worn in years. She smiled seductively, sensing my enthusiastic approval.

"Are you sure?" I asked, taking her gently into my arms. "The doctor said to avoid any strenuous activity for at least a month."

"I guess I'll have to leave the strenuous parts to you, then," she teased.

I stood up just long enough to get my clothes off, then returned to her warm embrace. She felt amazing in my arms, and my fervent desire for her became immediately apparent. As much as I had longed to be intimate with her, I'd been waiting for her to signal me, not wanting to rush anything too soon.

"Are you sure we aren't disobeying doctor's orders?" I asked.

"I promise," she said, melting into my chest.

We kissed deeply with the passionate tenderness of lovers long denied to each other, both of us lost in our mutual arousal, hands caressing backs, breasts, thighs, crevices, and more. Mary's sweet breath skimmed my face as she whispered, "I want you, Francis. I want all of you, now."

We united our flesh in pure ecstasy, both crying out in pleasure, our bodies blending as our souls had blended so long ago, timeless and forever more. We were one. Again and again throughout the night, we moved together, seamlessly, erotically, and ardently conjoined, until each of us was spent.

I drifted off to blissful slumber, realizing that whether I deserved it or not, I had my life back.

CHAPTER 7

"You guys were on fire!" Stephanie shouted as we all filed into our backstage changing area. Justus had never had such a successful tour, and we were all exhausted, sweaty, and happily basking in the adulation we'd just received from 20,000 screaming fans. It was the final performance of our Resurrection Tour, which we'd made every year since the inception of Justus during the forty days of Lent, culminating on Easter Sunday. I thought back to the first Resurrection performance, on Easter Sunday in 2000. There were fewer than thirty guests in the tiny sanctuary of Trinity Lutheran in Keeler, Indiana. Boy, had we come a long way!

We'd just wrapped up this year's tour with a sold-out show at Ak-Chin Pavilion in Arizona. Even though Rikki and Tracy were the only Catholics among us (I'd long ago abandoned my Catholic roots for the Lutheran Church), we'd always performed living Stations of the Cross for our Lenten concerts—something Christian music crowds had never experienced before, and they ate it up.

Rikki tossed me a wet cloth, and I gratefully ran it over my face and neck. The adrenaline of the stage was still coursing through me, and I paced the room, slapping my bandmates' backs and congratulating everyone on a phenomenal performance.

The dressing room door burst open, and Eddie and Heather ran into my arms, with Mary and Cindy following close behind. Everyone's spirits were notably high as we all hugged and celebrated.

"Give us a few minutes to get cleaned up and change clothes," I told them, "and I'm taking everyone out to Easter dinner at the Sanctuary!" Just hearing myself say those words brought me to a place of sincere gratitude. I remembered that after our first Easter show to those thirty fans, the band shared Easter dinner at the Waffle House. We'd gone there because the owner was a member of Trinity and had put a 15 percent off coupon in the collection basket, directing the usher to give it to our struggling band!

It had become a tradition. Every year, after the last concert of the Resurrection Tour, no matter how big or small it had been, all the band members and their families shared the Easter dinner meal, and this year we were celebrating in a far more luxurious place than Waffle House. Before long, Mary, the kids, and I found ourselves in Cindy's new Maserati as she drove us all to meet up with the others.

The Sanctuary was on Camelback Mountain, and as Cindy turned onto East Camelback Road, I realized it was the first time we'd been on this highway since our accident. I became increasingly uncomfortable as we got closer and closer to the spot where Mary had tumbled our Land Rover down the hillside.

"We were so lucky," I said. "It wasn't that long ago that our lives were spared on this highway. Let's take a moment to thank our Lord for His mercy."

Mary was sitting up front with Cindy, and I was in the backseat with the kids. With the exception of Cindy, who was driving, we all bowed our heads and fell deep into thanksgiving. "Heavenly Father, with a grateful and cheerful heart, we humbly thank You for the favor You showed to me and Mary in sparing—"

But before I could utter another word, just as we approached the exact curve of the road where the accident had taken place, my prayer was broken by a shrill cry from Mary.

"No-o-o-o!" she screamed, yanking us all out of our private reveries.

"What is it, sweetheart?" I urgently asked, leaning forward to rest my hands on her shoulders.

"Did you see it? Did you see her?" Mary's eyes were wild, and the terror in her voice shook me to my core.

"See what?" I asked.

Eddie started to whimper in the seat beside me, squeezing Rosey's four purple tentacles. Heather reached over my lap to hold his little hand.

"That woman standing in the middle of the road! With the long black hair, in the tight, black clothes!" Mary buried her face in her hands and sobbed. "I mean, I don't think anyone was actually there. My eyes were closed. But I saw her. Just for a second. I saw her, and I felt like Cindy was about to hit her. Oh, Francis, I know I'm not making any sense. I just—I just felt like I saw something . . ." Mary's voice trailed off as she realized how much she was frightening the kids. She shook her head as if clearing out cobwebs. "It—it was nothing, I guess. It just startled me. I'm okay."

Despite her words, Mary seemed far from okay. She repositioned herself to face forward in her seat so the children wouldn't see the tears still streaming down her cheeks. She dabbed at them with the sleeve of her sweater, offering me a weak smile as if to say, "I don't know what that was, but I will get control of myself now for the children."

"Who was the lady, Mommy?" came Heather's small voice.

"There was no lady, sweetheart," said Mary. "It was just Mommy's imagination—though I do feel like it was someone I've seen before."

Cindy put her hand over Mary's to comfort her. "I have never seen the calm and composed Mary Rose lose control like that!" she said. "Are you going to be all right?"

"Yes. Yes, of course," said Mary, still visibly shaking. "Let's go have dinner and celebrate that Christ has risen." Since it was clear that Mary didn't want any more attention on her, we shifted the conversation to other things until we arrived at the Sanctuary. I tried to appear as natural as possible, but inside I was reeling.

The woman Mary had described was Paulina. She'd had a vision of Paulina in the middle of the road. The intensity with which she had screamed no was unmistakable; it was the same shrill no she had uttered before we crashed a few months earlier. And now that she remembered that much, how long would it be until the rest of the memory revealed itself to her?

At dinner I immediately ordered wine and champagne for the table and poured Mary a glass to help calm her nerves. Stephanie and the other band members were still pumped up from the show, and lots of toasts were made to the sold-out Resurrection Tour. My own high had been deflated, however. All I could think about was Mary's vision and what might come of it.

How long would this indiscretion haunt me? It had been nearly three months since the accident, and I had gotten comfortable believing that I could put it all behind us. The reignited stress of being found out was almost enough to make me want to confess everything all over again. I knew I wouldn't do it, but I was desperate for relief from the nagging guilt.

"Now that the tour is wrapped up," said Cindy, "I guess your next gig will be at my place!"

"That's right," said Mary. "It's time for Francis and Rikki to make good on that auction promise to cook you an amazing meal. Then you'll get your private Justus performance."

"I've been counting the days!" said Cindy, who was sitting to my left. "It's all I can think about." She squeezed my knee under the table, and her clear blue eyes seemed especially sparkly as she smiled at me.

Cindy looked past me then to address Mary, seated on my other side. "This man is a gem. Looks, charm, cooking skills, wild talent, and he does so much good in the world! I hope you know what a lucky, lucky, woman you are, Mary!"

Cindy's right hand continued to pat my left knee while Mary rested her left hand on my right thigh. "That is one thing I never forget," said Mary, beaming at me. The activity under the table had gotten awkward, so I stood up to refill everyone's glasses yet again.

That night, after the kids were asleep, I asked Mary about her vision. I was tempted to never bring it up again, but I thought that I should be concerned enough to follow up, since it had obviously been so upsetting to her.

"It was the strangest thing," she said, shaking her head. "My eyes were closed as I listened to you pray, yet what I saw was so vivid, so sudden. It felt like a sharp pain through my heart, and I could clearly see a very glamorous woman standing in the middle of the road, looking right through the windshield at me. She had long, silky, black hair, and she was dressed in skin-tight black clothing. As soon as I saw her, it was like I willed the car to swerve to try to hit her on purpose. It's just a horrible thought. I've never had a vision like that before! What's happening to me? What do you think it could mean, Francis?"

The innocence and trust in her eyes were too much, and I had to look away. "It wasn't long ago that you were suffering from a brain injury, sweetheart," I said, despising myself for my lack of sincerity. "It could just be a random leftover effect, I guess."

"I suppose," she said. "But the pain was so real. It feels like it's left a scar on my chest, or my heart; I don't even know how to describe it."

I took her in my arms so she wouldn't see the tears welling up in my eyes. Would this nightmare ever end?

It took two more weeks for me to finally relax and stop worrying about Mary's memories returning. Ever since I'd left for the Resurrection Tour, Eddie had been in a phase Mary found troubling, and it was taking up nearly all of her time and attention. With all of Mary's focus on our boy, the vision of the woman on the road soon seemed to be completely forgotten.

I held up shirts in the mirror, planning my outfit for the dinner concert at Cindy's. "It's not a real concert," I said to Mary, as she pulled out my most outrageous Justus stage wear.

"Of course it is!" Mary declared. "Cindy contributed $25,000 to my Down on the Ranch charity, and she deserves the full Justus experience! Have you guys decided what you'll play tonight?"

"We thought we'd just let Cindy and her friends make requests," I answered. "Is there anything special you want to hear?"

"About that." Mary scrunched up her face as though she had something to tell me, rubbing my shoulders from behind. "Eddie's having such a hard time falling asleep lately with all these night terrors he's been having. If Rosey is out of his sight for even a second, he completely freaks out. You know those four tentacles he's always holding? He told me that they represent Mommy, Daddy, Heather, and little Eddie. Isn't that sweet? The other four tentacles represent other people he loves, and those change from day to day. Anyway, Rosey's the only thing that comforts him right now, and I can't expect a sitter to get that. Cindy has already said she completely understands if I need to miss her private concert. She even suggested it when I told her how hard it was going to be for me to leave Eddie."

"It won't be the same without you," I told her. "But sure, I understand."

"The kids and I are going to Chipotle. We'll miss you," she said, sliding her hands down my chest and kissing my neck from behind.

Stephanie and my bandmates were already at Cindy's getting the equipment set up when I arrived. Rikki was in the kitchen unpacking the filet mignon, onions, sour cream, noodles, and all the spices and other ingredients we needed to whip up my famous beef stroganoff for Cindy and her friends.

Rikki and I chopped, sliced, and stirred while Cindy popped in and out of the kitchen to offer us drinks and check on our progress. She looked especially good in a white lace dress, high-heeled boots, and a white leather Justus tour jacket. It was cute to see how excited she was as she showed us off to her friends.

As the house filled with the scrumptious smells of our cooking and the sound of the band tuning the instruments, I watched Cindy, happy to see her doing so well. I had never particularly cared for her now ex-husband, even though we had all socialized together for many years. He was an unhappy, critical man, and it seemed to their friends that he never gave Cindy a break, always complaining about her lack of sophistication and education, her country-girl ways, and her lack of any professional aspirations. According to Mary, Cindy had struggled hard to try to make the marriage work and was terrified to be on her own again. Tonight, however, she could not have looked lovelier—carefree and enthusiastically enjoying her party.

Once the feast was laid out, we all held hands and bowed our heads in prayer. Seated at the head of the table with me, Cindy concluded the blessing: "And thank you, dear Lord, for Francis. Although he doesn't know it, he has been my savior during these past dark months. I listen to the gift of music You have given him, and I feel alive again. I feel as though I'm seen and loved—something that has been difficult for me to feel in the past." She squeezed my hand as she said these words, and a mutual glance revealed that she had tears in her eyes. I had no idea that she had been leaning on my lyrics so heavily during her crisis, and it warmed my heart to know how much she was helped by them.

Soon all our bellies were filled with good food, and everyone else's heads woozy with wine, especially Cindy's. I had always chosen to avoid alcohol, preferring to keep my wits about me.

The performance went surprisingly well, considering it had been many, many years since we'd delivered our music in an unplugged format to such a small audience. Cindy and her friends danced like teenagers, all their strappy designer shoes abandoned to a pile in the corner. It was well after midnight when we wrapped up the final encore and the guests began to leave.

Cindy's once perfectly coiffed hair now formed a wild, natural frame around her pretty, flushed face. "Francis, how can I ever repay you? Not just for tonight, but for everything you are, and everything you've been to me all these years." Cindy teetered a bit as she leaned to get her boots back on, grabbing my arm for support.

"Just glad I could help," I told her as I looked into her azure blue eyes. "And I'm really glad you liked your dinner concert, I can't thank you enough for your over-the-top donation to Mary's charity."

The band packed the last of the gear and lined up to hug Cindy good-bye as they filed out with the remainder of the guests.

Cindy pulled me aside and said, "Francis, can you stay a bit longer? I'd love to talk to you. There are times when I feel like God is upset with me for getting divorced, and times when I feel I've lost my faith in Him. I just know you'll have the right words to help me find it again."

"Of course," I told her, motioning for everyone to go on without me.

"What's up?" asked Stephanie, lingering behind.

"There are some things Cindy wants to talk about, so I'm going to stay a while," I told her. "You guys go on home. It's late."

"I have some things to discuss with you, too," said Stephanie.

"We've still got recording to do for the new album, and we need to set up the studio schedule. I'll wait till you're done here, and you can drive me home so we can discuss it on the way."

"Can't that wait?" I asked her, bewildered.

Stephanie gave me a look I couldn't quite decipher and said, "I feel it's best that we talk about it tonight."

"Suit yourself, but I think Cindy wants to have a personal conversation with me, so why don't you wait here in the living room while Cindy and I talk in the kitchen?"

Cindy had already gone into the kitchen to boil water for tea, and was surprised when she came out and saw Stephanie there. "Oh, I thought Francis was the last one," she said, with forced politeness. "Would you like some tea, Stephanie, or will you be going?"

"I'll be staying," said Stephanie, "until Francis is ready to leave. I'll pass on the tea."

I followed Cindy back into the kitchen, and we sat at her table while she told me all the details of the final months of her marriage: how difficult it had been getting her two girls through the divorce and figuring out where she wanted to go in her life now that it was no longer built around trying to fix what had seemed from the start to be a doomed marriage.

"The Lord has been with you every step of the way," I reassured her, "and will never forsake you." I pulled up my Bible app on my phone. "Remember Deuteronomy 31:8: 'It is the Lord who goes before you. He will be with you; He will not leave you or forsake you. Do not fear or be dismayed.' Cindy, you are blessed, also, with many good friends who love you."

"Oh, Francis, how could I forget! Those are part of the lyrics to 'Forsaken,' one of my favorite earlier songs of yours. Just being around you and your energy makes me feel so much better. Do you think we could do this again? Maybe meet for a drink this week at the Sanctuary to talk a bit more?"

"Of course," I told her. "I'm happy to help in any way I can."

The ride home with Stephanie was tense. She barely mentioned scheduling the studio time. "What's up with you?" I asked.

"You're a big boy, Francis," she said. "I know it's not my place to interfere in your life. But I don't like the feeling I get from that woman when she's around you. I never have."

"What do you mean?" I asked. "I've known Cindy for years, and she's one of the sweetest people I know!"

"Just be careful, Francis. That's all I'm going to say."

CHAPTER 8

"**B**ut why Flagstaff, and why does it have to be for four days?" I asked Mary, as she packed her suitcase. "If you feel like Eddie needs a change of scenery or a place he could sleep better, why don't we all fly off to Hawaii for a long weekend?"

"You know how much my mom means to Eddie," Mary replied. "I really think some time with his grandma will do him wonders. She's such a soothing presence to him. Don't you remember the last time he went through a spell like this, how much she helped? God has blessed them with a special bond."

Mary's words were making sense, but the truth was I didn't feel like going to Flagstaff for four days. I had just come off the most successful tour of my life, and I wanted to be a rock star a little bit longer. Somehow it didn't seem like a rock star should have to go spend a long weekend sitting around his mother-in-law's house.

"Stephanie's been bugging me about setting up some studio time," I told her. "Maybe I'll stay here and work while you guys go."

Mary looked disappointed. "You really won't come?" she asked.

"I've got stuff to do here," I said. "I don't want to get behind on the new album. Plus, Cindy says she needs to talk to me some more. Apparently, I'm a source of inspiration for her."

"You're a source of inspiration for us all, *including* Eddie," said Mary, "but it is kind of you to give Cindy your time like that."

Mary was trying to say the right things, but I still felt her sting. I knew she was annoyed that I didn't want to go to Flagstaff. But I was annoyed, too. Sometimes it bothered me that she was becoming so hypervigilant to Eddie's needs, often to the point of neglecting mine. Because my mom had had a very difficult time showing me love, I knew that Mary's loving nature was one of the things that had attracted me most to her. But sometimes it was hard when she lavished more love and attention on the kids and her charitable causes than she did on me.

Mary looked at me with a shrug and a sigh of defeat. "Well, Heather didn't really want to go and miss her *Wizard of Oz* dress rehearsal anyway. I guess I could leave her here with you and Delia. Will you go watch her rehearsal on Sunday, to make up for me not being there?"

"Of course. I'm happy to go," I said, feeling I had been some-what redeemed for my decision.

After spending a few days with my daughter and my band-mates in the studio recording *Forgiven*, it was time for me to help Glinda the Good Witch get all ready for her big performance. Together we curled her hair and stuck cotton balls in the toes of her shoes to make them fit better. I got a first-row seat and recorded some of her fantastic performance so Mary could see it later. I beamed proudly from the audience as Heather stole the show. She had certainly inherited her dad's stage presence! I was glad I had silenced my phone, because it started vibrating just as the curtain fell on the first act.

Seeing that it was Stephanie, I answered the call, but the room was too noisy for me to make out what she was saying. Yet I could tell from the tone of her voice that it was important. Cindy had spotted me and was waving as she made her way in my direction. I'd forgotten that her daughter, one of Heather's best friends, was also in the show.

"There he is! Rock-star father of the year!" said Cindy, reaching out to hug me.

I held up my hand, letting her know I was on the phone as I stepped away to find a quieter corner of the auditorium. Finally I could make out Stephanie's words.

"Francis! You're not going to believe who I have on the phone. *The president of Haiti wants to speak with you!* The undersecretary is on hold right now, waiting to patch him through to you!"

Stunned, I told Stephanie to put him through as I hurriedly left the auditorium to find a private place in the hallway.

"Is this Mr. Francis Rose?"

"Yes, Mr. President. It's me. What an honor to receive a call from you!"

"The honor is mine, Mr. Francis. I do not have the words to thank you for all you have done for my people, the dear people of Haiti. You have saved the lives of thousands of Haitian children and filled their lives, and the lives of their parents, with hope."

"I'm so grateful that God has blessed me with the ability to do so, sir."

"I wanted to personally be the one to tell you that you are being awarded Haiti's National Order of Honour and Merit for your extensive humanitarianism in our country. It is the highest humanitarian honor ever bestowed upon a non-Haitian, and it is on a par with your country's Presidential Medal of Freedom."

Still stunned, I responded, "Thank you, Mr. President. I don't know what to say."

"Say you will come to my country. You are invited to the presidential palace to receive your award from me in the presence of my prime minister and the gathering of the entire National Assembly. After that there will be a formal reception for you in the village that was built with the proceeds from your last benefit concert. We will be naming the town François, Haiti, in your honor."

I could hardly catch my breath. How could I tell him everything I was feeling? How could I begin to express how much my heart broke each time I went to Haiti and how much joy it gave me to know we were able to change lives there—to save the lives of babies and young children? How could I make him understand that while I was touched to receive this award, it was nothing compared to the fulfillment I got from knowing how much good we'd been able to do?

"I am so grateful for this honor, Mr. President."

"And Haiti is grateful for you, Mr. Francis. My undersecretary will be in touch soon with all the details."

Hanging up the phone, I felt like I'd just been made king of the world. What an incredible honor! In the span of just a few moments I had officially become a legend to an entire nation. Walking on clouds, I made my way back to Heather's show, surprised that it hadn't started again yet and was still in intermission.

As I got close to my seat, I saw that Cindy was now occupying the seat next to me. "You're not going to believe this," I told her, still shaking.

"When it comes to you, Francis Rose, nothing would surprise me." she teased.

"I've just gotten off the phone with the president of Haiti," I said, enjoying her wide-eyed expression of shock. "I've been awarded a medal for all the humanitarian work I do there, and they're naming an entire town after me. He said it's an award comparable to our Presidential Medal of Freedom!"

Cindy grabbed my arm and squealed. "Francis, that is so amazing! And so fitting. They should name the whole *country* after you! You are finally being recognized as the super human being you are. You deserve that and so much more. Oh, Francis, I'm so happy for you."

I basked in Cindy's adoring gaze, noticing for the first time her tight red dress, salon-perfect hair, red high heels, and iridescent red nails. She was really pulling out all the stops these days. A diamond-encrusted unicorn glittered at her plunging neckline.

Just then the lights went down and the curtain opened on the stage setting for the second half of *The Wizard of Oz*. I don't know whether it was my daughter's performance or the news I'd just received, but I felt ready to explode with pride.

When the show was over, Cindy insisted that we go out to celebrate my exciting honor with a drink at the Sanctuary. I thought, *Why not?* This was kind of a big deal, and Mary wasn't here to celebrate. Cindy's daughter, Julie, and my Heather were staying at the school for a postproduction party, so I arranged for Delia to pick Heather up from the party and stay with her at the house until I returned.

I was driving a little faster than usual because I was jumping out of my skin to call Mary and tell her the news. Cindy's Maserati was following so close behind that I was nearly blinded by the reflection of her headlights in my rearview mirror. "Call Mare Bear," I told Siri.

"Hi, sweetheart!" Mary exclaimed.

"Honey, you won't believe what happened tonight while I was at Heather's dress rehearsal! During the intermission, the president of Haiti called and said I'm receiving Haiti's National Order of Honour and Merit in front of the whole government at the presidential palace! He wants me to bring the family and all the band members. Honey, this is like receiving the Presidential Medal of Freedom here in the United States!"

"Oh my gosh, Francis! God is so good! He's blessed you with this ability to help the poorest of the poor. I'm so happy for you. Dear God, thank you for bestowing on me the best husband in the world, and for giving him the gift of awareness and discernment to care for Your children."

I joined Mary in prayer, then told her I'd better run because I was meeting Cindy to celebrate.

"Have a wonderful celebration, sweetheart! I love you," she said as we hung up.

Once inside the Sanctuary, Cindy led me to the bar and said to the bartender, "See? What did I tell you?"

"Wow, it really *is* him!" said the bartender. "What can I get you, Mr. Rose?"

Cindy laughed at having won her bet with the bartender.

"Just a root beer for me, please." Then turning to Cindy, I said, "You must be quite the regular."

"I get here from time to time," Cindy coyly replied. "I told him I'd be coming here for a drink with you at some point, since you'd agreed to counsel me some more this weekend. But now just look at all we have to celebrate. Francis, you must be out of your mind with well-deserved pride. This honor is just fantabulous! I can't tell you how thrilling it is for me to get to celebrate it with you."

Cindy's red dress hugged her curves in all the right places, and I noticed a few of the male bar lurkers eyeing her up.

"It feels good to share it with you, Cindy. You look beautiful," I said. I sensed that her overall look had taken some extra care and planning, so I wanted her to know it had paid off.

A curled strand of her platinum hair fell across her face as she tilted her head to meet my eyes. "Francis Rose, you always know the perfect thing to say. Won't you join me in having a drink or two? Just this once? For such a special occasion?"

"You know that's not my thing. I can celebrate just fine with this root beer," I told her. We made small talk for an hour or so, and Cindy seemed much more interested in talking about me and my accomplishments than about her divorce troubles. She was more vivacious and charming than ever, ordering drink after drink and never running out of conversation.

She jumped up from her barstool when Justus's song "Salvation" started playing in the lounge, saying, "This is my favorite song of yours! Francis, dance with me!"

Sensing the bartender had played it on purpose, I laughed as she pulled me up, protesting. "You know I'm not much of a dancer, especially to my own music," I said, but she was having none of it.

"I'll dance for us both," she teased. "You just stand there and look good."

True to her word, Cindy handled the dancing, swinging her hips in wide circles and running her hands gently over my chest. She was the only one in the room dancing, and normally I would have been embarrassed, but her movements were so graceful, so professional, and so seductive that I found myself mesmerized by her delightful lack of inhibition.

When the song ended and I was able to finally coax her back into her seat, I said, "Cindy, it's getting kind of late. You know, I was away from the kids for more than forty days with my tour, and they really missed me. I feel like I need to get home now and check on Heather. It's been really fun."

"Of course!" said Cindy. "Julie and Brianna are sleeping at their dad's house, so I'll come with you. It's still too early to go home, and you promised to counsel me some more and help me regain my trust in God."

Cindy hadn't seemed like she was in need of counseling, but I really didn't want the night to end. It had been a long time since someone made me feel this good about myself. I wanted to keep my promise to her, too, so we headed to my house to see Heather. Since she'd had a lot to drink, I suggested to Cindy that we go in one car and come back for the other one later.

"Maybe the reason you don't like to drive is you've never driven the right car," she said, dangling her keys. "Wanna celebrate your success with something fast and sexy? This car oozes testosterone. It needs a man behind the wheel. Come on; show me how a real man drives this thing!"

I laughed. "Sure. Why not?" I got Cindy into the passenger

seat of her Maserati, adjusted my seat, revved the engine, and slammed the gas. Hitting the paddle shifter, chirping the tires as I ran up through the gears, I passed a 50-mile-per-hour speed limit sign doing 110.

"Yippee! That's the Francis I know and love," Cindy screeched, both hands plastered to the leather ceiling.

"Holy shit, what a rush!" I exclaimed, slowing down. "I haven't felt that excitement since racing my dad's '78 Camaro Z-28 on the way to the swimming hole with my girl, Gracey. Wow, I miss that feeling!"

I was snapped out of my hormonal high by a call from Mary. I was driving like I was in the Indy 500, so I decided to cool it a bit and pull over to the side of the road to talk to her.

"I hope you had a wonderful celebration, sweetheart!" she began. "I miss you so much, and I've been so excited about the news of your award. Everyone here sends their congratulations. We'll have to get you all spruced up and looking your best for the Haiti trip, not to mention the *Forgiven* tour coming up!"

At the mention of the tour, Cindy put her hands to her heart in a swoon gesture, letting me know she could hear Mary's voice on the phone.

"How is Eddie doing?" I asked.

"Oh, Francis, you should see him. He's doing so much better here. Catherine is the best medicine for him! He even let her hold Rosey and showed her which tentacle she was. Thank you for sending the video clip of Heather in the play. She was fantastic."

We chatted a bit more about the kids, Heather's dress rehearsal, and the sunset photos Mary had taken at the Flagstaff Arboretum.

After a while I noticed Cindy rolling her eyes. "Cindy's waiting to talk to me, sweetheart, so I'll see you a little later."

"Love to you both," said Mary. "It looks like I won't be home till tomorrow afternoon, so don't forget to make Heather's school lunch."

I hung up the phone and hit the road again, smoking the tires around the last few curves before my house. "You're all mine now," said Cindy. "You are such a saint, Francis. The time and care you give to your kids—it's really above and beyond! I mean, my Julie and Brianna are much more self-sufficient. I'm glad they spend so much time with their father, because it gives me a chance to do the things I want to do. Don't you ever wish you had more time for the things *you* want, Francis?"

"I guess I'm just a natural family man," I said, as I downshifted for the last time and pulled into my driveway. "But on this thrill ride, I sure didn't feel like Ward Cleaver!"

When we got in the house, Delia told us she'd just put Heather to bed, explaining that the little girl was tired from her long, exciting day.

"I'll go give her an extra tucking in," I told them, making my way to Heather's room.

Heather looked like an angel in the soft glow of her night-light. She was looking more like Mary every day. "How's my Glinda the Good Witch?" I asked, rubbing her back.

"Daddy!" Heather exclaimed, flipping over to see me.

"Don't get all awake now," I told her. "You need to rest up for the big performances ahead. Glinda needs all her rest to help Dorothy. I just wanted to tell you how amazing you were in the dress rehearsal today, and how proud I am of you."

"Thank you, Daddy," said Heather, her sleepy eyes fluttering. "I'm happy you saw me. Maybe someday when I'm big, I can perform to help people, like you do."

"You know what I think? I think that when you're big you will be able to do anything and everything you ever want to do, and you'll do it better than Daddy ever did."

Heather smiled as I kissed her forehead and pulled her covers up.

"'Night, 'night, my princess," I whispered.

"'Night, 'night, Daddy."

I returned to the living room to find Cindy draped artfully across my white sofa, one leg crossed over the other, holding a glass of champagne and leaning sideways just enough that her breast was almost entirely exposed. The image caught me off guard, stirring my senses.

"Um, where's Delia?" I asked, glancing into the kitchen.

"Delia left. She assumed you didn't need her anymore tonight. Come sit with me, Francis. I hope you don't mind that I poured myself a drink."

"Of course not," I said, admiring the play of her red dress against the white couch. I'd always known Cindy was a knockout, but she had never looked as intoxicatingly beautiful as she did in that moment.

"Cindy," I said, "I can't tell you how happy I am to see you doing so well. You're like a whole new woman."

"I'm glad you noticed, Francis," she said, leaning toward me. "That's exactly what it feels like. After all those years with Doug, I had no idea who I was anymore—no idea who I would be without him. But now, thanks to you, I've found me again."

I looked at her quizzically. "Thanks to me?"

She nodded emphatically. "You have no idea, Francis. You have no idea how I've studied you all these years. I thought I had to put up with Doug, because men like him were all I'd ever known. Then you showed me a whole new perspective. Your goodness, your kindness toward others, your big heart, just the excitement you seem to bring to every day and everyone you're around. And look at our wild ride home! I didn't know men like you existed. I listen to the lyrics you write, and I just weep, Francis. I weep over the beauty, the depth, the emotions you give me." Cindy had been leaning in closer and closer, and now she rested her head on my shoulder. Moved by her words, I put my arm around her.

"I'm glad I could help," I told her.

"I know. And, Francis, I'm here for you, too. I will confess something." She gently laid her hand atop mine as she set her drink down on the table. "I overheard you talking to someone on the phone. It was the day of the PTA meeting. Even though Mary hasn't said anything to me yet, I know that you two are having problems. And it's okay, Francis. It's okay to admit that. Believe me, I've lived through it, and you can, too. Sometimes it just turns out that you're with the wrong person. Sometimes it turns out that the right person has been right there in front of you all along, even when it's not the one you married." Cindy moved her lovely face closer to mine, her lips glistening, her eyes wet with love.

"Cindy," I said, resisting the direction my body wanted to take me in, "I'm sorry you overheard that. I knew someone was outside the door that day, and I regretted having that conversation on the day of the meeting. I know it sounded bad, but I didn't commit adultery with Paulina. I swear. I stopped it. I know it was still wrong, but at least I stopped it just in time."

Cindy looked at me with earnestness and adoration in her crystal blue eyes. "Francis," she said, her voice thick and breathy, "you don't have to explain yourself to me. You are a good man. A gift. You always have been, and you always will be. You're about to receive a big humanitarian award that proves what a good man you are." Cindy giggled at herself, having slurred the word *humanitarian*.

"Everyone knows it," she continued. "Don't worry about that. Don't worry about what you are led to do by your own natural impulses. You're a *good man*, Francis. Trust your impulses."

As she spoke, Cindy ran her fingers across my jeans toward my inner thigh. With a graceful, swift shift of her body, she slid onto my lap, straddling me and holding my face in her hands. "I've always loved you, Francis Rose. You can't deny the attraction, this chemistry between us."

I felt frozen to the sofa as Cindy pressed her mouth gently to mine. I flashed back to being in the hotel room with Paulina and seeing the Bloody Mary Mix behind her. I struggled to hold that image in my mind in an effort to stop my body. But it revolted, reacting wildly and uncontrollably to the tenderness of the vulnerable woman in my arms.

"But, Cindy, no. I can't. It's not right." Feeling my heart race, I flashed on Mary's heart-rate monitor in the hospital room. I gently pushed Cindy from my lap, but she quickly repositioned herself, clenching my hyper-aroused body between her thighs.

I couldn't stop; I couldn't fight the urge any longer. I closed my eyes, parting my lips to allow the sweet probing of Cindy's warm, wet tongue. My mind went blank. All I knew was the fire building in my body and the rush of desire, more intense and foreign than any I'd felt in a very long time.

Maybe Cindy was right. Maybe my relationship with Mary wasn't what it once was. Was my faith blinding me to the fact that I deserved more? That perhaps God wanted me with someone who truly appreciated me?

"But Heather," I protested. "She's right upstairs."

Cindy jumped up, closing and gently locking the living room door. "Don't worry, my prince. I won't scream . . . too loud." Cindy sauntered toward me, lifting her leg and straddling me once again. "Mary's not coming home until tomorrow, and Heather is sound asleep. Tonight is ours."

Unleashing my longing, I ran my tongue down her soft chin to her supple neck, all the way to the exquisite, snowy-white breasts that had tumbled from her dress. Cindy threw her head back, moaning in pleasure as I lapped up the perfumed, salty perfection of her bountiful bosom. Deftly, she unzipped and removed her dress, revealing a matching red thong comprised of the tiniest scraps of red lace.

She pulled my T-shirt over my head and kissed me hungrily, her erect nipples brushing my bare chest as my hands devoured her silky curves. Slowly, my fingers traced the lines of her thong, slipping underneath its straps, and gliding it down her tender thighs. Ravenous for more and more of her, I pulled her close to me, kissing every inch of her. "Oh-h-h, Francis," she moaned again and again.

Savagely, Cindy opened my jeans, liking what she found. She was eager to show me how much—with her eyes, with her velvety hands, and with her warm, luscious mouth. I'd never felt such unbridled ecstasy. When I didn't think I could hold back any longer, Cindy enveloped me in the wet, hot paradise of her hungry essence. We rode wave after erotic wave until ultimately rocketing together into a climatic explosion of oneness.

I don't know how long we stayed silently intertwined, our chests heaving, slowly regaining our senses. It felt as if we were under a spell, protected in our own impenetrable bubble, separate from the world.

Then, abruptly, our bubble was popped by Stephanie's voice *inside* the house.

"Francis? Where are you? Why is that car in the driveway?"

My eyes flew open as I pushed Cindy off me and frantically grabbed for my shirt. Without a word, we both got dressed in record time, just as Stephanie walked into the room.

No matter how badly Cindy and I wanted to appear casual and innocent, we both knew we were failing miserably. When I had given Stephanie a key to the house, I had never in my wildest dreams imagined we'd find ourselves in a situation like this. Stephanie glared at me with a steely, convicting stare as I looked down and realized my T-shirt was inside out. Cindy cowered like a scared child, her hair disheveled and her red lipstick incriminatingly smeared.

The three of us stood silently, shifting our gazes from one to the other, for a painfully long moment. It was clear to me that Stephanie knew exactly what had just transpired. Would she make a scene in front of Cindy? Would she disown me as a friend? Oh, dear God, would she tell Mary?

CHAPTER 9

Alone in my home studio, tears stinging my eyes, I let the rising sun coming through the window illuminate the words of Hebrews 6:4–6 in my tattered and torn Bible. "For it is impossible, in the case of those who have once been enlightened, who have tasted the heavenly gift, and have shared in the Holy Spirit, and have tasted the goodness of the word of God and powers of the age to come, and then have fallen away, to restore them again to repentance, since they are crucifying once again the Son of God to their own harm and holding him up to contempt." Staring at my old Bible, in that moment, I knew that nothing in there or out here could redeem me. All I could do was slowly close the worn cover and bury my head in my hands.

I had *really* done it this time. I had not only violated the seventh and tenth commandments, I had broken the covenant of marriage. Through the cracked open studio door, I could hear Mary's beautiful, joyful voice singing as she cleaned up the kitchen mess I'd made in her absence. I hadn't seen her yet because she'd gotten home late and I'd gotten up early to hide out in my studio, my safe haven. I knew I couldn't stay in there forever, but how could I go out and face her?

What would happen next? The possibilities tormented me. There were too many pieces in the puzzle for me to keep up with now. Would Stephanie say something to Mary? Would Cindy? Would Mary get her memory back from the crash? Hell, even the bartender at the Sanctuary saw me with Cindy. I felt like a cornered animal crouching against the bars of my cage. I'd committed mortal sins, and man, were they really closing in on me. There was no way I'd be able to come through my indiscretions unscathed.

Wanting to look busy in case Mary came in to check on me, I opened my e-mail to continue going through the barrage of messages that had accumulated while I was away on tour. Slouched lifelessly over my desk, my head cocked to the side in my hand, I tackled them, opening and deleting message after message, until one of them stopped my heart.

Paulina Zakharova.

It wasn't excitement or fond memories that stopped my heart, but a sharp pang of anxiety. I popped my head out of my hand and straightened up in front of my computer screen. How could I possibly face a message from Paulina right now? I played with the thought of deleting it unopened, but I couldn't do it. The subject line read "A Farewell Poem." I opened the message:

> *I could have been his Angel, and he my King*
> *Salvation in passion, created in a dream*
> *So sudden love found us—great destiny's call*
> *But fate's interruption took its lethal toll*
> *A script of lost hopes cuts through the bleeding wound*
> *We chased stars and rainbows, yet rain was so cruel*

My heart had been longing for King's tender soul
He opened it softly and it felt like home
My aura reflected in King's deep green eyes
Our souls were connected and hearts intertwined
Ethereal connection tied our life paths
And tapped into lightness of infinite faith
A tale of uncertainty stole future from us
Unbearable burden broke two loving hearts
Pain, fear, emotions—but life goes on
Your sacred devotion will help us move on
Fight the world for a reason; you'll win all your bets
Fight the world for a season; you might have regrets
God touched us so gently, and we felt alive
But life tore love lately, made our souls cry
I'll always be near in spirit with you
Give up on your fear, your wishes come true
The King holds his crown, and Angel will fly
Let go of your doubt as we say good-bye.

Любите вас всегда—Paulina

Paulina's intoxicating voice rang through my soul as I read her words. I copied and pasted the closing statement into Google Translate. It meant "Love you always."

My heart collapsed as I realized, for the first time, how much pain I had caused Paulina. She had come to me for help and I had abandoned her, both professionally and emotionally. Tears fell onto my keyboard as I hung my head in shame. I had hurt Stephanie, too. I saw her image in my mind glaring at me from across the white couch, her profound disappointment in me etched deeply into the lines of her face. The excruciating pain I'd inflicted on Mary was not only emotional but had been physical as well, nearly killing us both. And now there would be Cindy to deal with.

My agony was exacerbated by Mary's chipper voice as she chatted with Delia in the kitchen. I knew it was just a matter of time before I'd have to insert myself, with forced cheerfulness, back into the household scene. I hovered my finger over the delete button, in part wanting to banish Paulina from my laptop the way I'd banished her from my phone. But her declaration of lost love had moved me, and I decided to store the message in a miscellaneous file instead.

I was about to resume the task of clearing my e-mail when I heard Mary say, "An empty champagne bottle. That's weird; Francis doesn't drink." She must have opened the trash to throw something away as she was tidying the kitchen and seen the bottle there. She continued, "Delia, where did this champagne bottle come from?"

"It wasn't me, Miss Mary!" said Delia, a bit defensively. "Miss Cindy opened it when she was here with Mr. Rose last night. Then she insisted I go home right away. I guess she drank it after I left."

"Oh, right," said Mary, "they were going to talk some more. Francis is being such a good friend to Cindy. But he really shouldn't let her drink a whole bottle of champagne. That's not good for her, and it's only going to mask her pain. I'll call her today to check on her."

My chest contracted as I made sense of the words I was hearing. The first thing I registered was that Mary, in her innocence and unwavering trust in me, did not think anything of the fact that Cindy and I had been alone here together while Cindy drank an entire bottle of champagne by herself. Her concern was for Cindy and her pain! How many wives would be so selfless, so caring, so unsuspecting? It stung my heart, and it also ratcheted up my anxiety to know that Mary was going to call Cindy later.

My second realization was having a different effect. A slow hot anger rose within me as I registered the fact that Cindy had *told* Delia to leave. When I had come out of Heather's room and asked about Delia, Cindy said Delia had left, but she did not say that she had told her to leave. What happened between Cindy and me wasn't just a case of two friends getting carried away by a spontaneous moment of lust and bad judgment. Cindy had planned it—every bit of it.

Feeling a slight reprieve in my guilt, I was overcome with an urge to embrace my wife. I came out of the recording studio to see Mary standing in front of the open, half-filled dishwasher holding a champagne glass up to the sunlight. Even from the doorway, I could see Cindy's red lipstick stain on the glass. I walked toward Mary, but she seemed in a trance, peering into the glass as she twisted it in the beam of sun.

"No! No!" Mary shouted vehemently, causing my heart to stop in my chest. She shook her head vigorously. Seeing me in the kitchen, she put down the glass and ran into my arms. "Oh Francis, it happened again! That vision! I was looking at the red lipstick on the champagne glass, and it made me see that woman again—the same one I saw in the middle of the road, with the red lips and black hair. It was just a brief flash but, oh God, it startled me. Why do I keep seeing her? Why?"

I gathered my shaking, teary-eyed wife into my arms. "Honey, you know that Dr. Shapiro said you would be recovering from your brain trauma for maybe a year or more. You drove late at night from Flagstaff. Your texts said Eddie was having nightmares while he dozed in the backseat. The two-and-a-half-hour trip took you four hours. You're overtired, sweetie. Here, let Delia finish cleaning. You need to take it easy. Let's go sit down."

I took Mary's arm and led her to the living room. Out of habit, Mary veered toward the couch, but as soon as it came into view, I froze, remembering Cindy sprawled there in her red lingerie—and *out of* her red lingerie. I didn't want to sit there with Mary, right where so much had happened that would destroy her. I tried to steer her toward the leather loveseat instead, but she ignored my subtle directives and sat down in the exact spot Cindy had occupied.

If it was even possible for the anxiety I'd been feeling all morning to escalate, it did. Would this recurring vision be the thing to jar Mary's memory? I'd never been able to forget the moment I asked Dr. Shapiro if Mary would regain the memories she'd lost. "There's a fifty-fifty chance," he said, with a stare that pierced right through me. Memories of Dr. Shapiro competed in my head with the arousing yet nightmarish memories of what had taken place just twelve hours earlier on this very white couch.

How would I ever extract myself from the tangled web I'd woven? In that moment I just wanted it all to have been a bad dream. I would have given anything to go back to the time before I'd ever opened that letter from Paulina, before I'd ever betrayed my Mary.

As a way to force herself to feel back to normal, Mary, as usual, turned her attention to others. "How is Cindy doing, Francis?" she asked, her eyes wide with concern, her head resting on the fluffy tan throw pillow on which I could still see strands of Cindy's platinum hair.

"She's having a rough time," I said. "She's lonely, of course, and still troubled by all the trauma caused by the divorce. I think she just needed a male perspective."

When had I turned into such an unrepentant, piece-of-shit liar?

"You really shouldn't have let her drink so much. I worry about that becoming a problem for her. I'm glad she's turning to you, since you set such a good example in that regard."

"You're right," I said. "I shouldn't have let her drink so much." If only Mary knew how true that was.

In my pocket, my phone vibrated twice in quick succession. I pulled it out to see that I'd received two texts: one from Stephanie and one from Cindy. I opened Stephanie's first. "We need to talk. Meet me at the Brick Road Recording Studio at 2:00 PM." I swallowed hard. Facing Stephanie was the last thing I wanted to do.

The next text, from Cindy, said: "Hi, Rock Star Francis! Thank you for such a magical time. I haven't felt like this in longer than I can remember. When can I see you again?" Following the words were two hearts and two rock-guitar emojis.

I must have grimaced, because Mary immediately asked what was wrong.

Fumbling for words, I answered, "Stephanie wants to go over the remaining steps for wrapping up the new *Forgiven* album. The tracks still need to be mixed and bounced." I stuffed my phone back in my pocket. "The record label wants *Forgiven* to be released sooner now." I couldn't believe how easily I was still lying.

"You will meet the deadline, and the album will be amazing. Just like always," said Mary, kissing my cheek on her way out to the kitchen.

I pulled my phone back out of my pocket and typed a reply to Stephanie. "I'm kinda busy today with Mary and the kids."

Then I copied the words and pasted them directly into the reply-box beneath Cindy's text as well. Within seconds, a reply from Cindy came back. It was five crying-face emojis. Stephanie wasn't letting me off the hook, however. Her text said. "Make the time, Francis. This is serious. I will see you at the studio at 2:00." I didn't respond, but we both knew I would be there.

I arrived at the Brick Road Recording Studio about thirty minutes early, desperate to get this uncomfortable encounter behind me. Alone in the soundproof room, I prayed for the strength and courage to endure Stephanie's confrontation. Sitting on the same stool I'd often sat on to sing about virtue and the greatness of God, I hung my head over the microphone in grief. How different the seat and microphone felt under the weight of my sins.

I brought the dead microphone to my bowed head, leaned my forehead against it and said, "Heavenly Father, why have you allowed this to happen? Why have you forsaken me and put this temptation in front of me and let it grow beyond my ability to stop it? Please! Please! Don't let Mary find out, or anyone else. It will ruin my career and the good works you are doing through me. You know how it will hurt her, and she's not capable of bearing such a heavy burden. I am so sorry and will never make such a terrible mistake again."

Though still shaking, I realized I felt better after my makeshift prayer. Even if there were people walking the Earth with the power to destroy my life by telling my wife and the world the truth about me, I had a God who might protect me from that happening. The door slammed, and I winced at the sight of Stephanie barreling toward me like she wanted to hit me.

"What are you doing, Francis?" she angrily spat at me.

"I was praying," I answered.

"You better be," she hissed. "And you know I didn't mean right now. What are you doing with your life? How could you do this to Mary? Your children? Your fans? All the people around you—myself included—who would be devastated to know you are capable of such a thing?"

I'd never seen Stephanie so angry. Her face was red and her eyes were bleary from crying.

"I—I don't know how it happened," I started.

"Oh, please!" Stephanie interrupted. "Anyone could see the evil intentions of that woman a mile away. But *you*, Francis. You? I never would have believed that you would do this, and in your home, no less."

I saw an opportunity to relieve myself of some of the guilt, so I took it. "It was all her, Stephanie. I was just trying to help her. She said she needed my guidance, and then she forced herself on me. You know I'd never turn away a friend who came looking for my counsel. I was just being a good Chris—"

Stephanie shot her index finger in the air to stop me. "Don't you dare say it, Francis Rose!" she snarled at me. "Don't you dare claim to be a Christian at a time like this."

I knew she was right, so I hung my head while we both took a few breaths to calm down.

"I'm so damn mad at you right now," she finally said. I'd never heard her use such a word before.

"I know," I replied, defeated.

"I'm here in the full spirit of Matthew 18:15, Francis: 'If your brother sins, go and point out his fault, just between the two of you. If he listens to you, you have won him over.' Will I win you over, Francis? Will I? Huh? Tell me now! Will I?"

"Yes," I said, wanting it all to just go away.

"How long has this been going on?" she asked.

"It was the only time. I swear. It was the only time in my whole marriage that I've ever been unfaithful to Mary. I never would have done it, but Cindy was out of control—"

"Stop making BS excuses, Francis. You're stronger than that. You're Francis Rose! You have to tell her. You have to tell Mary," Stephanie stated, as though it were the most obvious thing in the world.

"No! No, I can't. I was weak, Stephanie, and I sinned. I'm sorry. I'm so, so, very sorry. But you have to promise me you won't tell her. She's fragile; you know that. With the accident, all her responsibilities to the Down on the Ranch families, Eddie's condition, and taking care of her mom who's all alone, she's been in a really frail state. She couldn't handle something like this. Please, please, Stephanie, I'm begging you."

Stephanie was silent for a long time, obviously wrestling with the moral implications of the decision she was about to make.

"I don't know. I'm inclined to share the truth with Mary, but if I choose not to share your sin with the most beautiful thing to ever happen to you, you must *never* do this again. *Never! And* you must seek forgiveness from God with a sincere heart," she said, her eyes boring into me as if trying to read my intentions.

"Of course it will never happen again! I swear to you. Never again, Stephanie" I said, profoundly relieved that she seemed willing to consider keeping my secret.

"That woman will be back. Mark my words. You are going to have to slay this monster right now, before it gets any bigger. And regarding all this nonsense about her forcing herself on you— don't you ever forget what the Bible says, Francis Rose." Stephanie fumbled with her phone, obviously looking for a passage she'd bookmarked for me. "1 Corinthians 10:13: 'No temptation has overtaken you that is not common to man. God is faithful, and he will not let you be tempted beyond your ability, but with the temptation he will also provide the way of escape, that you may be able to endure it.'"

"But there was no escape," I muttered sheepishly. "I didn't know how to escape her."

Stephanie's anger-flushed face loomed in close to mine as she said, "Stop right there. This was *your* indiscretion. *Your* bad decision. *Your* responsibility. Answer me this honestly. No, answer this to your mirror. How's your relationship with God, Francis? Your prayer life? You doin' it? Are you in the Word? What's gotten into you? Who do you think put those first twenty fans in the church in Keeler, and who do you think put those twenty thousand fans in the arena for our last show? Who gave you the ability to raise over a million bucks for the dying children in Haiti? You seem to have forgotten who to thank, or even who to turn to. Right now, you're acting more like Judas than Justus. Keep it up and you'll have the same tragic ending—for eternity."

With those words, Stephanie grabbed her bag and stormed out of the studio, the door slamming behind her. I waited long enough to make sure she was gone.

Then—shamed, humbled, and nearly broken—I headed out, not knowing where I was going, with the sting of Stephanie's words still ringing in my soul.

CHAPTER 10

I drove for several hours, unable to go home and unable to escape myself no matter how many miles I covered. Finally my car led me to the one place I thought might offer me a sliver of salvation: Scottsdale Lutheran church, where Mary and I had been members for more than a decade.

I pulled down the brim of my tattered Arizona Diamondbacks baseball cap, pulled up the hood on my white hoodie, and hid behind my mirror-lens aviator sunglasses, praying I wouldn't be recognized as I headed to the small chapel connected to the main church. I felt more like the Unabomber than the lead singer for a squeaky-clean Christian band. I took a back-row seat in the far corner, fell to my knees on the hard floor, and prayed to God for the answers to Stephanie's questions. How could a man like me possibly have put himself in a situation like this?

Stephanie had told me to connect to God, and I knew she was right. I was startled to realize how long it had been since I'd relied on prayer the way I had traditionally done throughout my life. From my knees, I asked, "God, why did you allow Cindy to take advantage of me? She used what she overheard on my call to your servant Pastor John against me! Why didn't you provide me a way of escape from this terrible temptation? Please help me right this wrong. What will this do to my career? What will my fans think? What will this do to Mary? As Jesus begged you in the garden of Gethsemane before his crucifixion, I plead with you for the same: 'Father, if you are willing, *please* take this cup of suffering away from me.' Father, if my poor decision with Cindy gets out, I, too, will be crucified! Please, please don't let this happen to me."

I had hoped that praying would make me feel better, but I felt just as shitty and alone as I had when I'd walked in. Why? Maybe I've fallen too far from God to be lifted by prayer anymore, I thought. Maybe this is just what I've become. Lost in my misery, I watched a family enter the otherwise deserted chapel. A boy and a girl about the ages of Heather and Eddie clung to their parents' hands as they solemnly walked toward the alter. I bowed my head as they passed, quickly pulling up my hood, hoping I'd be unrecognizable. I'd always worn my faith on my sleeve and been happy to greet others in the house of God. But that was the old Francis.

I watched this family, not unlike my own, sobbing and praying. Their voices echoed through the small empty chapel, letting me know they'd come to mourn the man's mother, who had just died. In their own ways, they were each praying that God would take her soul up to heaven. The boy (slightly older than Eddie) asked his dad if he could pray out loud for his grandma because "God will hear me better." The father agreed, and the boy began, "Dear God, thank you for letting us play with Grandmama. She always made the best chocolate chip cookies, with the melty cookie dough in the middle, and her hugs were the best in the who-o-o-ole world. I bet she'd let you lick the spoon and give you a big hug if you asked. But, God, Daddy was the luckiest of all, because he had Grandmama since he was a baby."

My head bowed, I watched my tears fall onto my sunglass lenses and roll down the rims before spilling onto the floor. Then, closing my eyes, I was emotionally carried away to a vision of my own mother lying in a casket as if she were the grandma being prayed for. It had been well over a year since I or anyone in my family had seen her. She hadn't known how to handle my fame, and even more important, she had never been able to relate to Eddie or the challenges that went along with his condition. She'd never been the warm and loving type, and becoming a grandmother had not done much to soften her. When I was young, there were even times I thought I was a mistake, because I never had any brothers or sisters. As Pastor John had pointed out, my mother's lack of love was probably the reason I craved love from women so much and probably had a lot to do with why I was in this mess.

Mary was good about speaking with my mother on the phone every few months and had always encouraged me to reconnect with her, but I'd gradually let the time between my visits get longer and longer. I couldn't remember exactly when I'd last seen her.

I grabbed a Bible from the pew in front of me and leafed through the pages to find Matthew 5:46–48: "If you love those who love you, what reward will you get? Are not even the tax collectors doing that? And if you greet only your own people, what are you doing more than others? Do not even pagans do that? Be perfect, therefore, as your heavenly Father is perfect." I had never understood that last part. How could I be perfect? Especially now!

Still, I felt as if the Holy Spirit were directing me somehow, nudging me to check in with my mom. At this moment, when

I could very well be about to lose my family, lose everything, how could I risk the additional tragedy of my aging mom dying before I'd had a chance to talk to her again? I decided that this family coming in with their prayers of mourning must be a sign from God to me—God nudging me to do right in at least this one small way, since I felt so powerless to do right in any other way. Flipping through the Bible again, I found Colossians 3:13: "Bear with each other and forgive one another if any of you has a grievance against someone. Forgive as the Lord forgave you." I closed the Bible and prayed for the courage to do as this passage suggested.

I stepped out into the bright light and pulled my phone from my jeans. It was now or never. I turned on the phone to dial my mom's number. When the home screen came into view, there was a number nine next to the green message icon, and a number four next to the green phone icon. Scrolling through to see who had been trying to reach me, I found that eight of the nine texts and three of the four phone messages were from Cindy.

"Hi, Superstar!"

"How's your day so far?"

"How's my Haiti hero?"

"When can I see your beautiful face?"

"Where have you been?"

"I've been trying to reach you all day."

"Why aren't you answering me?"

"Maybe you're at home. I'm out and am going to swing by and check on you."

Swing by my house? What the hell? Was she serious? I had to get there before she did! What if she talked to Mary?

The ninth text was from Mary, and it came in about thirty minutes after Cindy's last text. It read, "Hi, honey, hope you're doing great! I'm taking Heather to swimming and Eddie to T-ball. Cindy just got here, and she's riding with me. I love you, my dear."

The three phone messages from Cindy were similar to her texts, with the last one stating that she was going to my house. The final voice message was from Mary, who said, "I hope you got my text. Cindy and I are here watching Eddie's T-ball practice, in case you want to stop by."

Shit, they were already together! I took my hat off and ran my hands through my hair in desperation. How could I casually watch Eddie play T-ball with the two of them? But then, how could I leave the two of them alone together? And Mom! What about Mom? Realizing I'd been making all the wrong choices lately, I decided to do something right for a change. The Lord had directed me to call my mother, so that's what I was going to do first.

I texted Mary: "I'll be there in a little while. I'm busy right now in the studio putting finishing touches on a few songs for the *Forgiven* album." Lies, lies, lies. Now I'm even lying about having been in church!

Mary responded, "Okay, can't wait to see you. Eddie has been looking over to see if you're here. He's wearing the matching Diamondback hat you got him. Cindy says she has a gift for you to thank you for all you've done. She says you'll know what it is."

As I was reading Mary's message, a text came in from Cindy. "I guess I'll see you soon. Eddie just got his first hit of the day! Mary looks so tired." Cindy's text was punctuated with a red rose emoji.

Resisting the pull toward the parking lot and my car, I walked back behind the chapel, where there was a dirt path lined with a canopy of pink desert willow trees leading to a wooden bench. I sat down to dial the number I had avoided dialing for more than a year. I'd always dreaded reaching out to my mother as an adult; I preferred to keep plenty of space between my current life and my memories of growing up with a mother who seemed to have a heart of stone encased in lead, locked away in Fort Knox. I thought I had put all of that behind me, but now that I was about to hear her voice, I felt just like a love-deprived little kid again. Only this time I knew I didn't deserve love, not from her or anyone.

"Who is it?" she griped by way of answering her phone.

"Mom. It's me, Francis," I said.

"Francis. *Hmmph.* What are you calling me for?"

"I'm calling because I haven't talked to you in a long time, and I wanted to see how you're doing."

"That's not really why you called me. What's going on?"

Even though there was no warmth in her voice, I still felt a rush of emotion within me. She was my mother. I knew that somewhere deep down she cared about me. And maybe a mother's love was the only kind I still stood any chance of getting at this point.

"I've screwed up, Mom. I think I've just blown up my whole beautiful life. I'm scared, and I don't know what to do." It didn't take much prompting for me to come out with the whole sordid tale. I told my indifferent mother about Paulina. And about Cindy. And about how miserable and sorry I was. I told her how Mary and Cindy were at Eddie's T-ball practice waiting for me to join them, and how frozen and terrified I felt. She listened and waited patiently for me to get it all out, then left me hanging with a long, horrible silence.

"Mom?" I asked, worried that she'd fallen asleep or put down the phone.

"Just like your damn father," she said.

"My dad?" I asked. "What do you mean, just like Dad? Was he unfaithful to you?"

"When I was pregnant with you, we hired a midwife. Pretty young thing. Two days after you were born, he took off with her and I never saw either one of them again. You were to be named Gil Junior, but I changed it to Francis, after the saint, a week later when I realized he wasn't coming back. I never wanted to remember the man who broke my heart."

I held my breath, taking in her words. How could it be that I had never known this? All this time, how could I have never tried to learn the circumstances under which my father had left us? I guess part of me had been afraid to ask—afraid to hear something this terrible.

A series of realizations cascaded through my being. No wonder my mother had never been able to love me! It was my entrance to the world that had brought about her own devastation and heartbreak. No wonder she seemed not to like children in general. Yet in all my life I'd never heard her speak ill of my dad. She had done that for me. That was how much she loved me.

We stayed silent for a long time. Then, my voice cracking, I managed to say, "That must have been really terrible, Mom. I never knew. I'm so sorry." I was sure she could hear my emotion through the phone.

"Knock it off, then," she said, but with tenderness in her voice. "Don't be that, Francis. Be better than that. I know you're no saint, but you're no Gil Senior, either."

It was the best advice my mother had ever given me, and my heart swelled with love for her. I felt completely awash with compassion for this woman I had always known but never truly *seen* before. Beneath her cold exterior I could feel a tender soul who'd been crushed and forever scarred by a man just like me. A man just like the man I was becoming. I felt ashamed of that man, and also ashamed of all the judgments I'd been clinging to about my mom. She didn't deserve those judgments.

"Mom, we haven't always been close, and there have been things I've wished were different, but right now I just want you to know how much I love you. I apologize for the distance I've kept between us in the past. I forgive you for everything and hope you can forgive me, too."

"What's done is done," she said. "You don't need to worry about me, Francis. I never should have stayed with your father as long as I did. The midwife wasn't his first mistress."

"But, Mom, I don't want you to think I'm like my father. I haven't been keeping mistresses! These were isolated situations, and I didn't take the lead in either one of them! These women were sent by the devil to tempt me. I don't know why God keeps testing me like this."

"Francis Robert Rose, I've raised you to fight the deceptive schemes of the devil," she said. "Hold on, I'm going to read you James 1:13–15: 'When tempted, no one should say, "God is tempting me." For God cannot be tempted by evil, nor does He tempt anyone; but each person is tempted when dragged away by one's own evil desire and enticed. Then, after desire has conceived, it gives birth to sin; and sin, when it is full-grown, gives birth to death.' You are experiencing a slow, spiritual death, my boy—far worse than even physical death."

"That's how it feels," I said, recognizing the truth of her words. "But I don't know how to get it under control. What should I do, Mom?"

"For starters, hang up the damn phone and get to that T-ball field. Stop avoiding the mess you've made and start cleaning it up instead."

I knew she was right. I promised I would call her again soon—and this time I meant it. As I rushed back down the tree-lined path, branches knocking into my head, creating a trail of pink blooms in my wake, I glanced back at the chapel, where the family I'd seen earlier was just emerging. "May God bless your grandmama, little guy," I said under my breath. "May God's love save us all."

I started in the direction of the T-ball field, shooting Mary a text while I was driving. "I'm on my way, sweetheart."

As awkward as I knew it would be with Cindy there, I wanted desperately to make it in time to be there for Eddie. And Mary. My Mary. In my mind, I tried to simply erase Cindy from the picture. It seemed that every traffic light was red, and every car I got behind was driving infuriatingly slowly.

I finally pulled into the parking lot and stared, disheartened, at a nearly empty field. All that was left were a few coaches and parents cleaning up the equipment and empty Gatorade cups strewn across the dugout. I picked up my phone to text Mary, but before I could start typing, a message popped up from her number, complete with a kissy-face emoji. "Hey you! It's Cindy! Mary's driving, so I've commandeered her phone. We've gone for ice cream. Wanna come meet us at Fatty Daddy's?"

I hated that Cindy was now the go-between for me and my wife! I hated how casual and flirtatious she'd been acting. Didn't she realize what we'd done? Didn't she have any morals? Any regrets? Mary was her best friend!

My Mustang's tires kicked up clouds of red dust as I backed up, sped out, and headed toward Fatty Daddy's. I was determined to find them, yet unsure how I would possibly be able to calmly interact as if it were just another ice cream outing. My stomach had been in knots all day, and the thought of eating anything at all made me feel like puking up my breakfast toast.

I pulled up in front of Fatty Daddy's and scanned the parking lot for Mary's car or Cindy's. I saw Mary's new black Range Rover, so I jumped out of my car and nervously walked into the store. It wasn't her car, damn it!

On my way out of the store, from across the parking lot, I heard, "Hey, it's Francis Rose from Justus!" I was really in no mood for fans. Resentfully, I plastered on my rock-star face just long enough to shake hands, pose for a photo, and sign a few autographs.

Then I hopped back in my car to text Mary, even though I hated the idea of Cindy being the one who might answer. I had no choice. "Where are you all now?" I typed.

A reply came back right away. "Here, let me show you," it said. I didn't know who had Mary's phone at this point, but a sickening feeling of dread came over me as the next message came through—this time, a photo.

It was Cindy, her arm holding the phone out for a selfie. She was wearing a low-cut red tank top and white shorts, sitting on *my* white couch. Her head was tilted seductively to the side, and the smile on her face clearly said, *We have a secret.*

Repulsed by how much she was enjoying this, I slammed my foot on the gas and headed toward my house.

CHAPTER 11

As I walked through my front door, exasperated and near my wits' end, I could hear Cindy's kids and my kids laughing together in the playroom. The first person I saw was Cindy; her face lit up when I entered the room. "You found us!" she squealed.

"Hello, Cindy," I said. I tried to sound as normal as possible, but I was jarred by the sight of her in red again on my white couch, enjoying a glass of wine.

"Hello to *you*," she cooed, leaning forward just enough to make it clear she wasn't wearing a bra under her spaghetti-strap tank top.

I resumed my search for my wife and found her in the kitchen making peanut butter and jelly sandwiches for the kids. I tentatively kissed her forehead. I had no idea what might have transpired between her and Cindy, and I held my breath in agony while awaiting her response. Looking up from her sandwich prep and licking the grape jelly from the knife, she beamed at me. "You should have seen Eddie today!" she excitedly reported. "He was amazing!"

"I wish I could have been there," I said, relaxing my breath.

"I'm so sorry you had to run around looking for us!" said Mary. "I told Cindy to keep you posted on our whereabouts, but I guess we kept missing each other."

The kids came running into the kitchen looking for their sandwiches, and Eddie ran into my arms when he saw me. "I got a home run, Daddy! Me! Eddie got a home run, just like the Diamondbacks!" He pointed to his baseball hat. "We're champions of the World Series!"

"High-five, little man! That is awesome! I always knew you could do it. You're Daddy's champion!" I picked up my son and hugged him, delighted for a reprieve from my own dark thoughts. Eddie had always given the deepest, warmest hugs, and I let my heart melt into the pure, innocent heart of my son for as long as he'd let me.

My happy moment was interrupted by Cindy, who had joined us in the kitchen. "Eddie was the best baseball player out there today! Weren't you, Eddie?" She leaned in close to Eddie's sweet face and continued, "Eddie is as good at baseball as his daddy is." Her eyes moved from Eddie's to mine and she smiled coyly, adding, "And almost as good at scoring home runs." Cindy winked to make sure I caught her innuendo, but I turned away from her, sweat breaking out across my brow.

I shot a quick glance at Mary to make sure she hadn't been paying attention, but she seemed sufficiently distracted, just getting off her phone. "That was Heather," she said. "Swim practice ended early, and she's ready to be picked up. Would you mind going for her, sweetheart, so I can stay and visit with Cindy and her kids?"

Mary visiting with Cindy was exactly what I most wanted to keep from happening. "Me? No, I can't. I have to get back to the studio to work on *Forgiven*. You'll have to pick her up."

"Really?" asked Mary, looking disappointed. "I thought you were done for the day." She sighed. "Okay, I'll go for Heather. Cindy, thanks so much for keeping me company at T-ball today. You stay here and relax while the kids play. Or if you have something more fun to do, go ahead and let Delia watch them." Mary kissed Cindy and me both on the cheek and left. Her innocent love for us both made me feel sick.

Cindy looked at me wide-eyed, with an expression of *Good job getting rid of her!* I ignored the expression and said, "Cindy, we need to talk. But not here."

I saw Delia glowering at Cindy from behind the large Saguaro cactus in the corner and realized she had probably picked up far more than I'd have liked. "Delia, please stay with the kids for a bit," I said, taking Cindy's elbow and leading her out the door.

Cindy giggled as I opened her car door and ushered her into the driver's seat. "I like the way you're manhandling me, Francis. But you know I'd go anywhere with you!"

I got into the passenger seat and said, "Start driving and turn left once you get out of the driveway. We're going to the recording studio."

"Whatever you say," said Cindy, remaining flirtatious in spite of my coldness. "I've missed you so much! Why haven't you called me back? You felt so-o-o-o amazing, and it's all I can think about." Cindy's hand slipped onto my left thigh as she tried to make eye contact with me, veering the car slightly and jerking it back.

I was startled to realize we were just a block away from Camelback Road, where the accident had occurred. "Cindy, please just pay attention to the road. This is where I almost lost my life and almost caused Mary to lose hers. Not here. Not again. Not ever again!"

Cindy furrowed her brow. "What do you mean, you almost caused Mary to lose her life? Wasn't Mary driving that night? Mary almost killed *you!*"

I immediately wished I could take back the words. I removed Cindy's hand from my thigh and said, "We're almost there. Let's wait to talk until we get to the recording studio."

Once we were finally alone in the quiet studio, all the speeches I'd prepared had somehow flown out of my mind. Emotionally exhausted, I fumbled for a place to start. Not giving me a chance, Cindy wrapped her arms around me and started kissing me, but I took her hands forcefully in mine and held her at arm's length.

"That's not going to happen again, Cindy," I said. "Not now. Not ever. Do you understand?"

Cindy pursed her glistening lips into a pout. "No, I don't. I don't understand at all, Francis."

"It was a mistake," I said. "I love my family. I love Mary. I've been wracked with guilt, and you should be, too. I can't get Hebrews 13:4 out of my mind." I opened my Bible app and read, "Marriage should be honored by all, and the marriage bed kept pure, for God will judge the adulterer and all the sexually immoral."

"But, Francis, we aren't adulterers, because our love is *real*. The bond we've just forged is deep and undeniable. Its roots were planted many years ago. You can't tell me you don't feel it, Francis. You can't tell me you don't want me right now." Cindy's body moved with her words, undulating in subtle yet sultry waves, her hard nipples announcing themselves beneath the thin, silky fabric of her tank top.

"We sinned, Cindy. Mary thinks the world of you, and I want to keep you as a friend, but I just don't see how it's possible. We can't undo what happened, but we can never let it happen again. I love my wife."

"I'm sure in some ways it feels like you do," said Cindy, moving toward me even as I backed away from her. "But Francis, you know deep down that if you really loved Mary, all of this would never have happened. I wasn't even the first. That other woman—Paulina, I think her name was. She was the first sign that you and Mary are done. She was wrong for you, of course, because I'm the one you're meant to be with. Don't you see? It's all so clear."

"What's clear is that this is not going to happen, Cindy," I said firmly.

"It's already happened, my love," she replied with a smile of utmost confidence. "And even though I'm the second woman you had an affair with, I know ours is true love. When friends are lucky enough to turn into lovers, and lovers turn into soul mates, then that is the relationship that's destined to last. You know I will take good care of you, my prince."

Frustrated, I hung my head. "I don't think you're hearing me," I said.

"Oh, I hear you," Cindy replied, lifting my chin so that her shining blue eyes could lock with my eyes. "And I understand that you need time. I'm willing to give that to you, my prince. I'm willing, for now, to take whatever scraps you can offer me. I can settle for that at this point because I know, in the end, the whole package will be mine." Cindy's pronunciation of the word *package* was far from subtle. She bit her lip seductively before turning around and sauntering out of the studio, teasing me with the sway of her hips in her too-short white shorts.

After a week of painstaking diplomacy and dodging Cindy's texts and incessant visits to my house, I didn't know how much more my nervous system could handle. I spent as much time as possible at the studio, at a complete loss for what to do next. Wrapping up the recording for the *Forgiven* album was a good excuse for me to make myself scarce around the house, at least, but soon all that was left to do was to edit and refine the tracks, and I was worried about the next phase: going on tour. Although I avoided spending long periods with Mary, I had become consumed with multiple small check-ins throughout the day to make sure she was still herself and Cindy hadn't said anything to her. How could I leave the two of them alone together for all the months we'd be gone on tour?

At the studio one day, after we'd all high-fived and congratulated one another on finally completing *Forgiven*, Stephanie and I were the last ones to leave. We were all headed over to the Sanctuary for a wrap party, but Stephanie made sure that she and I would be alone in the studio first.

"Have you told her?" Stephanie asked me, her brows lowered and her voice stern.

"What? No! I'm not going to! I told you that! There's no way she could handle it!" I felt my pulse quicken at the thought of Mary knowing my secret.

"Relax," said Stephanie, sensing my panic. "I'm not talking about Mary. Have you told Cindy that she has to leave you alone?"

"I've tried. And I continue to try each time she haunts me," I said.

"Tried? Francis, that's not good enough! You have a worldwide tour coming up, and a visit to the presidential palace in Haiti to receive an amazing award. You can't afford to mess everything up right now! Don't you understand how important these coming months are to your career, to your life? You've been lucky up to this point that Cindy hasn't said anything to Mary. If you're not careful, this whole thing will blow up on you. You have to make sure this is firmly behind you."

"I told her, Steph. But she's been around our family for so long, I can't just banish her now. That would require an explanation, don't you think?"

Stephanie shook her head, disgusted with me. "But at least you've cut off all personal contact with her, right?"

I thought about lying. It would have been easier. But instead I took the opportunity to unburden myself to Stephanie. "She texts or calls me nearly every day," I admitted. "Sometimes a few times a day."

"I hope you don't answer her!"

"I can't get her mad at me, Steph! What if she tells Mary? I have to at least keep being polite with her. Throw her a compliment every now and then. She's a loose cannon, and I can't afford to find out what would happen if I didn't try to keep her at least a little bit happy."

"Francis, please tell me you have not been with that woman again." Stephanie looked like she could cry.

"What? No way! I haven't, Steph. I swear. I have not been physical with her, and I never will again, but I do have to be nice to her when she's at the house and try to keep her from going into bunny-in-a-pot mode on me."

"So, the plan is to let her keep distracting you with these nonsense texts and calls while you're preparing for your tour, or—God forbid—even *on* tour when you should be focusing on your fans and music?"

"I've thought about that," I said delicately. "And I do have an idea to run by you. I'm thinking maybe we should bring Cindy with us; let her come along as an assistant for the tour. That way I can be sure she's not talking to Mary, and I know it would make her really happy."

"Are you completely out of your mind?" Stephanie snapped.

"I know it sounds that way," I stammered, losing confidence in my plan. "But I was thinking I could get Rikki to ask her out. She's gorgeous and fun, and maybe if I could get the two of them together it would solve all my problems."

"You're delusional! Do you have any idea how ridiculous you sound?" Stephanie was practically screeching now. "Have you given any thought to how she would perceive an invitation from you to go on tour with you? Francis, are you still leading her on? Does she think she has a chance with you?"

I took a deep breath. I honestly didn't know how to answer that question. "No. Of course not. I mean, I don't think so."

"You have to end this, and end it now. I'm serious, Francis, you are in a downward spiral with no bottom. Just look at how long it took you to finish up the final song for the album. You struggled with it more than any of the others, and it's the title track, for God's sake! And yes, remember, this is all for His sake, Francis! You know that you had the hardest time with the song 'Forgiven' because your head was all caught up in this disgusting mess you've made. You've worked too hard and too long to build Justus to this level of enormous success and spiritual impact for me to let you screw it all up now. Get this behind you. Do it now."

I knew she was right, but I also didn't like the way she was telling me what to do. Feeling cornered, I lashed out. "I will handle it in my own way, Stephanie. In my own time. It's my band, my family, and my life!"

She looked hurt, and I immediately regretted my firmness. I watched her countenance shift from one of maternal concern to painful resolution. "I hoped it wouldn't come to this, Francis," she said. "But do you remember when I quoted Matthew 18:15 to you?" She opened her Bible app and read it to me again: "If your brother sins, go and point out his fault, just between the two of you. If he listens to you, you have won him over.'"

"Yes, I remember."

"You told me I had won you over, but now I'm not so sure. Do you know what comes after those lines, Francis? Let me read them to you. Matthew 18:16–17 says, 'But if he will not listen, take one or two others along, so that every matter may be established by the testimony of two or three witnesses. If he still refuses to listen, tell it to the church; and if he refuses to listen even to the church, treat him as you would a pagan or a tax collector.' Do you understand what that means, Francis? You could potentially be excommunicated over this."

Stephanie waited for me to absorb her words before continuing. "If you don't immediately get this mess under control on your own, I'm going to bring in Pastor Vance and the church elders to assist."

I searched her face in the hope that this was an empty threat, but she looked more serious than I'd ever seen her—and more troubled than I'd ever seen her. I was again reminded of the pain I was causing those around me by my actions.

"Stephanie," I pleaded. "I don't want Pastor Vance—or anyone else—to know about what I've done. I vow to you that I will take care of it. I'll call our old pastor, Pastor John from Keeler, again. Just please don't tell anyone!"

"Again?" Stephanie asked. "You've been in touch with Pastor John about this?"

"Yes. Wait, no . . ." My head was spinning with all the lies I was having to keep straight. Stephanie didn't know about Paulina, so there was no need to tell her the real reason I'd called Pastor John the first time. "What I mean is that I do keep in touch with him. We have a wonderful, open relationship and I called him to talk about the accident and Mary's condition." More lies.

Stephanie visibly softened. "I'm sorry if it feels like I'm being hard on you, Francis. I know that the accident and watching Mary suffer was traumatic for you. I know trauma can cause people to act out of character. It just seems like in these few short months you've changed so much, and I don't like to see that. Even physically, you look ten years older! Are you taking care of yourself?"

Grateful that the conversation had shifted in a new direction, I basked in Stephanie's loving concern. "It really has been hard," I said. "And I know I'm looking and feeling so tired. Mary found a few doctors who specialize in antiaging remedies. I'm going to look at their credentials and check a few references and make an appointment next week. She says I need to look my best for the tour and the Haiti trip."

"Good," said Stephanie. "Just try to get all this stress and sin behind you, Francis. If you don't, it's going to kill you. I miss the real Francis Rose."

"Me too, Steph," I said, telling the truth for once. "Me too."

CHAPTER 12

As much as I wanted to forget about my showdown with Stephanie, my conscience wouldn't let me. I couldn't sleep. I couldn't eat. I felt like someone else was walking around in my skin—someone foreign to me who had hijacked my soul. I realized the only way I was going to make any headway toward feeling better would be to call Pastor John, but knowing that Cindy had eavesdropped on my last phone call with him, I was paranoid about someone overhearing me again unless I went to a very private place.

I knew there was only one place in which I had felt the slightest hint of grace in recent months, where I could be as authentic, transparent, and vulnerable as I would need to be on this call. After lying awake for hours, I got up at 4:30 AM and drove once again to the small chapel behind my church. Knowing the chapel would be empty so early, I punched the security code into the keypad at the front door.

My footsteps fell heavy in the empty chamber as I took the same spot I'd occupied on my last visit, when the Holy Spirit had led that family in as a sign for me to reconnect with my mom. Falling to my knees and hanging my head, I prayed, scouring my soul for the right words to use with Pastor John. I dreaded the call with every fiber of my being. How disappointed he was going to be in me!

Thinking of Pastor John's disappointment reminded me of how much I had let my own mother down with my actions. Yet my confession to her had ultimately made me feel incrementally better. I decided to call her for one of her no-BS pep talks to give me courage before I called Pastor John. She was always one to tell it like it is, and I needed an unwavering push.

"What is it?" she answered, alarm in her voice.

"It's me, Mom. Francis." I whispered into the phone, respectful of where I was.

"Oh, Francis! What's wrong? Are you all right?"

"Yes, I'm fine. I'm sorry if I woke you up. I just really wanted to talk to you about something."

"You scared me calling at this hour! But go ahead. I'm listening," she said. It felt so good to hear her say those words. It occurred to me that it might be the first time I had ever truly felt she wanted to listen to me.

"I've been trying to fix the mess I made, like you said, but it hasn't been easy, and it hasn't been fixed."

"You're still being unfaithful to Mary?"

"No! No! Mom, I told you! I will never do that again! It's just that Cindy has been part of the family for so long. She's Mary's best friend. And that makes it really hard to keep her away from me and our family."

"Yes, I remember her, the blonde with the big boobs."

"I want to call Pastor John for advice, and to get all of this off my chest. But I'm so worried about what he'll think of me."

"I can certainly understand that."

Even though she wasn't saying much, I felt somewhat comforted by my mother's willingness to hear me out. I felt lighter. My phone vibrated, and I saw a text from Mary.

"Mom, I have to go," I said. "But I really appreciate being able to call you like this."

"Talk to your pastor, Francis. Talk to your God. And yes, you are always welcome to talk to me as well. Get that woman out of your life if you want to keep your marriage."

We hung up, and I read Mary's text. "Where are you? Is everything okay? I woke up and you're not here."

I snapped a selfie of me in front of the crucifix inside the chapel and sent it to Mary. Of all the condemning places I could be, I felt the need to prove to her that I wasn't doing anything wrong—not this time, at least. I texted back, "I couldn't sleep, thinking about the upcoming tour and visit to Haiti to get my award, so I came here." Still a lie, but at least only a partial one.

"Let God soothe your soul, sweetheart," was Mary's response. "You have so much on your plate. And please pray for Eddie, too. He had another night terror last night."

The chapel door click-clacked open as the custodian unlocked it for the early-morning worshippers. I had missed my window of solitude for calling Pastor John. Eager to follow through with my intention, I got up to find a new place to make my call. I walked past a few fellow congregants as they filed into the chapel. Taking off his sunglasses, one smiled broadly when he saw me. "Now I see where and when you get all your inspirational lyrics and melodies! I love your music, Mr. Rose! I can't wait for the *Forgiven* album!"

I thanked the man, shaking his hand. People loved me. I helped them through my music. How could I be all bad when I clearly had such a positive influence on my fans? I hopped in my car and turned toward the AK Chin Pavilion, where Justus had performed its last concert. The empty parking lot would be the perfect place for me to speak with Pastor John in peace.

As the pavilion loomed in my windshield, I recalled the euphoric feeling I'd had on Easter Sunday as 20,000 fans screamed my name. I seemed to be their savior. As Christ rose that day, the hopes and hearts of those fans soared as well. They needed me. All the excitement of the performance coursed through my veins once again, and it gave me the strength that had been eluding me. I parked the car, picked up my phone, and dialed Pastor John's number. He answered on the first ring.

"Francis! I've been thinking about you, my son. How are things going for you?"

"Am I getting you at a good time, Pastor? I know you're an early riser, with your prayers and all, but we could always talk later if this isn't a good time for you."

"Your timing is perfect, Francis. Tell me, how are things with you and Mary?"

I took a deep breath, conflicted over how much to tell him. How could I share the details of my shame with this man I respected so much—and who, up until now, had respected me as well? Part of me wanted to spin a different story for him, but an even bigger part of me felt so crushed and beaten down by all my lies that I knew I had no choice but to tell the full truth.

"I've sinned, Pastor John. Even worse than before. There is no easy way to tell you this, so I'll just come out and say it. I've

committed adultery. I've broken the covenant of marriage."
Hearing myself say the words aloud was mind-boggling. I felt
completely foreign to myself. Who had I become?

"I'm very sorry to hear that, Francis." Pastor John's voice was
not angry, not judgmental, but just so disappointed and so sad.
Why did I continue to make everyone around me miserable?
What kind of monster had I become in the lives of those who
loved me?

Pastor John asked me to elaborate, assuming I had taken my
indiscretion with Paulina to the next level. I guess that would have
made more sense to him, but I explained that it wasn't Paulina
who had pushed me over that line, but our family friend, Cindy.
I told him all about the evening on the couch, and how Cindy
had tricked me and taken advantage of my kindness toward her.
I could tell Pastor John was shocked that I'd been with a second
woman, yet he didn't reprimand me. He soothingly talked to me
about temptation, sin, redemption, and forgiveness. He didn't
scold me. He talked to me the way I'd always imagined a real
father would, if only I'd had one. I felt ashamed but also loved, as
if he believed in me. I needed him to believe in me. I felt a desire
rising up within me to redeem myself in his eyes.

"I know it was wrong, Pastor," I said, "but I want to make
sure you understand that I didn't pursue either of these women.
Mary had been ignoring me for so long, always doing everything
for Eddie. And then these women came along. They both tricked
me, Pastor. They were sent by the devil to find the crack in the
armor of God that I *always* wear. I really am a good Christian
and a good man, just like the Francis you remember."

"When you equate the two transgressions, Francis, are you saying that you committed adultery with both women? Even the first woman, Paulina?"

"No! Not at all! I barely sinned with Paulina, Pastor! I just meant that the devil sent both of them to bring me down."

"Remember James 4:7, my son: 'Submit yourselves therefore to God. Resist the devil, and he will flee from you.' You have not done this. Francis, from all you've told me, I believe you've created ungodly soul ties with these women. An ungodly soul tie is formed when you join your body with another in a sexually immoral act. You may think of the encounter as purely physical, but the truth is that any time you have sex, you are, in essence, gluing your soul to your partner's. When this takes place outside the covenant of marriage, it is ungodly and must be ripped apart. Now imagine gluing two pieces of wood together, letting the glue set, and then ripping them apart from each other. Would you be able to separate them with a clean break? Would either piece of wood be able to retain its original condition? No. Residual splinters of wood from each piece would remain conjoined with the other piece. In the same way, when you have sex, you conjoin your soul with that of your partner, and when the souls are ripped apart, fragments of each remain embedded in the other."

"But I didn't even have sex with Paulina!" I said.

"Intercourse happens on three levels—emotional, spiritual, and physical. As I hear myself explaining it to you, I come to believe even more that what transpired between you and Paulina was enough to create an ungodly soul tie. And certainly, in the case of the second woman, you have created one."

In my mind I could hear Cindy's words: *Even though I'm the second woman you had an affair with, I know ours is true love. When friends are lucky enough to turn into lovers, and lovers turn into soul mates, then that is the relationship that's destined to last.* Soul mates! Soul Mates! Oh my God, that's what Cindy believes!

"Pastor, what can I do? How can I cut and unglue these ungodly soul ties?"

"I am glad that is your intention, my son. And I can help you. Let us pray."

Pastor John prayed over me, then said, "Repeat these words, Francis: 'By the blood of Jesus Christ and with the sword of the spirit I command you, demon spirit of pride, lust, and adultery, to leave me now, and I cut any soul tie made by my sinful behavior.'"

I repeated the prayer several times, bringing more energy and volume to each round, and underscoring his prayer with my own silent, desperate plea to Jesus for the ungodly soul ties to be severed. I felt as though a mini-exorcism were taking place; my face was flushed with fever. I cranked up the air-conditioning in my car, trying to bring down the soaring heat I felt all around me.

Pastor John continued, nearly shouting now. "I ask You, Lord Jesus, to cut any and all ungodly soul ties between Francis and Paulina and Cindy, by their relationship, sexual or otherwise, for now until eternity. Repeat it with me again, Francis. With absolute sincerity and vigor! 'By the blood of the lamb, and with the sword of the spirit, I command you, demon spirit of pride, lust, and adultery, to leave me now, and I cut any soul tie made by my behavior!'"

I wanted to shout the words with the conviction I heard in Pastor John's voice, but I became light-headed and muddled in my attempts. I felt Paulina's silky warm hand sliding inside my shirt. I heard the popping of each snap as she opened it, all the way down to my navel. I felt her tugging at the button on my jeans, pulling me in close, our tongues hungrily encircling one another . . .

"Focus, Francis!" shouted Pastor John. "Stay with me! Repeat after me!"

Pastor John shouted the words he wanted me to recite, and I closed my eyes, struggling to hold the words in my head so I could do as he asked. But my head was filled now with Cindy. My body stiffened, aroused and ablaze with the memory of her naked curves, her velvety hands as they caressed me, her warm luscious mouth that had enveloped me, and the wet hot paradise she offered me so freely. I opened my eyes, trying to banish the tormenting thoughts! What were those words? What were the words Pastor John wanted me to say?

"By the blood of the lamb, and with the sword of the spirit— what? What the hell?" Why was Cindy's Maserati pulling into the parking lot? I panicked, ducking my head in the car as if that would keep her from seeing me. As the car got closer, I realized it wasn't Cindy at all, only a car similar to hers, but I was shaken to the core. I straightened up in my seat and, voice cracking, began again: "By the blood of the lamb, and with the sword of the spirit, I command you . . ."

The words trailed off as I was involuntarily distracted and stared, in evil amazement, at a billboard across from the arena. The ad was for Ciroc Vodka, and it featured a seductively gorgeous, black-haired woman leaning forward, holding a bottle between her legs, inviting passersby to "have some."

Pastor John's booming voice broke my reverie. "Francis! I command you to listen to these words and repeat them *now!*"

I'd never heard Pastor John be so forceful. I grabbed the steering wheel, closed my eyes, and firmly emptied my mind of anything other than his instructions. Finally, after several more attempts, I was able to honor his request. Again and again we repeated the words of deliverance together, until I was able to steady my breath and return my body chemistry to a state at least approximating normality. "By the blood of the lamb, and with the sword of the spirit, I command you, demon spirit of pride, lust, and adultery, to leave me now, and I cut any soul tie made by my behavior."

Even after we'd stopped uttering the words, I continued to let them loop around and around in my mind, praying they would keep all other thoughts at bay. Pastor John mumbled more prayers for me and read James 5:15–16: "And the prayer offered in faith will make the sick person well; the Lord will raise them up. If they have sinned, they will be forgiven. Therefore, you must confess your sins to each other and pray for each other so that you may be healed. The prayer of a righteous person is powerful and effective."

"Thank you, Pastor," I said, exhausted and grateful for my deliverance. "Thank you for being the righteous person praying for me. I can't tell you how much this means to me."

"You're most welcome, my son, but there's another righteous person who must hear from you. It's time for you to 'confess your sins to each other and pray for each other so that you may be healed.'"

"Please, Pastor John. You don't mean Mary?"

"Yes. I mean Mary."

"But it would kill her! I can't do it! What if she leaves me? I can't live without her!"

"The blood of Christ has already been shed for our sins, and while atoning to heaven is a must, it is equally a must that you atone to your wife. I understand how difficult this will be for you, my son. But there are only three ways for this situation to go: You will be caught in your lies; you will put your head in the sand and hope the whole thing goes away, knowing that it never can, as long as you're carrying the weight of it; or you will confess and work toward making things right."

"But the last time I tried to tell Mary about Paulina, it was too much for her to hear, and I nearly killed her. How will she possibly be able to handle a betrayal by both me and her best friend? Can't I at least just pick one or the other to confess to her? I can't do both!"

"My son, how can you be fully forgiven if you only confess with half your heart?"

I opened my Bible app and searched for a passage that had been haunting me. Too distressed to find it easily, and too frustrated to keep looking, I paraphrased. "But, Pastor John, Matthew 5 says something like, if a spouse commits the sexually immoral act of adultery, the other spouse has a right to a divorce! If I confess these sins to Mary, I will be confessing my sexual immorality, and she'll surely divorce me! Even if the Bible didn't say she could, I know that's what she'd do. I know it because if the tables were turned, it's what I would do. And I've made this same terrible choice twice!"

"My son, let me ask you a question. If a man robs a bank at gunpoint, is subsequently caught, confesses his sin to the Lord, and earnestly seeks forgiveness, will his sin be forgiven?"

"Of course, Pastor. God is loving and forgiving."

"That is correct. Now let me ask you another question, Francis. Will this man still go to jail for his crime?"

"I assume so," I answered, my heart collapsing as I began to understand the point that the pastor was illustrating for me.

"You must accept whatever the Holy Spirit moves Mary to do, my son."

I sucked in my breath, feeling the truth and weight of his words. I wanted to protest more, but I knew there would be no point.

I thanked Pastor John for his counsel and hung up the phone. The familiar parking lot now looked desolate and surreal somehow. All the excitement I'd felt earlier from the memories of the fans and the incredible performance at this arena was gone. Deflated, confused, and frightened, I opened my phone again to find texts from Mary and Stephanie and a missed call from my mom.

Stephanie: "When can you meet at the studio for final approval on the *Forgiven* tracks? I have to turn over the tapes to the record label in the next few days."

Mary: "When will you be back, sweetheart? Eddie and Heather are sitting on the front steps with their goggles and bathing suits on, waiting to go on the picnic you promised them at Oasis Water Park."

I ignored the missed call from my mom. I just didn't have it in me to talk about my desperate situation anymore. I hated what Pastor John had forced me to see. But deep down in my soul, I knew he was right: the only way out of my torture was to confess my sins, not just to Stephanie or Pastor John but to the person I had betrayed: the best person I'd ever known, my true soulmate, my Mary.

CHAPTER 13

Sleep eluded me, in spite of my having gotten plenty of exercise in the blazing Arizona sun with the kids, going on ride after ride and slide after slide at the water park. They'd been so happy all day, yet seeing their joy at spending time together as a family only served to drive a dagger of shame through my heart. Mary had looked so happy, too. It was hard enough to watch her play with the kids with such love in her eyes and in her soul. But each time she turned those loving eyes on me, I had to look away. It was becoming more and more painful to receive her loving attention. Thank God for dark sunglasses.

Tired of staring through the black of our bedroom toward the ceiling, I got up around 4:30 AM again and retreated to my home studio. It felt good to put some physical distance between me and the angelic presence sleeping so soundly beside me. I didn't deserve to share her bed. I needed to be alone with my thoughts, alone with God, and plan my course of action: my confession. I wanted to rehearse the words so thoroughly that I couldn't second-guess myself. Even though I continued to pray for strength and courage, each time I tried to gather my thoughts, I was consumed with the memory of how horrifically my first confession had gone.

I could still back out—at least partly. I could still just tell her about Paulina. That would probably be easier. After all, according to Dr. Shapiro, she seemed about to regain her memory anyway. Or I could just tell her about Cindy, which seemed the worse of the two options. Either of those options would be easier than making a double confession! But as I thought about what Pastor John had taught me, I realized that in order to cut both ungodly soul ties, I would need to confess to both sins. Yes, it would have to be done that way, I resolved. I would do it as soon as Mary woke up.

I went into the kitchen and brewed her a strong cup of coffee, hoping the aroma would wake her. Killing time by opening messages in my office, I read another reminder from Stephanie to meet her in the studio to sign off on *Forgiven*. I started rationalizing my plan to talk with Mary as soon as she woke up. Surely, I couldn't drop a bomb like that and then leave her alone while I was at the studio all day. I decided I'd better meet with Stephanie first, so that the rest of my day would be clear for consoling Mary, assuming she'd let me. I took care of mundane office tasks until after sunrise, left Mary's coffee in the microwave with a note on the kitchen counter, let Stephanie know I could meet her, and headed out for the studio.

I got to the studio before Stephanie. It was just after sunrise, and the early rays of sunshine splashed across the lobby walls, highlighting Justus's framed photos, awards, and platinum record for *Sanctified*. The rays reflected off that album back into my eyes, making me wonder how I had strayed so far from the path that had gotten me here. It was as if God was sending me a message. His light was what had gotten me this far, and I longed for it again. In my mind, I begged God to allow Philippians 3:13 to bear fruit: "I do not consider myself yet to have taken hold of it. But one thing I do: *forgetting what lies behind* and straining forward to what lies ahead." I so desperately wanted to leave this unfamiliar Francis in my past.

When Stephanie arrived, I was grateful to find her in total business mode, anxious to get the final time of listening to the album taken care of. As she fired up the equipment, I felt my phone vibrate in my pocket. I glanced just long enough to see that it was a call coming in from Cindy. *Really! This early?* Anger surged through me as I sent the call to voice mail and turned off my phone. The last thing I needed was for Stephanie to see Cindy calling me, giving her an opportunity to reopen that line of interrogation with me.

"I'm so excited!" Stephanie said. It felt great to see her smiling in my direction again. That hadn't happened much lately. "The press conference for *Forgiven* is all set up for next week, followed by a spectacular release party at the Beverly Hills Hotel! And the week after that, you're off to Haiti to collect your medal of honor. God is so good!"

"Wow, that's fantastic!" I said. "We sure have come a long way, haven't we, Steph?"

"I was just thinking about that," said Stephanie, wistfully. "Do you remember when we recorded our first song, 'Justus,' about the disciple who almost became an apostle? We didn't even have a record contract yet. We begged our way into that tiny makeshift studio in the back of the Sam Goody music store at 2:00 AM, when no one was around."

"I remember," I said. "Our only plan then was to sell the song after each Mass and at church festivals to anyone who would buy it! And even though we barely made any money, we had all agreed from the start to split the proceeds with the church's soup kitchen, which fed Keeler's homeless population. We went all over town stapling flyers onto telephone poles!" My heart melted a bit, thinking about our humble origins and how simple things were back then.

"Do you remember how we celebrated the wrap-up of that first recording?" she asked, the twinkle in her eyes telling me she remembered it well.

"I do!" I said. "We scraped together just enough money to take the band, families, and Pastor John out to a celebratory dinner at Applebee's!" I beamed at Stephanie, noticing her moist eyes and realizing how much our work together had meant to her all these years.

"I'll always remember that dinner," she said. "No matter how over-the-top amazing this Beverly Hills Hotel party turns out to be—and believe me, it will be amazing!—nothing will ever beat the excitement and innocence of that first celebration. I hope you don't mind that I told the catering staff at the hotel to have the same kind of Buffalo wings and nachos that we had that night."

"Not at all! Great idea! Can you imagine if we had had a crystal ball at that first celebration and could have seen what we were destined for?" Right after the words left my mouth, their full implications hit me. All the fame, all the money, all the good I'd been able to do in the world—that's what I was initially thinking about when I imagined my younger self looking into that crystal ball. But what if the crystal ball had also revealed the mess I'd made of my personal life? It would have shattered young Francis's heart.

We put on our headsets to begin the final listening. The rest of the band had already signed off, and it was always me and Steph who had the final say. The tracks sounded fantastic—even better than I'd remembered them. I turned up the volume to really feel their impact. At the end of each song, Stephanie and I gave each other nods and high-fives to indicate our approval.

But when the very last song came on—the title song—my insides began to churn. It was the most powerful song Justus had ever recorded and the most striking lyrics the Holy Spirit had ever moved me to write. But something just didn't feel right. Somehow the song didn't feel like it had felt when I'd written it. It felt sharp—painful, even. I listened to myself sing, "All I need is you to love. For you to set me free. All I need is your breath inside of me. To give me life. Bring me back to my knees." Unable to bear it any longer, I pulled the headset off.

Seeing that Stephanie had noticed my discomfort and wanting to avoid a conversation with her, I quickly said, "Yep! That's a wrap. Everything sounds great. Thanks for meeting me here today and getting this over to the label." I grabbed my keys and tried to make a beeline for the door.

"I understand why that song upset you, Francis."

Stopped by her words, I quickly turned around to face her. "I'm fine. All's good. This album is going to sell millions. Let's get it to the record label right away." I didn't want to talk about it anymore.

I got the sense that Stephanie wanted to question me. She wanted a status update on Cindy. I could feel it in her. But she must have also been able to feel *me*—my emotional exhaustion, my soul's ache, my remorse, and my shame. She walked over to me and put her hands on my shoulders.

Softly, she said, "You are stronger than you feel. You're a better man than it seems right now. And you will come through this season of your life."

She hugged me for a long time, allowing her friendship and her belief in me to sink deep into my soul. Unable to articulate my immense gratitude, I gave her a quick thank-you squeeze and left the studio. Blinking into the bright midday sun, I pulled out my phone to text Mary. I steeled myself, gathered my nerve, and typed, "Hi, sweetheart. Meet me at the Sanctuary for lunch?"

Mary's reply came back immediately. "So *Forgiven* is a wrap? That does call for a celebration! I'll be there as soon as I pick Heather up from swimming and drop her off with Eddie and Delia."

As I drove to the Sanctuary, I tried to rehearse my confession. But imagining Mary's face upon hearing what I'd done was too painful. I decided the confession would have to just come out naturally in the moment. If I kept trying to plan it, I was afraid I'd back out. It was like making a plan to saw off your own leg. The more you thought about it in advance, the less likely you'd be to actually go through with it.

I asked the hostess for a quiet table in the corner and ordered a root beer.

"You're in Justus, aren't you?" asked the shy waitress as she set a basket of chips on my table.

"I am," I said, extending my hand. "Francis Rose. Good to meet you."

"I'm sure people ask you all the time—so you don't have to say yes—but do you think we could take a picture together? My boyfriend will never believe this."

"Of course," I said, leaning into her photo. "Would you like an autograph?"

"Thank you! Could I have two?"

I fulfilled the waitress's requests, sending her happily off her shift. I nervously scanned the room. It was taking Mary much longer to arrive than I expected. My mind ambled down dark pathways of possibilities. Mary had said she'd be going by the house first. What if Cindy had been there, waiting to talk to her? Or what if Cindy had called her? Maybe Cindy was angry with me for ignoring her call and took revenge by spilling our secret to Mary. God, I would be glad when all this was over. Just a few more minutes and I wouldn't have to be tortured by this anymore—at least not by the keeping-secrets part.

Sensing commotion at the restaurant entrance, I looked up to see Mary barreling toward me with a terrified expression I'd never seen on her face before. Eyes wide, hair frazzled, she accidentally knocked over a chair as she rushed across the crowded restaurant. Adrenaline shot through my bloodstream. Oh shit. It had happened! She'd found out!

Two valets came running after her, calling "Ma'am! Ma'am!" One put his hand on her arm, and she twirled to face him, looking disoriented, as though she couldn't imagine why he'd stopped her.

"I need your car key, ma'am," he said—apologetically, because her distress was palpable. Mary gave him the keys and angrily took the stub offered by the other valet.

My heart stiff with fear and unable to breathe, I stood up, utterly unready for whatever was about to take place.

Mary lurched to the table like a zombie and leaned against it, staring at me.

"Honey—honey, say something," I said, bracing for the worst. When she didn't respond, I started rambling. "Mary, it's terrible, I know. God help me, I can explain. I talked to Pastor—"

Mary grabbed me around the neck and sobbed, "It's the worst thing, Francis! Why? Why?"

Shaking, I rested my forehead on her shoulder. How could I answer that question? It was the same question I'd been asking myself, but I'd never gotten any kind of answer that made sense. Why? Why? Why had I done this to her? My mouth dry, I pulled her away from me to look into her eyes. "Mary, please know how much I love you. I made a terrible, terrible mistake."

"Why did it happen? Why did it happen, again?" she sobbed.

Her question stunned me. She was finally remembering my first confession after all this time, and now she was asking how it could have happened again, with Cindy!

I struggled to get my response right. I opened my mouth to speak, but there was no air to even push out of my lungs. Before I could formulate an answer, she sobbed, "I guess I should have known better than to drive that route, but I wasn't even thinking about it. And then, just as I passed that spot on East Camelback where we crashed—oh God, I saw her again!" Mary fell into my arms, dissolving into tears, unable to continue.

Slowly it dawned on me. Mary didn't know. *She didn't know.* My shameful secrets were still my own. She'd had one of her visions, and that was what all this was about. The roller-coaster ride of my emotions was making me too dizzy to support her, so I led her to a chair at the table and scooted my chair right up next to hers.

"It was just a vision, sweetheart," I said, my hands shaking uncontrollably.

"But Francis, it wasn't the same! It was awful! It was the clearest one I've ever had, and *you were in it this time!* You were lying on the side of the road. It was so terrible; it looked like you were dead! It was you and that same woman I've seen before. Oh, how I've come to hate her, Francis! That woman with the skin-tight black clothing and the red lipstick and that long, shiny, black hair. Only—only this time, the hair started to *change*, Francis! It seemed to be turning from black to blonde! It was like the woman herself was changing into a different woman, starting with the hair, but then it all disappeared before I could see any more. Why? Why does this keep happening to me? I need to make it stop!"

My thoughts formed a tornado in my mind as I took my sobbing, trembling wife into my arms. "It's going to be okay, sweetheart. It's over now," I said.

Wiping her eyes and dabbing at her nose with a napkin, Mary asked, "Francis, why did you say you made a terrible mistake?"

I froze.

Mary continued, "It wasn't your mistake, honey. I know you don't like to drive. It was my mistake that we crashed that night."

Awash with more emotions than I knew how to process, I needed to step away to get my bearings. I said, "Let me get you a drink, sweetheart," and headed for the bar. What if this newest vision brought flashes of memory with it? What if she were about to remember the conversation in the car that preceded the crash?

I had to tell her before she remembered it on her own! But how could I tell her when she was in such a disoriented frenzy?

"Hey, look who it is!" said the bartender. It was Dave, the one I'd met the night I'd been here with Cindy.

"Just a glass of Chardonnay," I said, hoping my tone would let him know that I wasn't in the mood for small talk.

"That blonde you came in with the other night, Mr. Rose—wow, what a hottie! I bet women throw themselves at you like crazy! That Christian rock thing must really melt the chicks' hearts—and panties!" He winked at me, wiggling his eyebrows.

"Can you just get me the wine?"

"Sure, sure, I'm getting it. I bet it's for that other beauty you have lined up over there in the corner. I gotta hand it to you, man, it's a great gig! What an act!"

I threw money on the bar and took Mary's wine. "Cindy is a longtime family friend," I said, "and that beauty over there is *my wife*."

Dave smiled broadly. "Okay, Mr. Christian rock star! Your secret is safe with me! Rock on!"

Mary was still visibly shaken when I returned with her wine. Frustrated and at the end of my rope, I said, "Damn it, sweetheart, I'm so goddamn sorry this keeps happening. What can I do to help you?"

"Just please help me figure out how to make it stop, Francis. With all of Eddie's issues lately, and with you being gone so much working on *Forgiven*, I've really been struggling. I need you now more than ever."

Mary brought my hand up and gently laid it on the side of her cheek, searching my face for reassurance that I would be her hero and protector, just as I'd always been. Over her shoulder, I saw bartender Dave watching us. Catching my eye, he made a zipping-up-the-lips gesture, letting me know that his lips were sealed.

I slouched back in my chair, leaning my head on the headrest, dead and empty inside. All my hopefulness at being near the end of my self-inflicted torture, all my resolutions and pure intentions—I watched them all melt away like the ice in my root beer. The confession wasn't going to happen—not now, and probably not ever. I would never be unburdened of my sin. I had done the deliverance with Pastor John, and that would just have to be the extent of my repentance. Whatever weak, pathetic, sinful creature I'd become, it was time for me to accept the truth of it and move on.

CHAPTER 14

A few days after my failed confession attempt, Mary went to see Dr. Shapiro. We were hoping he'd be able to do something or prescribe something for the flashbacks that were becoming so frightening and dangerous for her. She called me on her way home.

"What did the doc say, sweetheart?" I asked.

"Nothing very promising," she sighed. "He said I should get more rest, avoid *any* further stress, and take any number of over-the-counter memory-enhancement supplements. But aside from that, there's not much he can do for dissociative amnesia. Oh, but he did have one exciting bit of news, Francis!"

"What's that, honey?"

"He said that these types of vivid and intense visions are a sign that I might be on the verge of regaining my full memories from the day I lost! Wouldn't that be wonderful? It really does bother me to have lost the memories of a whole day of my life. Especially such a lovely day!"

I was glad she couldn't see my face. I forced a cheerful voice and said, "Wow, that sure is good news."

"He asked me about everything going on in my life, and when I told him we were getting close to the anniversary of my dad's death, he said it's possible that something emotionally traumatic like that could provide the final trigger for the recovery of my lost memories."

"It has been a whole year, hasn't it?"

"Yes, and what an eventful year it's been! Francis, do you think the accident has changed me? Cindy keeps telling me how tired I look, and she even said last week that I look terrible."

I had to sit down. "Honey, don't worry about what Cindy says. You look beautiful to me."

"Thank you, Francis. But have you noticed how strange Cindy's been acting lately? She keeps saying she's worried about you for some reason and complaining that you don't call her back. Yesterday I found her sitting on the white couch with our wedding album, just staring at the pages. When I asked what she was doing, all she could talk about was how beautiful I once *was*, and how it looked like our marriage had taken a toll on us both. It was like she wanted to tell me something."

My blood ran cold inside my body. "How did you respond to that, honey?"

"I didn't know what to say! I told her about all the stress I've been under, with Eddie's night terrors, the crash and my crazy visions, you working all the time, and the anniversary of Dad's death coming up. I told her I was going to see Dr. Shapiro, that you were going to see a new functional medicine doctor, and that she didn't have to worry about us."

"That's right, sweetheart. No one has to worry. Especially not

Cindy. Everything's going to be okay." I couldn't tell if I was trying to convince Mary or myself.

"Did you select a doctor yet from the list I gave you, Francis? Have you made an appointment?"

"Yep. I'm going tomorrow. I picked Doctor Yvonne Salacia, the one with the best reviews. She seems to give lectures on the subject often, plus she graduated from the University of Florida, just like the kids' doctor, who recommended her highly. Dr. Jill actually made a call on my behalf to get me in because this doc was booked solid."

"I'm so glad you're going. We both need to start taking better care of ourselves. We must really be falling apart for Cindy to notice and mention it!"

I had become accustomed to the never-ending pit in my stomach, but as Mary and I chatted, I could feel it turning to solid lead. *Better get used to it*, I told myself.

By the next morning I didn't think my anxiety could get any higher. It seemed to be wrestling with depression for space in my consciousness. The only relief I felt was when I was thinking about *Forgiven*'s upcoming press conference, wrap party, and tour. All I knew was I needed desperately to get away from this mess, and the tour would give me a legitimate reason to do that.

Driving to my appointment with the new functional medicine doctor, my mind wouldn't let go of the fresh hell I'd been through—the one that had just occurred this morning. As we were waking up, Mary had wanted to be intimate with me. It had been a while since I'd shown that kind of interest in her—not because I didn't love her, but because deep down I didn't feel I deserved that privilege with her. I guess she was feeling less stressed after her appointment with Dr. Shapiro, and it had been so long that she decided to take matters into her own hands—literally. It had started out pleasant enough. I was glad she wanted to be that close with me. But then—*nothing*.

Throughout my whole life, no matter what was going on, I'd always been virile. Never before that moment had I failed to perform sexually. Questions haunted me. Was it the stress of the album's upcoming release? The guilt from the infidelities? Was God punishing me for my indiscretions? Or, worst of all, had I completely lost my desire for Mary?

With all these options spinning through my brain a forbidden idea slipped into my mind. It was the only thing I could think of doing to save the situation. I fantasized about Cindy—her silky, naked curves, her slippery-hot hunger for me. With those memories in full swing, it didn't take much to get my motor running. Mary didn't have a clue, and she certainly seemed pleased with the outcome. But in hindsight the whole thing was making me feel sick. That infamous passage from the book of Matthew popped into my head: "But I tell you that anyone who looks at a woman lustfully has already committed adultery with her in his heart."

"Fuck!" I shouted in my car, pounding my hand on the steering wheel. "Fuck!" Even now, I realized, I was again committing adultery in my mind.

I pulled into the parking lot and found the office with the gold sign above the door that read Salacia Health. There was a parking spot up front marked RESERVED FOR DR. SALACIA. In the spot was a brand-new bright red Porsche Panamera Turbo with the vanity plate BUTYDOC.

Booty Doc? I asked myself, wondering if I was in the right place. Wait, it must mean "Beauty Doc." I supposed that was fitting. Even though the title "functional medicine doctor" sounded health-oriented, I knew the main purpose of this kind of doctor was to get people looking better, younger, and less like victims of their lives. I knew because that was pretty much why I'd come.

"I'm here to see Dr. Salal—"

"It's pronounced 'Sa-LA-she-a,'" said the chipper receptionist, handing me a clipboard. "You can sign in right here, and I'll be with you in just a moment!"

The waiting room was luxuriously appointed, with slate floors, leather furniture, and tasteful accents. The wood-paneled walls were covered with expensive artwork, awards, diplomas, and accolades. There was a framed photo of Christy Brinkley that caught my eye. She was standing with her arm around a flat-out gorgeous woman who made Christy look like a plain-Jane in comparison. Another photo showed Raquel Welch with the same bombshell beside her, and a third with Sylvester Stallone and the buxom beauty. It had to be Dr. Salacia. Was she the secret reason all these celebs looked so great for their age?

I started to wonder if I belonged in this office. Sure, I was suffering from some premature aging, but I was only forty! I knew I had a few faint lines on my face, and self-induced stress had taken its toll, but maybe this appointment was overkill. As I gazed at the photos of Dr. Salacia, I wondered on a different level if perhaps coming here had been a mistake. I quickly put that thought aside as the office assistant called my name and led me back to the doctor's private office.

"Francis Rose? Wow, it really *is* Francis Rose!" the office assistant said, becoming flustered. "I heard you guys are releasing a new album! When will the first show be?"

I followed her down the corridor. "Can't let that information out too early! We're having a press conference next week to announce the tour dates and locations. I'll let you in on a little secret, though. The first show is close to home!" I winked, causing her to blush as she led me into Dr. Salacia's swanky office.

"Be sure to watch our Facebook page!" I told her. "We'll be streaming the press conference on Facebook Live from the Beverly Hills Hotel. *Access Hollywood* will be covering it, and maybe *The 700 Club*, too."

The doctor, who had been sitting at her desk going over a file, looked up. I sucked in my breath, seeing her face for the first time. Even with her lab coat, glasses, and pulled-back hair—she was astonishingly sexy. *What an excellent walking commercial for her business she is,* I thought.

"Do you think I could get a really quick autograph while Dr. Salacia reviews your patient profile?" the assistant asked, shoving a prescription pad at me. I signed it, and she scurried away as if she possessed the secret formula for Coca-Cola or the recipe for Kentucky Fried Chicken.

As Dr. Salacia stood up, I caught a brief glimpse of her full-figure curves beneath her lab coat. She extended her hand. "Yvonne Salacia. Pleasure to meet you."

Our eyes locked as a wisp of her reddish-brown hair fell across her face. I'd experienced chemistry with women before, but *wow*. Immediately I wished I'd chosen another doctor. The last thing I needed was to be led down this path again. It wasn't too late. I could still make sure this was my last appointment. I decided it would be best to choose the next doctor on the list as soon as I got out of here.

"You too," I said, trying valiantly to shut down the reactions cascading through my system. Instinctively I glanced at her left hand to see if she was wearing a wedding ring. She wasn't.

"You must be someone important for my med school girlfriend to insist I fit you in today. According to my assistant Grace, I should know who you are or at least have heard of your band. Sorry."

"No big deal here. Just an aging rock star who's never had his picture taken with Christie Brinkley, Sly Stallone, or Raquel Welch."

She smiled, sizing me up. I held her gaze, each of us seemingly daring the other to look away first.

"What brings you in, Francis?"

In spite of the palpable heat between us, I felt completely comfortable with her, as if we were old friends who had bantered many times before.

"I guess it's mainly stress from my touring schedule," I said. "Probably same as most of your patients, only without the touring."

"I'm not thinking about any of my other patients right now." There was the smile again—not an open, warm smile exactly, but a wry half smile, as though I amused her. "Anything other than the touring causing your stress?" she asked.

Such an open-ended question. I couldn't help but wonder if she had this kind of initial connection with everyone who came in for a first appointment. She motioned for me to sit with her in the ornately carved mahogany, velvet-upholstered chairs in the sitting area adjacent to her desk.

I started with a few mild medical issues I'd had in the past (dehydration and a hernia), and then I told her about the grueling forty-day tour around Lent, Mary's dad's death, and the car accident, making sure to include many references to "my wife."

"Some of my patients are shy about what they disclose in their profile questionnaire. Drugs?" she asked, without a hint of judgment.

"Other than an occasional Tylenol or baby aspirin, none," I replied. "Not ever. Not prescription or street."

"How often do you drink alcohol?"

"Don't touch it. I may be a rock star, but that scene was never my thing."

"Well, Francis, none of this is raising any major red flags. You said you were feeling stress, but you haven't shared anything recent that sounds particularly stressful for a man as young and vibrant as you appear."

She was right. I hadn't told her about the parts of my life that were actually responsible for nearly all my stress.

"Really? How about that excessive touring?" I blurted out, relieved to have come up with a legitimate stress-inducing condition of my life. "It wasn't that long ago that Justus did that forty-day living Stations of the Cross tour for Lent, and now we're getting ready to go on tour again. It's incredibly physically demanding to be on the road for long stretches, doing shows night after night."

"*Mmmm.* I'm sure it is," Yvonne said, scribbling in my file and not looking the slightest bit impressed by my glamorous rock-star obligations.

"Is that all?" she asked, leveling a knowing glance at me over her glasses.

There was something so comforting about her—inviting, even. I somehow got the sense that she understood me, wouldn't judge me, and was perhaps even more *like* me than the people I ordinarily surrounded myself with. As harshly as I'd been judging myself, I got the feeling with her that I wouldn't be judged, and since this was going to be my last visit with her, I craved the relief of unburdening myself to her.

"Nah, that isn't all. There might be one more thing," I said.

Her eyebrows shot up with renewed interest, as if to say, "I thought so."

"I mean, I do feel stress about the upcoming tour. That's part of it, believe me. But there's another part. In two separate situations in the past few months, I've done something I deeply regret; something I never thought I'd do, something so out of character that it has really taken a toll on me. It's not who I am, believe me. It's—I've—I've been unfaithful to my wife."

Yvonne nodded, not looking at all surprised. Was it something she'd already guessed about me? Was I really that transparent? Or was she just that good at sizing up her patients?

"And you're feeling stress over these marital indiscretions?" she asked.

"Wouldn't anyone?" I countered.

Yvonne declined to answer, but her slight shrug told me all I needed to know about her position on the topic.

"Have you and your wife been to a marriage counselor?" she asked.

"No. My wife doesn't know about this, and I don't plan on her ever finding out. It's destroyed me! It goes against my religion, my songs, and everything I stand for. I still can't believe it happened. But it's all behind me now, and I just have to learn to live with it."

Yvonne studied me coolly. She wasn't going to absolve me, but I could tell she wasn't going to condemn me, either. Finally she said, "Ah. Well. According to my medical observations of you, you're a human being."

My eyes fell on the diamond cross glittering at the cleavage point of her blouse. "I see your cross. Are you a Christian? You're such a good listener."

She laughed. "So only Christians are good listeners?"

Hearing her say it made me feel foolish for suggesting such a thing, even though there were many passages in the Bible about Christians being good listeners.

"As for your question, I like diamonds and pretty jewelry," she said evasively. "Now let's see what we can do for you. While I don't condone your affairs, you're a very attractive man, and I'm guessing your testosterone levels are probably quite high, so having low T is out of the question. If I thought you weren't having enough sex, I'd give you this pamphlet to read."

Yvonne handed me the pamphlet. It was titled *15 Science-Backed Reasons to Have More Sex*.

"Sex reduces stress," she continued. "So keep having sex. Maybe try sticking to sex with your wife." There was no humor, nor judgment in Yvonne's delivery, and it almost seemed she was enjoying my situation. I felt mildly embarrassed by her suggestion.

"Also, you'll benefit from some vitamin IVs. You're run down, and you have a history of dehydration. I'd like to start you out on an intense detox-and-regeneration IV cocktail as soon as possible. It'll do wonders for your stamina and make your skin glow for that press conference."

"Thank you, Dr. Salsa—"

"Call me Yvonne."

"Thank you, Yvonne. This sounds exactly like what I need before my trip to Beverly Hills and also before I hit the road for my six-month *Forgiven* tour." Why did I feel the need to remind her once again that I'm a rock star?

"Shall we schedule you for next week, then? I'm presenting at a medical conference at the Beverly Wilshire next weekend, and I'd like to see you in here before I go so I can personally monitor the IV treatment. Didn't you say your press conference was at the Beverly Hills Hotel? I love that place, and it's just a mile away from the Wilshire. I'll have a few IVs with me, so let me know if you want a treatment in Beverly Hills right before your event."

I could tell it was my cue to leave, but suddenly I didn't want to go. She knew the worst there was to know about me, and she wasn't making me feel like a monster. It felt like she cared. "Yeah, I'd like to come back as soon as possible," I said.

"Check with Darlene on your way out for next week's availability," she said.

Yvonne seemed to be done with me, so I reluctantly headed out.

"Thank you for everything," I said.

"Of course," she responded.

Then, as I was halfway out the door, she added, "You'll like my treatment plan for you. I promise."

CHAPTER 15

Stephanie clapped her hands to get our attention. "Your skills are legendary, Rikki, but lay off for a sec, okay? I can't hear myself think!"

Rikki sheepishly raised his drumsticks in a surrender pose after having rattled them across every surface in the recording studio for the previous twenty minutes. I guess we all had a little excess energy built up.

"Friday is the big day in 90210-town," Stephanie continued. "And we all have to bring our A-game to this press conference. The international media and our fans are expecting something amazing, this being the release of our twentieth-anniversary album, and we can't let them down. We know *Forgiven* will blow them away when they hear it, but let's elevate the gifts God has given all of you to a new level and take the opportunity at this press event to make sure we let them know how really special it is!"

We burst into a cacophony of shouts and whistles, all of us excited to see the fruits of our hard labor about to be unveiled for our fans.

"Can I bring this beauty to show off?" Tracy asked, holding up her guitar. She'd had an image of the band hand-painted on it with Jesus looking over all of us, and she was so proud to show us. I loved seeing how dedicated my bandmates were to Justus and all it stood for.

"Only if I can bring *this* beauty to show off," countered Mike, lifting his T-shirt and flexing his pecs. He'd recently had *JUSTUS* tattooed across his chest in large black gothic letters, with the *T* made of two spikes similar to those used to nail Christ to the cross. The whole word danced when he flexed.

Stephanie laughed, pointing at each of us in turn with her admonishments. "Tracy, yes. Mike, keep your shirt on, dude. Rikki, keep those sticks still and silent during the press conference. And you—"

Stephanie paused, looking into my eyes. For a brief moment I worried about what she might say. "You—I want you to eat well these next few days and get plenty of sleep. Don't let yourself get any more run down than you already are. You have Beverly Hills, then Haiti the following week to receive your medal. I want you looking and feeling your best."

Mike let out a low whistle. "Francis is just tired from keeping up with all that fan mail," he teased.

"Yeah," said Tracy. "And sniffing all that perfume on the letters from the lady fans has made the color drain from his face."

Everyone chuckled, but I wasn't in the mood for that line of joking. A few months ago maybe, but not now. "I hear you guys. I'm going straight from here to the doctor to make sure I'm in good shape for next week. Don't worry. I won't let you down. I'll be ready."

"Whoa, so serious, dude," said Mike. "Relax, fearless leader."

As I grabbed my keys, Stephanie said, "I've set up a few one-to-one interviews for you early on Friday. I want you to check into the hotel on Thursday so you'll be all ready, okay?"

"Yep. Got it," I assured her, heading out. She walked with me, as if she wanted to say something more, but we both were silenced by what we saw when I opened the studio door. Cindy was leaning up against her car, obviously waiting for me to come out. She was wearing high heels, short shorts, and a halter top, all in tattered red, white, and blue.

An exacerbated groan rumbled from Stephanie's throat. She inched back into the studio, shouting, "Do the right thing, Francis. I mean it," with plenty of volume for Cindy to hear it.

My eyes adjusted to the bright sunlight and glare coming off Cindy's car while I silently prayed, "Oh, Saint Jude, patron saint of desperate and lost causes, please help me with what is now a totally desperate and lost cause."

"Hi, handsome," said Cindy. "You getting ready for your big tour announcement?" I detected an undercurrent of anger and sarcasm in her chipper voice and demeanor. "You know, even though I'm not nearly as Christian as you are, I did look up Matthew 7:12. You probably already know what it says, but I wanted to share it with you." She held up her bedazzled iPhone and read, "'So, in everything, do to others what you would have them do to you, for this sums up the Law and Prophets.' What do you think of that, Francis? You've been avoiding me, and I don't think you'd like it if I did that to you."

I'd like that very much, I said in my head, but I thought better of speaking it out loud. I nervously tried to recall the specifics of my conversation with Pastor John. I was counting on his deliverance to make this dreaded exchange easier for me.

"Look, Cindy," I said, in what I hoped was a relaxed, friendly tone. "I haven't been calling you back because what we did was wrong. I'm asking you to put it behind us now, like I've done. Let's just return to being the friends we've always been, okay?"

"Oh, I can be friends. But you know what friends do? They return their friends' phone calls. I get that you want to do the friendship thing for now, but we both know our friendship could evolve into so-o-o much more." Cindy ran her finger down my arm seductively. Then, motioning toward the backseat of her car, she added, "Hop in, and I'll remind you how friendly we can be together."

My body lurched to attention at her suggestion, but I angrily shut it down. Taking a moment to cement my intentions, I firmly replied, "Cindy, I value our friendship and all you have meant to me and Mary over the years. Our kids love playing together, and your Julie is so good with little Eddie. I want things to return to the way they were before we . . ." I struggled for the right words.

"Before we *what*, Mr. Christian rock star? You know, you profess such love in your songs. Love for God, love for your fellow man. The lyrics are so beautiful, and you know, I've always had a theory about one of your songs, Francis. Whenever I hear 'Sea Rose' I think maybe you secretly wrote that song in code, just for me. The future Mrs. Francis Rose. Cindy Rose. C Rose. Admit it, Francis—you haven't stopped thinking about me. I know you have our night burned into your memory, just like I have it burned into mine. We're soul mates, and we both know it."

Hearing the term *soul mates* brought me back to Pastor John's efforts to cut the ungodly soul ties I'd formed with Cindy and Paulina. Angrily, I told her, "Cindy, we are *not* soul mates. We never will be! We're *friends*, but if you can't put our poor decision that night behind you, we won't be friends anymore, either. And that song 'Sea Rose'? It's about a ship that carried flowers donated from Jewish and Christian congregations to troops fighting overseas in World War II. That's what it's about. Nothing more. I have to go!"

I tried not to linger on Cindy's tearful expression, afraid to be sucked into further conversation with her. I felt strong and empowered, having finally said what I'd been wanting to say for weeks. I got in my car and drove out of the parking lot, leaving Cindy standing by her Maserati until she was just a speck in my rearview mirror.

I wanted to stay angry, but as I drove I felt myself softening toward Cindy. She really seemed to have lost touch with reality. And her fantasy obsession with me was at least partly my own fault, I reasoned. As I started to worry about having been too harsh, a text from her came through. "Francis, I'm sorry if I upset you. I love you, and I always will. If it's only friends we can be, then I'll be blessed to have you as a friend in my life."

Relief washed through me as I typed back, "I'm sorry if I spoke harshly to you, Cindy. You mean the world to me and Mary, and I, too, am blessed to have you in my life. Thank you for understanding." I hit send, thankful that I'd finally gotten through to her.

Immediately Cindy's reply came back: "I'll be here for you when you're ready, superstar," followed by a winky-face and two heart emojis. My hopes collapsed. I wished I hadn't responded.

As I pulled into Yvonne's office parking lot, I noticed her red Porsche again. Grabbing my jacket from the back of the car, I smoothed my hair, put a few eyedrops in, and checked myself in the rearview mirror. So what if I'd dressed a little nicer than usual? It was an upscale medical office, and I simply wanted to fit in. As I walked by the Porsche, I ran my finger along the shiny exterior and noticed that it didn't have a speck of dirt on it. I felt good, looking forward to seeing Yvonne again but mostly looking forward to the boost I hoped to get from the treatment.

It felt like all eyes were on me while I signed in at the reception desk. One of the employees behind the counter pointed to his earbuds, then pointed at me with a big smile and a thumbs-up. He seemed to be telling me he was listening to Justus, and I assumed the office staff had Googled me after my last visit.

"Right this way, Mr. Rose," said the pretty, young nurse, leading me to a treatment room. "Dr. Salacia will be in soon, but I'm going to get you started. You must be getting ready for a world tour or something! The doctor has concocted a very potent detox-and-regeneration cocktail for you. How are you with needles?"

"I get light-headed at the sight of a pushpin," I confessed. "Go easy on me." I looked away as she plunged the needle into my arm and adjusted the flow. Squirming anxiously in my seat, I saw a familiar figure in the hall heading toward us. Yvonne's high heels clipped the marble floor as the doctor approached me, looking stunning in her tailored lab coat with a white shirt and white pants underneath. The consummate professional, she sat down next to me and re-took my pulse. Peering at me over her glasses, she said, "Just relax and take deep breaths."

Looking at the nurse's notes, she pointed out that, in addition to my heart racing, my blood pressure was a bit elevated. I suspected that this was a result of her close proximity to me, but I told her it must be because of my fear of needles. Scooting in closer to check the IV flow, she adjusted it and said, "The drip will take over an hour. By the way, did you get a chance to read the pamphlet I gave you? Or better yet—have you had a chance to put its advice into practice?"

I felt my face flush at her blatant question.

"It's the high concentration of Vitamin C that makes you blush like that," she said with a sly wink.

I leaned in close and whispered, "No, I didn't read it. And we really don't need to talk about it."

She flashed me the wry smile I was starting to enjoy and said, "Okay then, Francis. You just sit here and drip. You'll feel fantastic in about an hour. Your fans will thank me."

I couldn't help but watch Yvonne as she walked out of the room to see another patient. Authoritative and confident, her strut added to her sex appeal. Just then my phone rang and I saw that it was Mary. Feeling like I'd been caught red-handed watching Yvonne's body in motion, I answered immediately.

"Hi, sweetheart."

"How is the treatment going? Feeling strong yet?"

"Getting there, I think."

"Good, honey. I want you to feel your best for the upcoming big weekend. And this weekend is actually what I wanted to talk to you about. I've given it some thought, and I've decided what will be best for me and Eddie. You know how much I've been struggling with this first anniversary of my dad's death. Well, I talked to Mom today, and she's having a really hard time with it, too. I've decided I need to go be with her, Francis. We'll be able to comfort each other and honor his memory together, just as he would have liked."

"But—but what about my press conference and the party?"

"I know, sweetheart. I know you wanted me to be there. But you'll be so busy with the band and reporters and paparazzi. You wouldn't have had any time for me and the kids, anyway. They'll get so much more out of being with me in Flagstaff. Eddie always does better when we're there, and he keeps saying he misses Grammy. This way the kids and I can focus on remembering and honoring their grandfather."

"This thing is a really big deal, you know. It's Justus's twentieth anniversary." I couldn't understand how she could fail to see how important the weekend was to me.

"I've been there at all the other anniversaries," she said. "I think you can get through this one without me."

I was frustrated and angry but unsure about my right to be. "I just don't see why you have to go *this* weekend," I whined.

"I can't exactly change the weekend of my father's death anniversary," Mary countered, a bit of an edge to her voice. "Maybe you should have thought of that before scheduling your big party."

Seeing Yvonne on her way back to check on me, I hastily wrapped up the call. "You're right. Of course. I understand. Got to go," I said.

"We can talk about this later," Mary answered as we hung up.

Yvonne sat down next to me again. Sensing my distress, she

said, "You know, there's a reason they call this a rejuvenation IV. You should really try to relax."

For a moment I was tempted to tell her about Mary and her unreasonable decision to make her own selfish plans for the weekend, but I thought better of it. Yvonne's hands were warm as she checked my blood pressure and leaned in close to listen to my chest with her stethoscope. She smelled amazing—crisp, fresh, and inviting. With the stethoscope still pressed to my heart, she said, "I read up on you this week. Your work in Haiti; all you've done for the poor—you have a big, beautiful heart. I find that more attractive than anything else in a man. So hard to find."

"Thank you," I said, wondering if she really needed to be listening to my heart this long.

"I'm actually going back to Haiti in two weeks."

"I saw that. Congratulations. A well-deserved award." Yvonne stood up and began writing in my file, apparently having finally heard all she needed to hear of my heartbeat. She didn't look at me or give any outward sign of being especially impressed with me, in spite of her words.

I overheard the secretary booking Yvonne's reservations for the Beverly Wilshire and remembered her saying it was only a mile from my hotel. Not that it mattered, I told myself. Or maybe it would be a good idea to get a treatment just before the press conference, like Yvonne had suggested. After all, I was already feeling better from this concoction. I let my disparate thoughts wrestle inside my head. Was the treatment just an excuse? I tried praying my thoughts away, but they wouldn't budge.

I reflected again on my painful soul-tie extraction with Pastor John. Now that the old soul ties had been broken, shouldn't this kind of temptation be easier to quell? But Pastor John had said I wouldn't truly be free of my sinful state unless I repented to Mary, which I had not been able to bring myself to do. Was this really who I'd become? Why was I even fighting it?

"You're about done here, Francis," Yvonne said when she was finished writing. "I'm leaving next Thursday morning for Beverly Hills. Do you want to ride with me? I've chartered a plane for the day, and you're welcome to join me. Anyone else in your band, too, if they're going. The flight is about an hour; you could take an IV on the way and arrive refreshed and ready for your big event."

I didn't know what to say. Her offer sounded amazing. My phone vibrated, and I saw that Mary was calling me back, probably concerned that we'd hung up on such a sour note. My eyes fell on her contact photo. It was a family portrait, taken for our last Christmas card. Heather and Eddie's hands were clasped as Mary and I beamed at them lovingly. Choked up, I sent the call to voice mail and looked at Yvonne.

"Thank you for the offer," I said. "That's really nice of you. I'm actually the only one flying in on Thursday. The rest of the band arrives Friday. I wouldn't want to inconvenience you, so I better pass."

Yvonne blinked back her surprise that I had declined her offer. She held out her hand. "Can I have your phone?" she asked.

I hesitated for a moment, then unlocked it and handed it to her. She opened my contacts folder, typed in her number, and handed the phone back, smiling. I saw that she had given herself the first name *Doctor* and the last name *Yvonne*.

"There," she said. "In case you change your mind or want that IV while you're out there."

Fascinated by her confidence, charm, and beauty, I tucked my phone back in my pocket.

"See? I told you. You look better already," she said with a wink.

CHAPTER 16

Raising my sore arm to retrieve my duffel bag from the top shelf of the closet, I noticed the vein bruise from the IV needle. Enticing images of Yvonne sitting next to me with her stethoscope against my chest danced across my consciousness, then were chased away by Heather's sweet voice gently chiding Eddie.

"Daddy has enough shoes, now. He doesn't need any more."

In his eagerness to be helpful, Eddie had brought seven pairs of shoes from my closet and lined them up with the clothing I'd laid out to pack. Undeterred by Heather's logic, he continued to run back and forth between my closet and my bed, selecting footwear and accessories for my trip.

Heather patiently replaced the unnecessary items while Eddie, wearing a tattered T-shirt with an iron-on photo of him and Grammy, ran into the bathroom. He came out proudly waving my toothbrush, toothpaste, and a bar of soap. "Daddy brush his teeth and wash his face," he said sternly, dangling Rosey by the cherished four tentacles that to Eddie represented our family of four.

Watching the kids help me pack made my heart hurt again at the realization that they wouldn't be with me. After twenty years of struggle, Justus had finally made it big. I was at the pinnacle of my success, and my family wouldn't be there to share it with me. It just didn't seem right. I knew Mary had valid reasons for wanting to go to Flagstaff, but she hadn't really been talking to me about them, and I still couldn't quite understand why it was important enough to her that she would abandon me when I needed her most. I wished she would be more open and vulnerable with me, like she had been at the Sanctuary after the vision that had really scared her. As soon as the thought crossed my mind, I registered the unfairness of it. I certainly hadn't been open with her, either, lately.

Oblivious to my dissatisfaction, Mary came in and plopped down a warm basket of fresh laundry. "Clean underwear and jeans for the rock star," she teased. "You two need to leave Daddy to his packing and get to work on yours," she told the kids. "We all leave bright and early in the morning!"

"Eddie loves Grammy!" said Eddie, running off to fill his own little suitcase with shoes. But Heather lingered, twisting her toe on the ground as if she had something she wanted to say.

"Aren't you excited to see Grammy, too, sweetheart?" I asked her.

"Yeah, I guess," she replied unconvincingly. "It's just—I really wanted to go with you, too, Daddy. Mommy, why can't we go see Grammy after Daddy's show in California?"

Mary was upbeat but in no mood for negotiations. "Heather, sweetie, it's not really a show. You'll get to see Daddy's new *Forgiven* show soon. Grammy needs us there tomorrow, and Eddie is so excited."

"Then can't you just take Eddie to see Grammy and let me go with Daddy? You did it last time, and Daddy and I had so much fun. Remember, Daddy? Glenda the Good Witch will click her heels and be with you in California."

I looked at Mary. "Heather's right," I said. "Your mom isn't going anywhere. She'll be right there in Flagstaff after our Beverly Hills events, and Eddie won't know the difference for a few days. This twentieth-anniversary release will only happen once. All the other band members' families will be there. I'll tell you what—how about we leave early Saturday morning for your mom's, right after the release party on Friday night?"

Eddie ran back into the room holding his blanket around his shoulders like a cape. "Eddie Superman!" he shouted.

"Just look at him, Francis," said Mary. "He's been wearing his favorite shirt with her picture on it for two days straight now. I can't break his little heart. They really need each other. And Mom and I need each other, too, on this painful anniversary."

Mary's inflexibility was triggering the envious anger I always felt bubbling within me when she obsessed over Eddie. "Heather, please take Eddie and help him pack," I said.

Heather flashed me a conspiratorial grin, obviously hoping I would convince her mother to let her stay with me. "C'mon, Superman," she said, taking Eddie by the hand not occupied by Rosey. "I'll be Wonder Woman. Let's see whose packing super-powers are the best."

Once they were out of earshot, I said, "You're being unreasonable, Mary. The next few days are a really big deal, and I need you and the kids with me."

"With you? Or lurking in the background?" Mary shot back. "Francis, this is all about *you*. All about you and Justus. It's not about us. It's selfish of you to try to keep me from being where

I need to be on the anniversary of my father's death. You know you'd barely have any time for me and the kids if we were there."

"That's not the point," I argued. "The point is that you should want to be there for me. Even my *mother* said she would try to be there!"

Mary set down the shirt she was folding and stared at me in disbelief. "Madeleine? Seriously? Francis, when did this happen? I didn't know you'd been in touch with Madeleine!"

"Well, I have," I said, thankful that I'd finally gotten her attention. "I've talked to her a few times in the past month, and I feel like I've made some real headway in repairing our relationship."

My big revelation disarmed Mary's indignation. She'd been begging me to make things right with my mother for a long time. "Francis, that is wonderful," she said. "Why didn't you tell me?"

"I was hoping to surprise you when you saw her in California this week," I said, covering up the real reason I hadn't told Mary about my conversations with my mom.

"She's really flying in from Indiana?" Mary asked in amazement.

"Well, she didn't say she'd come for sure," I said. "But she did say she'd try. That's a pretty big step, considering the level of contact we've had these past years. And of course, all the other band members' families will be there. Hell, even Cindy wants to go. But not my wife."

I was hoping to guilt-trip Mary into changing her mind, but she just rolled her eyes at me as if to say, *Oh, please.*

"Well, I'm thrilled that you and Madeleine have been able to put the past behind you, and I hope you get a chance to spend some quality time with her out there. That would be so special," said Mary.

I felt like she was avoiding the subject, so I looked to scripture for an argument to use. "As I've told you before," I said, "I've always seen every line of Proverbs 31:10–31 as describing you. You are that wife, that gift, that treasure. But right now—Mary, I guess I just don't understand why you're making all this fuss over Eddie and your mom."

Mary looked sad, and for a moment I thought I might have penetrated her resolve. But she didn't cave. She finished folding the jeans in her hands and laid them on the bed. "I don't want to fight about this anymore. I am truly happy you've rekindled your relationship with your mom," she said, leaving the room.

The next morning, even though we all planned to leave early, I was scheduled to get out before Mary and the kids. I made Mary my special French Press coffee and left a note saying, "Good morning, sweetheart. I'm sorry we fought last night. I understand you needing to be with your mom on this emotional day. It's where you belong, and I'm sorry I was so selfish. I do hope you are able to comfort each other and that you have fun with the kids. Take lots of pictures and tell Mom I love her and will be thinking about you both and praying for you on this anniversary. Tell her I miss Ernie, too. I do love you. Francis."

I tiptoed into Heather's room to kiss her good-bye ever so lightly. She heard my footsteps, though, and rolled over, sleepy-eyed, to greet me. "I wish I could be with you on your big day, Daddy," she said, reaching her arms out to hug me.

"I know, sweetheart, I know. I'll miss you, but I really need you to take care of Mommy, Eddie, and Grammy. Will you do that for me?"

"Okay, Daddy. I will."

Seeing her sad face broke my heart. I slowly pulled her door closed and headed for Eddie's room. Eddie stayed sound asleep as I kissed his sweet cheek and tucked Rosey under his arm.

I stepped out onto my front porch to wait for Stephanie, humming our song "Forgiven" in my head. The first rays of light rising over Camelback Mountain filled me with gratitude for this momentous juncture in Justus's long journey. I was glad it would be just me and Stephanie flying out together ahead of the band. Even though Stephanie had lots of work to do before the press conference and party, her presence had always had a positive, stabilizing effect on me, and I cherished her friendship and loyalty.

After a short uneventful flight and what seemed like a longer limousine drive in the snarled California traffic, I found myself surrounded by fans in the lobby of the Beverly Hills Hotel. "You press some flesh and sign some autographs, superstar, while I get you all checked in," said Stephanie. She scooted through the growing throng that had instantly surrounded us and made her way to the front desk.

I felt bad that the record label had put her in a cheaper hotel nearby, reserving rooms at the swanky Beverly Hills Hotel only for me and the other band members. As the fans were starting to disperse, she held up a room key and said with a satisfied smile, "Presidential suite! The label is taking extra good care of its hot commodity!"

"I'll say! It's a far cry from the Red Roof Inn twenty years ago! Let's grab a bite here before you go."

"Too much to do. I have more to coordinate than you can imagine."

"What's on your list? Can I help?" I offered.

"Nope. I might even have a surprise for you up my sleeve. You don't get to know *everything* that goes on around here, mister." Stephanie's eyes sparkled. It was great to see her looking so happy again.

"Okay, okay," I said. I remembered her saying that she was arranging for some of the appetizers we had eaten at our very first release celebration to be served at this far grander release party. Who knew what else she had come up with along those nostalgic lines? "Well, don't work too hard. I want this to be a memorable fun few days for you, too."

"Oh, there's no doubt about that!" she said. "Your job right now is just to get plenty of rest and take care of your vocal cords." I watched Stephanie get back in the limo and cheerfully chat up the chauffeur as they pulled away.

I was excited, too, but I couldn't shake the sense that I was all revved up with no place to go—abandoned by my wife, ditched by my manager, and alone in a gorgeous landmark hotel in an exciting city. I wasn't hungry and didn't really want to go to my room yet. What to do? I cruised around the hotel for a bit, stopping in to check out the gym and the gift shop. I sat outside the shop sipping a root beer float and took my phone out of my pocket, acutely aware that Yvonne's number was lurking in there and that she had probably arrived by now.

I opened my contacts list, then quickly closed it and decided to call Mary instead.

"Hi, honey! Are you and the kids there yet?

"Um, just about."

"I wanted to see how you're holding up today. I know you'll be with your mom soon, but I wanted you to know I'm thinking about you on this anniversary and wishing we could be together."

"That's so sweet," said Mary, sounding distracted. "Honey, we're just pulling up to Grammy's house, so I have to go. Talk to you later, okay?"

I felt a little resentment and frustration rekindling at the mention of Grammy's house, but I tried to keep my voice in check. "Sure, I understand. Go take care of your mom and have fun. Hug Grammy for me."

I didn't feel like heading up to my lonely hotel room just yet, even if it *was* the presidential suite, so I went back and wandered around the lobby and decided to check out the legendary Polo Lounge. As I walked into the bar I felt my phone vibrate in my pocket. It was probably Mary calling to apologize for being so short with me.

I looked at the screen and saw that it was Doctor Yvonne. The text read, "Hi, Francis. Hope you're feeling good and ready for your big press conference. I'm here at the Beverly Wilshire. I brought an extra rejuvenation IV. If you're interested, you could come over, or I'd be happy to bring it there."

I read and reread the message, trying to sort out my mixed feelings. I couldn't deny the charge I got from seeing her name and reading her words. Her suggestion seemed professional enough. She was a doctor, and I was her patient. The IV I'd gotten from her previously had done wonders for my energy level and overall state of wellness. It only made sense that I'd want to get that treatment again before such an important event. I had time to kill, and this seemed like a good use of it.

I thought about how best to respond. The word was out about Justus's big tour announcement tomorrow, and I was afraid that traipsing around Beverly Hills might require me to fend off even more fans. I hit the reply button and typed, "Hi, Doc. Thanks for thinking of me. I'm here at the BHH. Of course, a needle stuck in my arm for an hour is just what I was wanting. Kidding. I'd love to see you and your needle again. How about I meet you in a few hours, at 4:00 PM, in the Polo Lounge, and we'll take it from there?"

I held my breath, waiting for her response. Finally, three dots indicated she was typing. "Perfect" was all she wrote, but she included a doctor emoji and an emoji that seemed to picture a syringe with blood dripping from it.

Unusually excited about having a needle stuck in my vein, I went upstairs to shower and shave. Staring into the mirror, I heard Pastor John's voice in my head. "Repeat these words, Francis. 'By the blood of Jesus Christ and with the sword of the spirit I command you, demon spirit of pride, lust, and adultery, to leave me now, and I cut any soul tie made by my sinful behavior.'"

I shook the thoughts out of my head, saying aloud to the mirror, "Don't worry. I've got this."

At around four o'clock I entered the Polo Lounge to find Yvonne sitting on a high-back maroon velvet couch by the back wall. I had half expected to see her in her white lab coat, but it was nowhere to be found. Instead she was wearing a beautiful white designer pantsuit and clear acrylic high heels. Her long auburn hair bounced freely around her shoulders, and the Louis Vuitton doctor's satchel at her side had Dr. Yvonne Salacia embroidered on it.

I approached her, unsure whether our greeting warranted a hug, and decided instead on an awkward handshake. "I'm clearly underdressed," I said. "I didn't want to get blood on my nice clothes, hence the T-shirt and jeans. But you look—" I searched for the words. "Well, you look very nice."

She flashed me that signature smile and said, "I thought I'd distract you a little bit while I put the needle in." Her tone was both playful and professional. It put me at ease. She sat on the far end of the plush velvet couch, leaving room for me to sit next to her. I opted to sit in the chair on the other side of the table.

The decor and aroma of the Polo Lounge was almost as intoxicating as the stunning woman sitting across from me. The opulence of this iconic, 1912 California landmark made everything feel like a movie. "What can I get you two?" asked the platinum-maned waitress.

I looked at Yvonne. "How about it, Doc?"

Yvonne glanced at her diamond Rolex watch and said, "Why not? With the exception of your treatment, I'm on vacation until my presentation tomorrow." I motioned for her to order, and she told the waitress, "I'll have a Bullet Rye Scotch with a splash of ginger ale."

Impressed by her bold choice and authoritative manner, I added, "And I'll have a root beer."

The waitress looked up from her notepad with a raised eyebrow. "Root beer for a guy who looks like he should be drinking Jack Daniel's?"

Yvonne seemed amused, too. She chimed in, "Yeah, don't you know there's a lot of sugar in root beer?"

"Don't you both know there's a lot of alcohol in alcohol?" I playfully snapped back.

"Right," said Yvonne. "And some doctors are the unhealthiest people on the planet." Glancing at me out of the corner of her eye, she asked, "Do I look unhealthy to you?"

"Nope!" chirped our waitress, before I could respond. Anyone looking at Yvonne would have to agree she appeared to be an impeccable example of radiant health and vitality.

We made small talk about our flights, our Beverly Hills commitments, and other banter-sprinkled topics that were clearly just excuses to spend some time sizing each other up. After about an hour, with Yvonne well into her second drink, she asked, "Where's your wife?"

"One of the biggest days of my life, and she decides she needed to be with her mom," I said, feeling the weight of it all over again. "I guess I understand. Today's the one-year anniversary of her father's death. But I just don't see why she couldn't have gone to be with her mom on Saturday. It will just be the band and me here."

Yvonne offered a consoling look. "Well, you have me and my needle for today," she said.

On the table, my phone rang. We both saw the name Mare Bear, along with the family photo I'd assigned to Mary. Yvonne looked at me. "I assume that's your wife. You want me to step away?" she casually asked.

I hesitated. "No, I'll call her later," I said, sending the call to voice mail.

Yvonne didn't argue; she seemed to have anticipated that I'd say that. Even though she was showing some evidence of feeling the effects of her two strong drinks, she maintained an air of supreme confidence. "Well, Mr. Francis," she said. "This IV treatment has your name on it." She reached into her Louis Vuitton satchel and pulled out an IV bag that, sure enough, had my first name neatly written on it with a red Sharpie, followed by an intricate hand-drawn rose to represent my last name.

"It literally does," I said. I was impressed with her artistic talent, remembering all the remarkable artwork in her office that bore her signature. Among her many charms and gifts, Yvonne was undoubtedly a talented artist.

"Yes, and although it might blend in, we can't risk spilling your precious blood on this beautiful couch," she continued. "Plus, the IV drip won't reach *all the way* over there where you're sitting." We both knew she was making a point about me choosing to sit across from her when I'd arrived.

In an authoritative and straightforward tone, Yvonne said, "I would prefer to administer to you in your room."

Her choice of words instantly aroused me. "Okay," I said. I felt a moment of virtue shoot through me, but it was gone before I could grab onto it.

Yvonne tossed her hair and pushed a strand behind her ear as she leaned in close and whispered, "I promise it won't hurt. It *could* even feel really, really good."

I nervously shrugged and said, "Doctor's orders, I guess. This way to the operating room." My attempt to defuse the mounting sexual tension with a little humor did nothing to defuse it. I threw some money down on the table and motioned toward the elevator outside the Polo Lounge.

As I followed Yvonne, my eyes lingered on her hips swaying with each stride of her stiletto-heeled designer shoes. I fought the urge to slip my arm around her waist. Could I be imagining her intentions?

I didn't have to wonder long.

Once we were inside the elevator, I inserted my key into the slot for the presidential suite as Yvonne's hands slid into my front jeans pockets from behind. I swung around to face her and she pressed her body against mine, forcefully pushing me up against the elevator buttons, momentarily triggering the alarm. Yvonne giggled and lifted her leg to half straddle me as she plunged her Scotch-flavored tongue into my salivating mouth.

I glanced at the concealed camera on the ceiling, which amused Yvonne. With her face close to mine, she brought her wet lips to my ear and whispered, "Don't worry. If a sex tape of you turns up online, it'll just help you sell millions more albums." I quickly positioned Yvonne in front of me, making sure her high-heeled stature obscured my face from the camera. As our embrace intensified, the elevator dinged our arrival on my floor. Before the doors were even fully open, Yvonne was pulling me through them, her jacket and shirt already unbuttoned.

Images of Cindy stripping off her red lingerie flashed through my mind, along with memories of Paulina and the intense lust I'd been able to overcome in the hotel room with her. This time, in this hotel, I knew there would be no point in fighting my desires. What good had it done me to throw away my shot with Paulina? I'd ended up an adulterous sinner, anyway. Was this really who I was now? If so, I was gonna like it. And judging from the ease and nonchalance with which Yvonne was embracing our carnal desires, there were plenty of people who lived this way and simply accepted this part of themselves. Now I was one of them. Like she said before, I was human, after all.

Once inside the room, I met Yvonne's aggressive passion with a burst of my own, much to her approval. She didn't even bother with my shirt, going straight for my jeans, deftly unsnapping and unzipping them and reaching boldly for her prize. She let out a satisfied cry when she saw and felt what she was looking for, falling to her knees and ravenously relishing her feast. I arched back against the wall, knocking down a picture frame and a vase on the adjacent shelf, sending them shattering on the floor. I surrendered, offering myself to her, reeling in the sublime bliss of her voracious appetite.

When I'd nearly reached the pinnacle of pleasure overload, I reached under her arms and picked her up, thrusting her onto the dining room table. Delighted with my show of forcefulness, she allowed me to undress her, peeling away layers of silk until nothing but the palest pink lace stood between me and her ample breasts and glorious, beckoning mound.

Savoring the moments, I gently removed her sheer Agent Provocateur bra, freeing her hard nipples as I caressed them lightly with my lips. Moving my attention downward, I peeled away her matching thong, already soaked with her hunger. Drunk with lust, I fervently payed homage to the fantastic bounty I uncovered there. Yvonne unleashed her orgasmic enthusiasm, writhing on the table as she raked her fingernails through my hair.

I scooped her up, honeymoon-threshold style, stumbling over her satchel and spilling the now-forgotten IV bag and needle onto the floor as I carried her to the gold brocade sofa. I sat us down as she wriggled into position on my lap, letting me know it was her turn to take charge. My head fell backward as she ran her tongue along my neck, tearing off my shirt from bottom to top, rendering me as naked as she was. Our flesh came together in ecstatic aliveness as she plunged me deep into her decadent mystery.

Countless penetrating engorgements later, she slowly stood. She crawled like a lioness to the opposite end of the couch, spreading her high heels and peering back at me over her shoulder, inviting me to penetrate her tunnel of love from a different angle as she draped her arms and breasts over the arm of the sofa. I fell into the exquisite rhythm of our choreography, letting the surreal waves of intensity cascade through me, over and over, as Yvonne burst into yet another orgasm.

Preventing my own ecstasy from coming to an end, I withdrew and turned her around. Our eyes locked as I again picked her up, Yvonne wrapping her legs tightly around me, conjoining our bodies like puzzle pieces that had finally found their perfect counterparts. I carried her to the bedroom, lowering her gently onto the satin-draped bed without ever losing our electric, full-body contact. Yvonne moaned her encouragement as I slowed down our dance, each parry growing more urgent and thrilling than the last.

Finally, Yvonne screamed out in primal abandon, her fervor exceeding her prior climaxes, and I knew it was my cue to just let go. I ravaged her, my bestial instincts leading the rhythmic parade, thrusting myself without restraint into her opulent chamber. I'd never felt so free, so physically alive, so on fire with passionate gluttony and unbounded lust. The explosion between us was like nothing I'd ever imagined. I fell next to her on the bed, both of us covered in sweat and fluids, both of us gasping for air. Laughing together and crying together, utterly depleted and staring at the ceiling, I groped for her hand, both our chests still rising and falling in rapid unison.

Moments passed, neither of us having the energy even to speak.

Then the silence was broken by the loud click-clack of the suite door opening.

I froze.

A chorus of happy, familiar voices shouted, "Surprise!"

It all happened in an instant, yet my experience of it was one of slow-motion horror. My eyes went from face to face: Mary, Cindy, Stephanie, my mom. I could hear Heather and Eddie's joyful voices until Mary's scream drowned them out.

In her shock, Stephanie tripped over Yvonne's satchel, spewing needles all over the floor and breaking the IV bag. Deep yellow fluid seeped into the white rug just outside the bedroom as Eddie reached down and picked up one of the uncapped needles. Violently shaking it from his hand, Stephanie quickly turned to scoop the children out into the hall before they could see me. My mother stepped past her to glare at me. "I guess you turned out like your father after all you, you lowlife jackass."

Yvonne pulled the covers around us both; I couldn't move. I watched Mary's eyes scan the pink lingerie and clothing strewn about the floor, the broken picture and vase, the tipped-over satchel with Yvonne's name embroidered on it. Her face took on a zombielike countenance, and her voice quivered as she said, "Francis, what are you doing? Who is this woman?"

My mind was a tornado. "What—what are you doing here?" I stammered. "You were supposed to be—"

"We decided to surprise you. I thought that was what you wanted. And now—this? You're doing this? To me? To our family? Oh, God, how long has this been going on?"

Cindy rested her hand on Mary's shoulder. "My dear Mary,"

she said in a sickeningly comforting tone. "Oh, Francis hasn't been the man you married for a long while. The last time you were visiting your mom he seduced me in your own house on your sofa. He told me he loves me. Just ask Stephanie; she witnessed the whole thing."

All the color had drained from Mary's face, and her eerily calm demeanor was terrifying. She slowly removed Cindy's hand from her shoulder without looking at her.

Yvonne indicated she'd had enough, gathering the coverlet from the bed and wrapping it around herself as she slunk out of the bedroom area to find her clothing. As she passed through the crowded doorway, Cindy uttered, "Slut" under her breath. Yvonne rolled her eyes, utterly unaffected by the fact that my world was shattering into excruciating, irreparable shards all around me.

Stephanie's sobs were the only sound in the otherwise silent microseconds that followed. She had apparently handed the kids off to my mother in the hall and was making her way into the bedroom. Her eyes—the eyes I'd counted on for compassion throughout my whole ordeal—bore into me with unbearable contempt. "How could you have done this? You've betrayed those who love you, Francis. But more important, you've betrayed the one who loved you most: God. May He have mercy on your soul." Stephanie motioned for Cindy to come with her, but Cindy seemed to want to stick around to witness the suffer fest. Stephanie said to Mary, "I'm here if you need me," then grabbed Cindy by the elbow and yanked her out of the suite, leaving only Mary standing at the foot of the bed.

Words swirled through my brain, but none were adequate for what I needed to say. I wanted Mary to cry, to scream, to hit me, but she had become a version of herself I'd never seen. It was as if the Holy Spirit had entered her, rendering her composed beyond reason, although it was clear to see the agony raging just beneath the surface of her veneer-thin composure.

She slowly backed into the settee across from the bed and sat down gingerly, her spine erect. It was as if she were watching a movie inside her mind, seeing all the pieces come together. She stared blankly out the window above my head. As if reciting lines from a play, she said, *"It's about Paulina, Mary. The woman I've been helping who wrote the musical . . . I'm afraid our professional relationship grew into something forbidden, something I deeply regret. I was not a good husband to you last night, Mary."*

My blood turned to ice as I began to make sense of her words. She was remembering the long-buried conversation we'd had in her white Range Rover the night my confession had caused her to drive us off the road. Her memory had fully returned.

Without emotion, she continued, *"I did. Yes. I kissed her and went to her hotel room. Hotel room . . . hotel room . . ."*

Her monotone recounting of the exact words I'd used sent chills through my body. Part of me wanted to stand up and grab her, to make the agony stop. But the futility of my situation had rendered me utterly unable to move or speak.

Finally Mary turned to look at me, her stare still vacant and her voice like death. Slowly, deliberately, she said, "It's all clear to me now. That woman you went to help with the musical, Paulina. You were with her. My best friend, Cindy. You seduced her in our own home. And now, in front of our children, there's this woman I assume is your doctor. You've slept with her. Francis, my heart. You've broken it into a million pieces. Wasn't I enough for you?

Wasn't my love enough? I'm sorry, I'm going to . . ." As her words trailed off, Mary's head tilted to the side, as if someone inside her had changed the channel.

"Actually, Francis, I'm not sorry for anything." The color started returning to Mary's face.

I sobbed, watching her numbness recede and her full-throttle pain begin seeping to the surface. She swallowed hard, stood up, and turned toward the door. She looked back at me and said, "I'm sad for you and the life you've chosen to throw away. I lost my dad a year ago. And today I lost my husband."

Terror shot through me as Mary walked out of the bedroom.

"Mary," I cried in horror. "Oh, Mary!"

Quietly, slowly, she closed the suite door behind her.

And I knew my Mary was gone.

CHAPTER 17

I barely slept, jolting awake from nightmare after nightmare in which I relived the horror of the "Surprise!" moment— the moment when the people I loved the most in the world discovered the filthy, disgusting truth about me. As the first rays of light bounced across my sweat-soaked pillow, I tried, for what felt like the hundredth time, to call Mary. At first she had ignored all my pathetic voice messages and texts, but at least I could see that they'd been delivered. I couldn't blame her for ignoring me, though, and eventually it became clear she'd blocked my number.

I even tried calling and texting my mom, and all I got was a scathing return text: "I raised an idiot for a son, Francis. At least your father was smart enough to take his mistress away. You just ruined your family and scarred your kids for life. Don't bother ever calling me again." Her words shot daggers through my heart, especially since our relationship had just so recently become what I'd always wanted it to be.

Why hadn't I run after Mary? That question had haunted me all night. But I knew the answer. I didn't chase her because I didn't have the guts to. I wasn't worthy of her consideration or attention. "You stupid idiot! You coward, Francis!" I shouted at myself, alone in the hotel room.

After hours upon hours of tears, I miserably tried to pull myself together. I ordered room service but couldn't eat a thing. First things first. There was no way I could deal with the interviews, press conference, and party. I had no idea what I would do with myself on this bleakest day of my life, but talking to the press and partying afterward certainly wouldn't be it. I picked up my phone to text Stephanie, and the memory of her face and last words to me started the flood of emotion all over again. I typed, "Hey, Steph. I'm so sorry. I'm a wreck. Please cancel my interviews and my appearance at the press conference and party today. Also, postpone my trip to Haiti next week to receive the award. I don't deserve it, and I can't handle any of this right now."

Lying back on the bed, staring at the ceiling, I waited for Stephanie's response. When my phone buzzed, though, it wasn't Stephanie's name lighting up the screen. It was Mary! Mary was answering me at last! I shot up like a cannon, flooded with gratitude and hope, adjusting my bloodshot eyes to read her precious words. "I'm unblocking my phone for this message only. I'm taking the kids, and we're going to be with my mom for a while. When you're done in Beverly Hills, please stay away from our house. Heather is hysterical, and Eddie won't eat or talk. He's completely unresponsive. He just clutches Rosey with one hand, holding only three tentacles, and his baseball glove with your photo in it with the other hand, just staring out the window. I can't see you. Don't try to contact me. I'm deleting you from my phone until I can sort out what's next."

I immediately tried calling her, with no luck. It was true. She really had cut ties with me. I raged internally at not even having a chance to explain myself, but at the same time I knew I had no explanation whatsoever to offer. It was just so painful to be cut off from her and the kids and to imagine my sweet little boy dragging around his favorite toy by only three tentacles. I sat in misery, praying for her to have a change of heart. Then, as if in answer to my prayers, my phone alerted me to a new text message.

I leaped up in excitement, but this time it wasn't Mary. It was Stephanie, answering my earlier message. "If you want to cancel your commitments, Francis, cancel them yourself. I haven't decided whether I will continue working for Justus, but if I do return it won't be for you; it will be for the other band members, who shouldn't have to suffer for your sins. I need some time to think."

My tear ducts were empty. My eyes only burned. I had been supremely blessed to be surrounded by wonderful people who loved me. And now there was no one. I had never felt so alone. My own reflection in the hotel mirror disgusted me. I smashed it with my fist, blood dripping into the sink and onto the white marble floor. Wrapping a towel around my hand, I tried to find God, but I only found the many ways He had attempted to help me and protect me, all of which I had failed to heed. I even cursed the memory of 1 Corinthians 10:13: "No temptation has overtaken you that is not common to man. God is faithful, and He will not let you be tempted beyond your ability, but with the temptation He will also provide a way of escape, that you may be able to endure it."

"Escape!" I shouted. "There were escapes all around me, all along!" Mary's call, which I'd ignored when Yvonne asked if she should step away in the Polo Lounge, had been an opportunity for escape. Even before I'd gone down to meet Yvonne, I'd clearly heard Pastor John's voice offering a warning and deliverance as I was shaving. That had been another opportunity for escape. I was given two crystal-clear opportunities to do the right thing, and I'd failed to heed them, along with every other sign and escape route God had offered me.

My mom was right. Not only was I being an idiot, I now deserved to burn in hell for being one.

At the thought of Pastor John, though, I paused, feeling a minuscule glimmer of the potential for rescue. Watching the blood soak through the many layers of towel on my hand, I knew it wasn't safe for me to be alone. Pastor John might be the one person in the whole world who would not forsake me at this darkest time. Although it pained me to think about the conversation that would be necessary to bring him up to speed, I knew he was my only hope for guidance out of this hell I'd created for myself. It was past noon, and I'd clearly blown off my morning interviews. Resting the phone on the blood-soaked towel, I pecked out a message with my left forefinger. "Pastor John, it's Francis. I have done the unthinkable, and I fear my life is ruined forever. I've never needed you more than I do now. I have no one else to turn to. I'm so alone."

I paced the hotel room with no idea where to go or what to do next. The demo tape for the song "Forgiven" was cued up in the player I'd brought to use for the press conference later, and something led me to push play. Hearing the lyrics, I suddenly understood why I had gotten so emotional the day I'd listened to this song in the recording studio with Stephanie. "Forgiven" was about God's love and forgiveness shown toward the other thief on the cross, who was crucified for his terrible crimes at the same time Jesus was. I realized now that *I was* that thief. I was desperate for God's forgiveness, but I would never be worthy of making such a request, especially not now. I listened to my own voice washing over me: "I forgave, for they knew not. I loved, though he deserved not. My son, my kingdom was waiting. One entered, the other fading." My heart convulsed as I realized I would *never* be the one who entered, but only the one who faded—into a flaming inferno for all eternity.

Even in my overwhelming grief, my music gave me an increment of weary solace. I thought about how much the music had always meant to me, and I thought about Stephanie saying that if she continued to work for Justus it would be for the rest of the band. I owed them everything, and I knew what I had to do next. As wretched and shattered as I felt, I got up, called the front desk and asked for a first aid kit, and dressed for the press conference.

As I was walking down the hall on the way there, Pastor John returned my call. I stopped and went into the stairwell between floors so no one could hear me. Through clenched teeth, I played him the highlight reel of my atrocity. I could tell he felt the enormity of my colossal error in judgment.

"I'm at the lowest point of my living life, Pastor, and in the afterlife, I'll descend even lower. I have no place to go and no one to turn to."

"I'm going to text you an address, Francis. It's imperative you meet me there tomorrow. Come prepared to spend several weeks."

Twenty-four tormented hours later, I was sitting on a hard concrete bench outside the entrance gate of the Spirit in the Desert Retreat Center in Sedona, Arizona. Since Mary and the kids were still in Flagstaff, I'd gone by my house just long enough to pack a few things, then come directly to this place and waited for Pastor John to arrive. Exhausted, I twirled my wedding ring on my finger, praying no one would recognize me in my white T-shirt, jeans, and Diamondbacks hat.

Toggling my gaze between the rocky ground at my feet and the family photo on my phone, I was relieved when a taxi finally pulled up and Pastor John's frail frame emerged from the backseat. Relief washed over me as I rose to greet him. "Oh, Pastor John, I can't thank you enough for doing this for me." I hugged him hard, holding our embrace for as long as he let me. I didn't want to let go.

"Of course, my son," he replied, holding my shoulder as he looked into my eyes. He had aged quite a bit since I'd last seen him, but he was still in good shape for a man in his late seventies. "This Christian retreat center is known for its healing, and so is Sedona itself. This is the place for you to be, to begin your soul's healing journey. I've called and arranged for your stay, but I'll let them know we're here now and get you checked in."

I followed Pastor John as he greeted his friends and took care of the details of my stay. I was scared. I had no idea what to expect, but I placed all my hope and trust in my old mentor, in awe of the fact that he had dropped everything in Keeler to fly all the way here. I knew he'd seen plenty in his fifty years as a pastor, but I doubted that he went to these lengths for all his parishioners, and I felt honored that he'd made this special effort for me.

The retreat center was plain and functional, no swank or whimsy to be found. Once the arrangements had been taken care of, Pastor John asked me to walk with him through the facility's rock gardens. Eager to spend time with my savior, I allowed myself to be led wherever he wanted us to go.

"There are reported to be vortexes here in Sedona, Francis," he said, with a sparkle in his eye. "Nothing Christian about them, and I don't pretend to understand how they work, but I do know that a strong Christian faith combined with the natural beauty of God's great mysteries can create a powerful synergy. Miracles have been occurring here since man inhabited this desert."

"A miracle is what I need," I said.

"How are you holding up?" he asked, his blue eyes piercing my broken soul.

I took a deep breath. "Not too well," I admitted. "Yesterday was agonizing. For the sake of the band, I had to go through with the press conference and release party. At first the band didn't know what had happened the night before, why my hand was wrapped in gauze, or why Stephanie wasn't there. I couldn't bring myself to tell them. The press conference was a complete disaster, between their confusion and the chaos raging in my mind. I tried to make a showing at the party, but by that time Cindy had told my bandmates all about the previous evening, and I couldn't face them. Rikki and Tracy came up and really let me have it. I dodged any meaningful contact with them for as long as I could, and then I had to bolt. What should have been one of the best days of my life was one of the worst."

"I'm sure it was difficult for you to be there yesterday," said Pastor John. "But it was good of you to not let your bandmates down."

"I've let *everybody* down!" I snapped. "The tour is scheduled to kick off in less than a month, and I don't know if I can do it, or even if they still want me in the band. I don't know what's going to happen with Justus, and even more important, I don't know what's going to happen with my *life*. I was a basket case yesterday. When they played 'Forgiven' at the press conference, I couldn't stop shaking or stop the tears running down my face. The press wrote that I was moved by the lyrics, but I can't keep up this charade any longer. All those people glorifying me all day just made me feel even more vile and worthless than I already felt."

"Your worth is not yours—or theirs—to judge, my son." Pastor John lifted his eyes heavenward.

"I don't even know who I am anymore. I'm not the man you knew back in Keeler, Pastor. Far, far from it. I've turned into something else, something dark and sinister, something unrecognizable to me. I thought it would be better after you helped me cut the ungodly soul ties, but it didn't work. How could I have done this? How could I have brought such heartbreak and devastation to the ones I love most in the world: my Mary, my children, my mom, even Stephanie?"

"I must urge you, Francis, not to give up on yourself, your family, and especially not your God."

"But, Pastor, how could I ever expect to have my life back? How would Mary ever find it in her pure, tender heart to forgive me? The book of James says something like 'If anyone knows the good he ought to do and doesn't do it, it is sin for him.' I knew what was good! I had what was great! And now I'll pay eternally for betraying the commandments of my God with this evil sin I've repeatedly committed."

"You are right to seek forgiveness, Francis, but I fear you are seeking it from the wrong source. This is not about you sinning against Mary, but against God. It is not about trying to gain forgiveness from Mary. It is about honestly and sincerely seeking it from God. Take a moment, my son, and consider whether this is an avenue you have explored."

I felt light-headed as Pastor John's words slipped through the cracks in my brain and seeped down into my soul. I thought about the way I'd justified and rationalized my actions, starting way back with Paulina. I remembered all the blame I'd leveled on others—particularly Cindy—instead of owning my part in my indiscretions. From the very beginning of my nightmare, I'd been running away from the truth of my sin. Even when I had prayed, I'd selfishly prayed that I not be caught.

Astonished, I said aloud, "Not once have I genuinely taken full ownership of my wrongdoing and sought true forgiveness from God."

Pastor John smiled as if I'd won the spiritual lottery.

My epiphany continued. "Had I done that, right at the beginning, with purity of heart and soul, I would have received God's mercy and forgiveness. And if I had truly known, in my heart, that I'd received that grace, I would have called upon that grace and love when confronted with any temptation, to give me the strength to avoid it."

Pastor John put his hand on my shoulder. "I think you know now what to do with your time here, Francis. Indeed, if God forgives you, who are you to hold on to your sin?"

We had reached the back end of the rock garden and come upon a beautiful gazebo draped in white roses whose sweet scent filled the air. "Sit here with me for a moment, Francis, and let me rest my legs." As we watched the bees pollinate from bloom to bloom, Pastor John remarked, "A serendipitous gift from God—this spot he's created for us. We're surrounded by a beautiful array of one of His most breathtaking creations. Do you know what the color white represents in a rose?"

"No, but I'm pretty sure the color white doesn't represent *this* Rose."

"White roses represent innocence, purity, and new beginnings. I remember many bouquets of white roses at your wedding with Mary. It was a time for you both to embark on a new path together. And now it's time for you to embark on another form of new beginning. This journey will be one of the soul. It will be made complete by the purity of God's love for you and the innocence that returns through His grace."

Pastor John reached into his shoulder bag and pulled out a rolled-up piece of old parchment paper. Across the top, hand-written in beautiful but shaky calligraphy was "Francis Rose." He handed me the scroll, saying, "I'm going to leave you with these four Bible passages to ponder. I want you to imagine you and Jesus reading them together. In addition to your own prayers for forgiveness and healing, every day you will read these passages with Jesus and pray upon them. If you do this, and follow the lead of the Holy Spirit, you will find the peace that has been eluding you."

I took the scroll from him and carefully unrolled it. "Thank you, Pastor. I will follow your instructions with all my heart and soul."

"Let's pray them aloud now, imagining Jesus sitting here in this lovely rose garden with us. Go ahead, Francis."

I began to read 1 Peter 5:8–10: "Be alert and sober of mind. Your enemy the devil prowls around like a roaring lion looking for someone to devour. Resist him, standing firm in the faith, because you know that the family of believers throughout the world is undergoing the same kind of sufferings. And the God of all grace, who called you to His eternal glory in Christ, after you have suffered a little while, will Himself restore you and make you strong, firm, and steadfast." I paused to let the significance of this passage sink in. Could it be true that my suffering was temporary? How long was "a little while"? Could it be true that God would restore me?

Imagining Jesus right beside me on the bench in our rose-covered pergola, I went on to the second passage, Romans 3:23–24: "For all have sinned and fall short of the glory of God, and all are justified freely by His grace through the redemption that came by Christ Jesus." Surely not *all* had sinned as I had done. Would even I be justified freely by the grace of God?

I then read aloud the third and fourth passages on the scroll—1 John 1:9: "If we confess our sins, He is faithful and just and will forgive us our sins and purify us from all unrighteousness" and Isaiah 43:25–26: "I, even I, am He who blots out your transgressions, for my own sake, and remembers your sins no more. Review the past for me, let us argue the matter together; state the case for your innocence." It was as if I were hearing these passages for the first time. *Purify. Blot out. Innocence.*

My tears fell on the parchment paper and the ground. The words deeply touched me, yet the piercing sting of my transgressions still prevented me from finding comfort in them.

Pastor John put his arm around me and said, "It's time for me to go."

"You're leaving?" I asked, hoping to have had more time with him.

"Yes, my son. It's time for your walk with the Lord to begin."

The following two weeks were among the most intense of my life. Each day was spent in deep prayer, exercise, and group work. During one of the group sessions I learned about the vortexes Pastor John had mentioned and that Sedona was famous to many of all faiths and walks of life for the results these vortexes reportedly generated when combined with prayer. I wasn't sure I bought into the whole vortex premise, especially seeing them tied in any way to my Christian faith, but I was so desperate to be healed that I was ready to try anything.

Stephanie finally reached out to me to let me know she would stay until the tour kicked off, which was only two weeks away. She was open to only minimal contact with me, however, and I still wasn't sure if I was up to performing or even if the band wanted me back. I felt completely removed from my regular life. Cindy had tried to reach me early on, but I had immediately blocked her number. I'd gotten one text from Yvonne, which had simply said, "I'm so sorry. It will all work out. You won't hear from me again." I deleted her number as well.

Of course, the person I ached to connect with was Mary, and she was still blocking my calls. I understood why, and I didn't blame her, yet I painfully missed her and the kids. I thought about them and prayed for them every second of every day.

One night, imagining that Jesus was right there praying with me as I read the four Bible verses that Pastor John had given me, I was led to open my Bible to Matthew 4:1–11:

> Then Jesus was led by the Spirit into the wilderness to be tested by the devil. After fasting forty days and forty nights, he was hungry. The tempter came to him and said, "If you are the Son of God, tell these stones to become bread." Jesus answered, "It is written: Man shall not live on bread alone, but on every word that comes from the mouth of God." Then the devil took him to the holy city and had him stand on the highest point of the temple. "If you are the Son of God," he said, "throw yourself down. For it is written: He will command his angels concerning you, and they will lift you up in their hands, so that you will not strike your foot against a stone." Jesus answered him, "It is also written: Do not put the Lord your God to the test." Again, the devil took him to a very high mountain and showed him all the kingdoms of the world and their splendor. "All this I will give you," he said, "if you will bow down and worship me." Jesus said to him, "Away from me, Satan! For it is written: Worship the Lord your God, and serve him only." Then the devil left him, and angels came and attended him.

I was deeply moved after reading this passage in combination with those Pastor John had recommended for me. As I spent time imagining Jesus in the desert, being tempted and prevailing over the devil, I started to feel the Sedona desert calling to me. The next morning I decided to go for a long walk to explore its mysteries.

The small bottle of water I'd packed didn't last long in the stifling, 100-degree heat of a sunny summer day without a hint of cloud cover. Parched and sunburned, I wandered aimlessly until a glittering vision caught my attention. About half a mile away from my hiking spot, an image of a cross seemed to be projected onto the entrance to a small depression in the mountainside.

I blinked my weary eyes, assuming it was a mirage, the effects of sunstroke, or simply my imagination, but the image persisted. I turned my head and looked far off in the opposite direction to see the Chapel of the Holy Cross, a famous, tiny chapel built into a red rock mountainside. This simple historic chapel was reputed to be situated in the area of one of Sedona's strongest vortexes. I had heard people at the retreat center talking about it and had read a pamphlet on it that had been left in my room there.

Trying to make sense of the vision I was seeing, I noticed how the windows at the front of this chapel were separated by wooden beams in the shape of a cross. It seemed as if the giant cross from this place of worship was projecting its image far out onto the side of the mountain in front of me. I headed toward the shadowy, projected cross that seemed to be summoning me as it moved ever so slowly with the change of the sun's position in the sky.

The closer I got to the side of the mountain, the farther away the hazy projection seemed to be. Was I hallucinating? The sun baked my entire body, my tongue stuck to the roof of my mouth, and my lips began to crack. I had long ago run out of water. Starting to feel queasy, I decided to head back.

Just as I was turning toward the retreat center, a mountain lion appeared from behind a collection of large rust-colored boulders. The beautiful yet terrifying creature gracefully and purposely started moving toward me. I froze, but my fear quickly turned to panicked disbelief as the beast transformed before my eyes. A woman's face emerged on the creature, framed by a long black mane. As she started to speak, she stood on her hind legs and . . . and . . . it couldn't be . . . it was Paulina, her fur turning to tight black leather! As I rubbed my eyes trying to clear what had to be an illusion, she started to speak with her thick Russian accent.

"Come to me, Francis Rose. You are the one I want. We have the chemistry to make this unforgettable. I want to act out a beautiful new love poem, a new script with you. Come back to my hotel room." As she walked toward me she slowly dropped the leather strap from her top, revealing her breast.

"I am finished with you!" I yelled toward the beast woman. Just as I did, she screeched a howling scream like a banshee and disappeared in a ball of fire. It was the most terrifying and blood-curdling sound I'd ever heard. Shaking, I stared at the spot where she had disappeared.

I knew in that moment I could not turn around. I would not go back—not to the retreat center and not to that life! Mustering what little strength I had left, I powered on toward the shadowy cross.

Then the fiendish screech came again! Was it her? I squinted up through the blazing sun to see a huge black vulture sitting atop a rocky outcropping a few hundred yards from the projected cross. With another ear-piercing screech, and with the spasmodic writhing of a demon, the horrific vulture grew to human size, convulsing one more time as it turned from black to white. Standing with the sun exploding rays from behind her shapely silhouette was Cindy.

"You don't need that Russian bitch. It's me you've always loved. I'm the one who has always known how to make you feel like the prince you are. Come to me, my soul mate." As she spoke, she turned to black again, opening her arms and spreading her ten-foot wingspan as she descended from her perch toward me.

"You can *never* have my soul, and you will *never* put me to the test again," I screamed with absolute certainty. As my words fell on the creature's feather-covered ears, she contorted in midair one last time, disappearing into a blast of black ash and smoke just above me. I covered my head and fell to my knees as the ash and soot rained down and stuck to my sweaty body.

I knew what was next but didn't want to face it. Running out of energy, and low on the faith that I could deal with any more, I was unable to stand. I was now less than a hundred yards away from the projected image of the cross. Crawling, I brushed against the base of a large saguaro cactus. One of its spines pierced deep into my shoulder, sending a copious flow of blood cascading down my arm to my hand and onto the ground. Before I could gather my strength to address the wound, a beautiful hand reached out to wipe it for me. It was Yvonne. She scooped up my blood and put it into her mouth, allowing it to ooze out and spill down the front of her pink lace bra, past her belly button and into the front of her matching panties. It wasn't a cactus spine that had pierced me; it was the oversized needle she was holding, now full of my bodily fluid.

With blood dripping like honey from her lips, she said, "You don't need that bleach-blonde floozy; you need a doctor to care for you and administer to you whenever, wherever, and however you want."

"Get behind me, Satan. I command all of you demons, get behind me now!"

As my words of conviction rang through the arid desert air, the image of Yvonne turned back into a cactus covered in beautiful red flowers.

Completely spent, yet growing in confidence, I knew I had to get to that cross. Making my way closer, I realized that the area marked by the cross was a chasm, a natural cave-like opening in the mountain large enough to drive a truck through. My energy level soared, and goose bumps erupted across my body in concurrence with an inner knowing that I was being given a sign. Was it the magical healing vortex energy I'd been hearing about? I felt a burgeoning sensation of peace and connection to the beautiful nature that surrounded me. The reflected image of the cross continued to slip toward the entrance of the cave wall as the sun made its way toward the horizon.

Finally at its mouth, I looked behind me to be sure I had overcome the power of a desperate and pathetic enemy. I cautiously entered the cave and was immediately overcome with a tremendous sense of a holy presence. The cave was wide at its opening and narrowed as I slowly walked in farther. Toward the far back corner, two smooth seats were artfully carved into the red sandstone walls. The seats were placed about six feet apart, facing each other. I was intensely drawn to this area of the cave, where the pleasing aroma of burned-down candles and campfire remnants still lingered. Even though it was dark in this innermost region, an alluring, mystical ambiance was created by the narrow rays of dusty light that found their way through the scents of burned juniper, pine, and mesquite.

I slid into one of the seats and noticed three bare crosses carved roughly into the opposite cave wall. The center cross was much larger and more prominent than the other two, yet the cross to the right of it was uncannily bright. It seemed to have been etched into the cave, then painted with a luminescent paint I'd once heard about ancient tribes using. The cross to the left looked like it was shaded dark with charcoal. Looking across the black void of the cave, I was mesmerized by the grouping, unable to tear my eyes away from it, particularly the striking difference between the smaller crosses, one light and one dark.

I felt weightless, light-headed, like I'd entered a surreal plane of existence. I wondered briefly whether I was on the verge of passing out from dehydration, heatstroke, or the battle I had just waged, but the dizzy sensation was pleasant enough that I was able to put those concerns aside.

"Don't be afraid, Francis." The voice was low and warm and seemed to emanate from the darkness surrounding the empty seat in front of me. *"I've heard you. I've watched you. I love you."*

I swiveled my head in both directions, scanning the dimly lit cave. "Who's there?" I asked.

"I've loved you since the moment you were born. I've followed your every footstep, every stumble, stride, and shuffle. Every victory and every loss. I shared them all with you. I've always been here, ready for you to seek me and ask for my grace, my mercy, my forgiveness."

"Wha . . ." I stammered. "Who? Is . . . Is it you? Is it really you?"

"Free will causes much joy or much pain. Francis, I have felt your deep pain along with you. Your hurt is my hurt. As I was made in your image, so you were in mine."

Electrified from the inside out, I couldn't find words to express my joy. There was no fear whatsoever. I felt only a hushed, sacred warmth radiating clearly from the empty seat across from me.

The glowing cross on the wall commanded all my attention as it slowly intensified in hue.

"Lord, if this is You—or even if it's not—Lord, I cry out to You. Oh, I do seek You. I do seek Your grace, Your mercy, and Your forgiveness for what I've done to You and to my family. Dear Jesus, I confess to You, at the foot of your cross, my terrible sins. Although I'm not worthy, much like the thief that was crucified to Your right on that horrible day, I ask that You take me down from this cross on which I've hung myself. Redeem me, Lord! I want to walk in Your light again! Redeem my soul!"

Clinging to the parchment scroll from Pastor John, I sobbed and pleaded, knowing that I was finally doing what I should have done from the start. From the purest depths of my soul, I begged Lord Jesus for His precious healing and redemption.

Exhausted by my emotional display, I stopped to quietly catch my breath, waiting to hear the incomparably compassionate voice of the Lord again. I sat, breathing and anticipating.

Then, just as I began to wonder if my divine conversation were over, the cave burst into a glorious riot of illumination. The cross that had been glowing all along began casting impossibly iridescent beams of light onto the larger cross, filling the cave with unbearable grace and beauty. I squinted into the radiance, amazed to find that the darker cross had become nearly invisible. A beam of sunlight flickered across my watch, revealing that it was 3:00 PM, the exact hour that Jesus had died on the cross.

I felt an intense peace wash over me that could only be described as the peace that surpasses all understanding. There was no doubt in my heart what this peace represented. It was the rarest of sensations, undeniably generated by the love of God and the grace found in God's forgiveness.

Like the dazzling light cast from the smaller cross onto the larger one, the emotion building in my soul was one of complete purity and restoration. Was I being washed clean of my transgressions, cleansed from my sins? I was held in the hand of God, elevated to the heavens, and returned to Earth with all the glory of heaven embedded within me.

"Thank You, Lord Jesus. Thank You." Tears fell freely from my eyes, but this time they were tears of inexpressible joy, lightness, and freedom. "Thank You for Your love, Your grace. I feel it, Lord. Thank You for this new life You have breathed into me."

Awash with the resplendent grace that filled and surrounded me, I picked up a partly burned mesquite twig. I carefully unrolled the parchment scroll I'd been clutching, turned it over, and used the branch to write "The Other Thief" across the top.

Words tumbled out of me as I rewrote the lyrics to "Forgiven," this time not from the perspective of God but from the perspective of an enormously grateful "other thief" who received God's grace, mercy, forgiveness, and redemption, even when he didn't deserve it.

CHAPTER 18

I raised the bronze, faith-fish door knocker and rapped on Stephanie's front door, shifting my duffel bag up higher onto my shoulder. It felt lighter than it had when I set out on my journey, but then again, everything felt so much lighter at this point. I felt such strength of mind, soul, and spirit now.

She flung open the door but didn't fling open her arms for a hug, as I had secretly hoped she might. "Francis," she said, nervously motioning me inside. "How was your trip from the retreat center?"

"It was great, but hard to leave such an enlightening place," I said. "Thanks so much for letting me crash here for the next few days until the tour kicks off. It really means a lot to me."

"I won't lie, Francis. I'm still heartbroken over all of this. But I'm a Christian, and you were a good friend to me for many years."

I brought my duffel bag to the spare room Stephanie had offered me, and we sat down in the kitchen to catch up.

"How are they?" I asked. Stephanie had been graciously serving as a go-between for Mary and me, and I was always desperate for another update on Mary and the kids.

Stephanie seemed unready to have that conversation with me, however, pretending to assume I was talking about the band. "Well, I told you about Rikki breaking his foot, right? He was able to have a special cast made that will allow him to play bass drum even with the injury. He's been practicing with it, and it looks like we'll have no problem with that." Stephanie was talking fast. She rattled on, "They've all been rehearsing the new songs together, but it's not the same, of course, without you here, and I'm concerned about the fact that we've had no practice time with you in more than a month. We're still in agreement that we'll incorporate a lot of the songs from Sanctified, right? Because that's what we had talked about before you . . . before you—"

Stephanie seemed at a loss to complete her sentence, so I jumped in. "Yes! Yes, I still think that's a great idea. I don't want you to worry about our lack of cohesive rehearsal time. We've played together for twenty years. We'll do just fine. I'm so grateful that you've held things together in my absence and continued to take care of the band."

"It hasn't been easy," she said. "They're understandably very concerned. We need to talk about the opening sets."

"I know," I said. "I know. We will. But first, Steph, how are Mary and the kids?"

Stephanie reluctantly met my gaze. "They're doing as well as could be expected," she said. I could tell my very presence in her home was making her uncomfortable, and I longed for a way to change that. She added, "Mary said she did correspond with you by text."

"Yes! She did, but only once. Let me read it to you." I took out my phone to read Stephanie the text exchange, hoping she might be able to add more detail for me, given that she was now more present in their lives than I was. "Hi, Daddy, it's Heather. I'm using Mommy's phone. I miss you so much. I hope you're doing okay. I keep clicking my heels, hoping you'll come home." My voice cracked as I imagined my baby girl saying those words.

I cleared my throat and resumed. "Hi, Francis, it's Mary. As you can see, the kids miss you terribly. Eddie has been dressing like you every day, in jeans and a T-shirt. He won't take off his sunglasses or his Diamondback hat, and he walks around with a microphone in one hand and Rosey in the other. You've broken everyone's heart. I hope your time away has allowed you to find yours. We'll have to figure something out soon, because they're really suffering." I looked at Stephanie for her reaction. She wouldn't meet my gaze and just stared uncomfortably at the floor.

"May I read you my response?" I asked her. Without waiting for a reply, I began. "'Mary, I'm beyond sorry and remorseful for my horrible sin against you and the kids and against God. I'm at your mercy and will do what you ask of me to bring peace back to your life and the lives of our children. I would love to see them soon, and maybe we could talk, too.' Steph, I understand why it would be hard for you to believe my words, but they're true. This time, I really have returned to the person I know God wants me to be. It's a peace that says I'll never hurt anyone again, never go back to that horrible life."

"What did she say?" Stephanie tenuously asked.

"She said, 'Yes, soon. Not for you, but for them. I can't see you. I'll have Madeleine or my mom bring them to you.' I replied, 'Okay, I'll be ready when you are.'"

Stephanie sighed deeply. I couldn't stand to see her so distraught, knowing that I was the cause of it all. I took her hand, squeezing it between both of mine. I looked intently into her eyes and said, "Stephanie, thank you. I mean that from the depths of my soul. Thank you for all the compassion and patience you've shown me throughout these past months. Thank you for your strength of character, your determination to bring the truth to light, and for your faith in me. You have done the right thing every step of the way, and I'll never be able to repay you for being a lighthouse for me, a touchstone of integrity and purity when I needed it most. Thank you, also, for being there these past three weeks for Mary and the kids. And for agreeing to let me stay here for a few days. I had nowhere else to go, aside from a hotel."

Stephanie's eyed welled with tears, and I could see her wrestling internally, wanting to believe that I'd truly changed but also cautiously needing to protect herself from being hurt by me again. I continued, "I know you have no reason to trust me right now, and that's okay. I wouldn't trust me, either, from where you're standing. But if you'll give me a chance, I know that with the passage of time you'll see that I'm a new man. I know that everything is going to work out for the best. Steph, I have full faith in Proverbs 3:5: 'Trust in the Lord with all your heart and lean not on your own understanding.' I've come to believe that even this whole nightmare has been part of God's plan for all of us. I'll never understand it, and I'm not sure I'd even want to, but through His grace it's made easier."

After a long silent pause, Stephanie asked, "What will be different now, Francis?" Her tone was not accusatory or angry. She seemed to genuinely want me to provide an answer she could feel good about.

"I received a miracle, Steph. There's a newfound calm in my soul, a peacefulness. I do know that my actions must have consequences, and I take full responsibility for them now. If my marriage is over, I will accept that and make the best of it, although I continue to pray every day with all my heart that it won't be."

"I pray that for you as well, but I've been praying a special prayer daily for Mary, Heather, and Eddie," said Stephanie. "Tell me about this miracle."

I hadn't spoken of it to anyone, not even Pastor John yet, because I was still trying to process the events in my own mind. But Stephanie's invitation unleashed an excitement in me to spread the word of my miraculous interaction with the Divine, so I began describing for her how I'd felt the calling to go out and wander the desert. I told her about the surreal projection of the cross on the mountainside that had pulled me toward it and how I'd gotten the feeling it was God's personal invitation to me. I told her how the devil had tried in desperation to tempt me out there, assuring her that I had been able to recognize it in the desert and would always be able to recognize it from now on. I told her I knew now that I was no longer powerless and that I had the power to banish him and whatever thoughts he tried to plant.

Stephanie listened intently as I painted the scenery inside the cave for her: the crosses on the wall, the seats carved into the sandstone, the intoxicating aromas, and the otherworldly illumination of the cross on the right that felt like God was putting on a light show just for me. I recounted Jesus's words to me and the overwhelming bliss of the peace that penetrated my broken soul, restoring it miraculously to its former shine, restoring me as a Christian and a man of God.

"Stephanie, I know it all sounds crazy, but I now fully know what God's mercy feels like. I recognized my utter helplessness to save myself, and like the other thief, I was a dead man. There was nothing I could do to save myself. All I could do was call upon His name and throw myself on His mercy, and that mercy is real! I've experienced the most beautiful gift—the cleansing of my soul through God's forgiveness. I felt the deep, tortuous pain of my sin against my family, against you and the band, and most important, against God. But that pain doesn't compare to the gift of redemption, of eternal salvation, that Jesus gave us when he died on the cross for me, for us. I now know what the thief who was crucified with Christ must have felt when Jesus promised him paradise, because, Stephanie, my life had reached that level of despair. And that despair turned to unfathomable joy upon my confession."

Stephanie's eyes were wide as she took in my words. "Francis, I do sense something different in you. No, actually it's not different; it's familiar. It's the Francis I knew and loved. He was still in there, but the evil of sin was keeping him captive. Something must have really happened to you in that cave."

Flooded with gratitude to be seen and validated by my old friend, I said, "Steph, what you sense is a peace that, as Philippians 4:7 says, 'surpasses all understanding.' I can't tell you how anxious I am to get back to my life, to finally get to Haiti, and give everything I've got to my music."

"Do you actually think you can bring that peace, that gift, that Francis that I know and love, back to the stage on opening night, and more important, to all the opening nights for the rest of your life?"

"I don't just think it, Steph. I believe and know it," I promised. "Yet I understand my actions must speak louder than my words. And they will. You'll see."

Stephanie smiled, and for the first time in a very long while, things felt right between us.

"I've got a favor to ask," I said. "I know it's a long shot, but would you save the traditional three seats in the front row on opening night? Just in case—well, you know." A single tear rolled down my face.

"Francis," she said. "No matter how unlikely it ever is that they'll be used, I will always save those three seats."

The band was already there when Stephanie and I arrived at the AK Chin Pavilion escorted by two security officers. On our way through the backstage hall to get to the dressing room, dozens of intrepid fans who had somehow gained entrance to this private area clamored to see me, touch me, and beg for my autograph. I stopped and talked to as many of them as I could, but there was no way to satisfy them all.

"I know you're nervous about seeing everyone, Francis," said Stephanie, sounding far more nervous herself than I felt. "I'm going to smooth this over, I promise. Just like I've always done whenever there's been a rift between any of the band members. Just let me do the talking. We have exactly one hour before we open. That's enough time to get all of you comfortable with one another again. I need you to focus and get into your performance mode."

I could already hear the roar of the fans filling the sold-out arena. "You know what I think, Steph? I think it's time for you to step down from this role of taking on my burdens for me. You've done it so well for so long, it's become habit for us both. But from now on, stuff like this is up to me. I will talk to the band. I haven't seen them in a month, and I owe them an explanation, in my own words."

Stepping in front of Stephanie, I entered the dressing room, my head held high. Rikki stopped rapping his drumsticks. Tracy put down her guitar. Mike stopped chewing, holding a half-eaten chicken wing in midair.

Looking at the custodian and attendants, Stephanie said, "Would you guys mind giving us a moment alone?"

"No, you're fine," I told them, nodding in Stephanie's direction to let her know I appreciated the gesture but welcomed these strangers to stay among us.

"Hi guys," I began. "Well, I've missed you and I love each of you very much. I've got something I gotta say. When we formed our band and named it Justus, you might remember that we'd done so because I wanted to take the same approach to following Jesus that the forgotten, yet faithful disciple Justus had taken. I didn't want any special attention or fame, I just wanted to express our faith and love for Christ through our music. Now just look at this sold-out arena.

"Anyway, for the last few months leading up to the Beverly Hills Hotel press conference and party, I acted more like Judas than Justus." I glanced at Stephanie as I repeated her words from long ago. "A few weeks ago, in a cave in the middle of the Sedona desert, I realized I had two choices. I could continue to throw my life away, like Judas, after an unthinkable and sinful act. Or I could seek God's forgiveness—which was available even to Judas, had he asked. In the recesses of that cave I pleaded for God's great mercy. And guys, I've received it. It's a love unlike any other. I ask the same of you, and in due time I pray you'll offer me the same grace.

"You know, it's funny, for all these years, I've seen this line from our song 'Love Never Fails' in a certain way." I sang the line for them: "I'll always love you near and far away. You alone occupy my heart, a love so deep I could never betray." Well, today, I see that line totally differently. I see it from Christ's perspective, as if he were singing it to me. Guys, I ask that you bear with me tonight when we perform 'Forgiven.' I love all of you, and I'm sorry for the hurt I've caused you."

I looked from face to face. I saw tears, love, and perhaps even forgiveness. One by one, I hugged these people who meant so much to me. Even the attendants and custodian appeared to be choked up, and I hugged them, too.

We were all still wiping tears from our eyes as we stood holding hands on stage behind the curtain, listening to our local celebrity radio deejay from KISS 105 FM say, "I give you the biggest band to come out of Keeler, Indiana: Justus!"

The curtain went up, the spotlights hit us, and we broke into "Love Never Fails," our hearts filled with camaraderie and the never-ending passion we shared for doing what God had put us here to do.

The roar of the crowd was deafening, and it seemed that everyone in the audience had stood up to dance and sway along to this classic favorite. I squinted through the glare toward the three seats Stephanie had saved in the front row, marked with Mary, Heather, and Eddie's names. I was not surprised to see that they were empty, but I continued to hold out hope for a miracle.

Throughout the first few songs, I kept a close watch on those seats. Then, not wanting my distraction to affect my performance, I made peace internally with the fact that they would not be coming. I turned to the right of the stage to look at Stephanie, and she just shook her head no. I knew it would have been a long shot, and I knew I would happily spend the rest of my life proving to them that I was still the man they'd once seen me as. I let go of watching the seats, dedicating myself instead to delivering the best performance of my life, on fire for Christ, and for my fans.

Toward the end of our two-hour set, blinded from fatigue and the glare of the spotlights, I thanked God for giving me the continued opportunity to serve Him in this way. It had clearly been the best performance in Justus's history.

We'd saved "Forgiven" for our final song. I turned to the roadie and signaled for an acoustic guitar and a stool. My bandmates looked confused, because I hadn't given them any advance warning about my plan. As I approached the stool in the center of the stage, our tech wizard fixed a single spotlight on me.

I removed the mic from the stand and slowly lowered to my knees. I brought the mic to my mouth and said, "Phoenix, I want to thank you for all the love and energy you have provided me, Rikki, Tracy, and Mike for the last twenty years. What started in little Keeler, Indiana, before a crowd of twenty, has grown into this crowd of twenty thousand, all because of the big promoter in the sky. I do this for you, but I do it all to glorify God, a God that loves you and wants you to seek Him. He's waiting for you to turn more fully toward Him, to receive a grace and mercy that knows no limits. I'm just a sinner saved by the forgiving power of God, and I know firsthand God's redemptive love, just like the other thief on the cross. I'm him. I'm forgiven."

Although the band stood ready to play what was supposed to be a song with full electric instruments, I rose to my feet, slid the stool underneath me, and began singing a version of "Forgiven" they'd never heard. With my heart full, I sang the lyrics I'd written in burnt mesquite on the back of the scroll Pastor John had given me—the lyrics that had poured out of me in a cave in the desert, after I'd sat with the Lord and been blessed with His healing love, mercy, and redemption. The original song had been written from the perspective of God, but I'd changed it to be from me, the other thief, singing the words to Jesus.

Rikki had attempted a soft percussive accompaniment, but he stopped, realizing this was a message I needed to deliver on my own. Tracy stood mesmerized, her pick in her hand. Mike sat down cross-legged on the stage. I felt all their eyes on me as I sang:

> *Here you patiently wait for me*
> *Through my pain and my suffering, you've seen me*
> *I've mocked you, deceived you*
> *Unleashed my sin against you*
> *But in the end, believed in you*

Your grace, it feels so pure
A forgiven man I didn't deserve
Your loving mercy forever endures
Redemption you offered, I needed to bleed

All I need is you to love
For you to set me free
All I need is your breath inside of me
To give me life
Bring me back to my knees

You forgave, for I knew not
You loved, though I deserved not
Your son, your kingdom is waiting
One entered, the other fading

All I need is you to love
For you to set me free
All I need is your breath inside of me
To give me life
Bring me back to my knees

I love you, Jesus, I love you
At the recesses of my dark cave
You let your light shine on me
I, yes, I, the other thief before you.

As the crowd leaped in unison to a standing ovation, Tracy, Rikki, and Mike converged upon me, wrapping me in a tearful group hug. Even Stephanie, who had never wanted to be on stage with us, came out from the behind the curtain and joined our embrace. Bouquets of roses rained onto the stage all around us.

As we locked hands for our final bow, I glanced one last time at the three seats in the front row. They were empty, of course, but something new caught my eye. Wiping the sweat away, I squinted in amazement. It was Rosey! Right there, draped atop the middle seat, was Eddie's tattered octopus, four of her eight tentacles hanging over the side of the seat.

LUKE 23:33–43:

When they came to the place called the Skull, they crucified him there, along with the criminals—one on his right, the other on his left. Jesus said, "Father, forgive them, for they do not know what they are doing." And they divided up his clothes by casting lots. The people stood watching, and the rulers even sneered at him. They said, "He saved others; let him save himself if he is God's Messiah, the Chosen One." The soldiers also came up and mocked him. They offered him wine vinegar and said, "If you are the king of the Jews, save yourself." There was a written notice above him, which read THIS IS THE KING OF THE JEWS. One of the criminals who hung there hurled insults at him: "Aren't you the Messiah? Save yourself and us!" But the other criminal rebuked him. "Don't you fear God," he said, "since you are under the same sentence? We are punished justly, for we are getting what our deeds deserve. But this man has done nothing wrong." Then he said, "Jesus, remember me when you come into your kingdom." Jesus answered him, "Truly I tell you, today you will be with me in paradise."

ABOUT THE AUTHOR

Frank McKinney is a true Renaissance man, six-time best-selling author (in five genres), real estate "artist," actor, ultramarathoner, aspirational speaker, and an usher for twenty-plus years at his 7:00 AM Mass.

Upon attending his fourth high school in four years (he was asked to leave the first three), Frank earned his high school diploma with a less-than-stellar 1.8 GPA (it would have been lower, but he got an "A" in creative writing). Then, with $50 in his pocket and without the benefit of further education, Frank left his native Indiana for Florida in search of his life's highest calling.

As a "philanthro-capitalist," he has made an unfathomable humanitarian impact in Haiti through his Caring House Project, where he has created twenty-eight self-sufficient villages in twenty-five Haitian cities in the last sixteen years, impacting the lives of 12,000-plus children and their families. Frank, his wife, Nilsa, and their daughter, Laura, make their home in Delray Beach, Florida, where Frank wrote *The Other Thief* in his oceanfront treehouse office.

Share the Profound Message
of *The Other Thief*

Give copies of
The Other Thief
to family, friends and co-workers . . .

Hardcover book (HCI, 2018)
Available at TheOtherThief.com • $20

Other Exciting Offerings from Frank McKinney

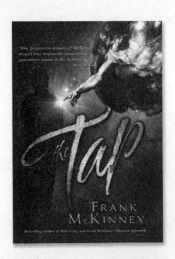

Bestselling author Frank McKinney introduces *The Tap*, a profound spiritual practice leading to success in the business of life. Your prayers for more are answered! *The Tap* shows how to sensitize yourself to feel and then act on life's great "Tap Moments," embracing the rewards and responsibilities of a blessed life. Feel it, follow it and find your highest calling. This book is about accepting the responsibility, and it gives you confidence in your ability to handle your "more," whether it's more wealth, health, happiness, or relationships.

Hardcover book (HCI, 2009)
Available at The-Tap.com • $25

Burst This! Frank McKinney's Bubble-Proof Real Estate Strategies continues Frank McKinney's international bestseller tradition of delivering paradoxical perspectives and strategies for generational success in real estate. Tired of all the "bubble" talk, all the doom and gloom? Here comes McKinney in his unassailable fear-removal gear and hip boots to help you wash away the worry—the anxiety that financial theorists and misguided media constantly dump into the real estate marketplace. During his 30-year career, this "maverick daredevil real estate artist" has not only survived but thrived through all economic conditions by taking the contrarian position and making his own markets.

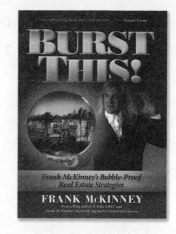

Hardcover book (HCI, 2009) • Available at Burst-This.com • $30

With **Dead Fred, Flying Lunchboxes, and the Good Luck Circle**, Frank McKinney boldly enters young reader fiction in this fantasy novel charged with fairy tale wonder, enthralling magic, page-turning suspense, and the deep creativity he's known for. It will both race and gladden the hearts of readers of all ages. This classic was inspired by real-life Laura McKinney's 1,652 walks to school with her friends and her father, Frank McKinney.

Hardcover book (HCI, 2009)
Available at Dead-Fred.com • $25

Frank McKinney's Maverick Approach to Real Estate Success takes the reader on a fascinating real estate odyssey that began more than two decades ago with a $50,000 fixer-upper and culminates in a $100-million mansion. Includes strategies and insights from a true real estate "artist," visionary, and market maker.

Paperback book (John Wiley & Sons, 2006)
Available at Frank-McKinney.com • $25

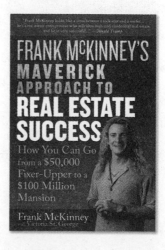

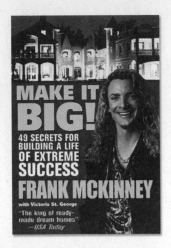
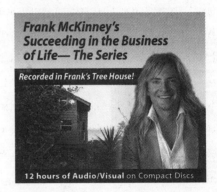